ClickMate

TIA KELLY

HONEY BLOSSOM PRESS

Copyright © 2025 by Tia Kelly

Cover Illustrated by Destiny Darcel
Cover Design by Qamber Designs
Cover Copyright © 2025 by Honey Blossom Press LLC

Print book interior design by Qamber Designs

Honey Blossom Press
www.honeyblossompress.com
@honeyblossompress

ISBNs: 9781967565023 (trade paperback),
9781967565030 (ebook)
Printed in the United States of America

HONEY BLOSSOM PRESS

For my sweet, strong girl, Rhyan. You bring me joy.

Off the Record

BELLAMY

ONCE UPON A TIME, BECAUSE WE ARE GOING FULL fairytale here, I thought I could spot a story coming from a mile away.

Trolls in my comments? Please. Ghosting? Been there, wrote the monologue. Trends? I clocked them before hashtags were even a thing. That was my edge. I told other people's stories, chewed them up, and served them with a punch line.

What I did not see coming was starring in one myself. And not the kind that ends in a kiss before the credits.

If you came here expecting bows tied on every conflict and a romance that glides in like a Hallmark Christmas movie, let me stop you now. I am not that girl. I never waited for glass slippers. I bought my own, pairs that do not pinch when life gets real.

I am five foot four with hips that file HR complaints, and I have learned how to make space before anyone offers it. No damsels here. Though if you are looking for a little distress, I have had my moments. Maybe that is why I dated men who never asked for more than I was willing to give. No rescues, no promises, no heartbreak I did not see coming.

If you prefer your stories neat and shallow, where no one blurts the wrong thing or makes a fool of themselves in public, you might want to close this book gently and walk away. Think of me as that friend you adore but never invite to a cocktail party, because I cannot answer a question without taking the long way around the block and narrating every landmark on the way.

And just so we are clear, I am more "Picture it, Atlanta, 2025" than I am neat exposition. I like a little flair in my facts and a little truth tucked inside the comedy. It is how I make sense of the noise.

So put your phone on Do Not Disturb. Grab a snack, maybe two. This is how two sworn enemies, or one sworn enemy and one very grumpy man who swore he did not care, crashed into each other's lives. And if I wander before I get there, just know it is part of the story.

Because if you think you have heard this one before, you have not. The only predictable thing about me is that I never am.

Chapter 1

BELLAMY

STUDIO LIGHTS FLATTENED EVERYTHING—SKIN, NERVES, even lies—until all that was left was the voice you'd trained people to trust. I kept mine steady, even when my stomach disagreed. Each light was adjusted for the livestream as the crew counted down. Three cameras, two cohosts, one shot to make it all look easy. Like none of us were faking it. What was happening here was radio too pretty to only be heard.

Maybe that was why the smoothie in front of me looked like ambition I never asked for. It was too green and far too confident. It also smelled like grass and guilt, like it was judging me for skipping yoga.

Across from me, my cohost Dani Rivera looked up from her notes. "Bellamy, you really drinking the Lord's landscaping at six in the morning?"

"It's Wellness Wednesday," I said, fighting a grimace. "Detox day."

"Your body's fine. It's your life choices that need the cleanse."

I traced slow circles with the straw, my voice dipping into something steadier than I felt. "It's about balance."

"Girl, please. Liquified spinach don't balance nothing but the trash can."

I sighed, dug into my tote, and pulled out my real energy

booster—a travel-size Hennessy bottle I'd packed this morning. The cap twisted off with ease and I poured a shot right into the cup.

On my left, Malcolm "Mac" Collier lowered his mug to its coaster without looking up from the rundown. He did not talk much, but as our anchor, when he did, it landed. He didn't even look at me when he said, "Add therapy to the detox."

"I go to therapy," I muttered, trying not to sound defensive.

Dani tipped her head, that knowing look returning. "Then maybe stay a little longer next time."

The studio moved around us with the practiced sounds of routine. Interns whispered behind the glass, cameramen adjusted angles for the livestream, and I fell into a pace I knew by heart.

Mondays meant Motown classics and sweet potato muffins, my way of making peace with the week ahead one warm bite at a time. Taco Tuesdays brought oxtail tacos from Miss Shirlene's, the soul food spot I put on the map after a viral segment. Throwback Thursdays hit with nineties jams and shrimp and grits, a nod to those Atlanta brunch spots with grass walls, DJs in the corner, and mimosa towers taller than your self-control. Fridays were indulgent with Uncle Nearest caramel éclairs and rotating themes that shifted between New Orleans bounce and Soul Train anthems. Whatever it was, even the stiffest execs loosened by eight forty-five.

This platform had my name on it because I'd earned it, not because of the one printed on my birth certificate. People loved celebrity math. Famous father equaled easy career. They skipped the mornings when I was here ahead of everyone else, watching the lights flicker.

That was because my father was Terrence Barnes. In the nineties he signed CDs at Lenox Mall until the Sharpies quit. Women left phone numbers on random scraps of paper from electric bills to ATM receipts, and once, a lacy *hello* tucked into my Trapper Keeper during after-school pickup. I was eleven, mortified for a week, and still told Kierra during the bus ride home because my daddy had R&B in a chokehold back then. A decade later she popped up in my DMs asking if I could hook her up with him now that she was grown. I gagged so hard I hit block by reflex. Some memories don't need sequels.

I was a daddy's girl, sure, but love didn't explain my grind or justify my name headlining the show's roster. And pride didn't book guests, write rundowns, or keep a show upright when everything tilted live on air, even when people tried to tuck me back under his legacy. They saw Terrence Barnes, icon. I saw the man who taught me to parallel-park in a tour bus lot.

If that weren't enough, my mom was famous*ish*. She did her own harmonizing micro-stint in the music business back when *A Different World* had all the ladies thriving in a true girls' girl era. She was the reason my press looked polished and my breakdowns never made it to camera.

That was the ecosystem I was born into. But this show? This one I'd built by hand, brick by brick? None of who my people were kept *Wake Up, Let's Brew* on the air. *I'd* done that. I showed up when my sleep, my concealer, and my patience called in sick. I'd fought for this platform through early mornings, endless rewrites, segments that bombed, and the rare magic ones that reminded me why I stayed. Maybe the doors had opened easier, but they hadn't stayed open without proof of what I brought to the table.

Warm cinnamon rolls and rich coffee scented the air as interns hurried past the glass. Mac argued with the sound tech over intro levels. This was our usual morning soundtrack. It was easy to forget we were live at times until someone said something wild and it hit the feed, clipped and trending by lunch. The cameras never stopped here; they were always streaming straight to the channel like it was gospel.

Karen suddenly breezed in with a look that always knotted my stomach before she even opened her mouth. She was the network-appointed executive producer of *Wake Up, Let's Brew*, a leftover from the original deal that greenlit the show. Back then, having her on the team made sense. She had the connections, the résumé, and the polish they trusted. I had the concept and the voice. We were not always at odds, but it did not take long to learn that Karen's ambition had sharp elbows. She was cutthroat in a way I was not, and worse, she had more actual power than I did. This might be my show in spirit and name, but Karen was the one with pull in the rooms that decided our future.

"Team." Her voice cut through the morning calm, too bright to trust. "We have a last-minute surprise."

Dani's gaze slid away from Karen a hair too fast as she reached for her notecards to update them. "We don't have a guest segment today."

Karen's grin widened. "Oh, but we do now."

Mac narrowed his eyes at the schedule. "Not on the rundown. Who is it?"

Karen clapped like she'd just booked Oprah. "Just a little surprise."

My pulse jumped. The last time she'd said that, it involved a live snake and a psychic who claimed I had blocked ancestral energy. I did not do surprises, especially hers.

"Karen." My voice dropped. "What did you do?"

Before I could brace myself, in walked LaMya Croix, reality TV goddess and professional orchestrator of mess. She was also, unfortunately, the very public ex of Troy Alexander, Hollywood's reigning rom-com prince and, technically, my man. Or at least he still called himself that when he was trying to convince me we were "working things out."

The hell?

Karen greeted LaMya with a hug that looked far too friendly for two people who just met. "Just shaking things up."

Even Randy, our intern who once misspelled Beyoncé as

Bayonsay, perked up and tried not to stare.

LaMya slid into her seat across from me in a white jumpsuit that announced itself before she did. Her gaze swept the room, smug and deliberate, like she knew she was the moment and dared anyone to disagree.

Me? I was usually that girl, the one who made the camera recalibrate. Skin luminous, makeup layered like strategy, wardrobe designed to negotiate a deal. I did not just arrive, I entered as both the face and the franchise.

Today, though, I was underdressed and underwater. Clean sweats and moisturized, but not slayed. My braids were pulled into a high ponytail because I'd missed my hair appointment the other day. Just gloss and concealer, a light attempt to keep the chatter online quiet. No earrings. And next to LaMya, who looked like a budget approval in heels, I resembled someone's cousin who'd wandered on set looking for a charger. Her outfit said premiere. Mine said real life.

"We are live in ten," Karen chirped from the control room, her voice bubbling with glee she did not bother to hide.

I tightened my grip on the cup. "Karen."

"Five," she cut in.

I had handled plenty of disasters on air, from technical glitches and wardrobe malfunctions to guests who confused us with their therapy sessions. This was different. This was betrayal in real time, and I was not camera ready for it.

Dani glanced at me, wary.

"Three."

Mac exhaled through his nose, audible and resigned.

"Two… one."

The ON AIR sign flooded red, casting the studio in its glow. The light always carried weight, a silent demand for performance. Mac cleared his throat, his voice steady, though his fingers tapped once against the desk before he stilled them.

"Welcome back to *Wake Up, Let's Brew*. Today's episode comes with a surprise guest… LaMya Croix."

Silence stretched across the room like plastic wrap pulled too tight. Not from us, but from the crew on the other side of the glass. Their murmurs bled through the comms, a ripple of disbelief that confirmed it. No one knew this was happening.

Across from me, LaMya smiled like the news wasn't news at all. She adjusted in her seat, all poise and practiced ease, like she was reclaiming a throne instead of borrowing a chair. "Bellamy, you look surprised."

I straightened, shoulders back, spine locked like I'd trained for this. "Pleasantly," I replied, curving my mouth into a smile sharp enough for broadcast but not yet sharp enough to cut.

She adjusted her mic with a flick, like settling a crown. "This show's always kept it real. I figured I'd return the favor. Clear the air. Since, apparently, I've been living in the fog."

Beside me, Dani's pen hovered mid-note and Mac froze halfway to another sip of coffee, setting his mug down slow. His silence felt heavy.

I leaned in, matching her composure. "We're glad you're here." My voice didn't tremble, though my chest felt tight.

"I wish I could say I receive that, but…" Her teeth flashed, all warmth rehearsed. "Well, my husband Troy and I were discussing you last night."

The air shifted. Silence did not fall. It slammed down and settled heavy. Even Mac's mug made a soft clink that echoed louder than it should have.

"Come again? Your who?"

I blinked once, slow, like the floor had given out but the cameras were still rolling.

She smiled wider, the trap snapping shut. "My husband."

From her Dior tote, she pulled out a white three-ring binder, thick, tabbed, and already screaming drama, each page tucked into a plastic sleeve like evidence in a federal case. She flipped to the first tab labeled *Exhibit A*, revealing a marriage certificate, crisp and notarized.

"Oh God," Dani whispered. "Not the binder."

"Oh yes," LaMya crooned, her smile curved and pleased. "Receipts."

Mac leaned forward slightly, his voice calm. "You brought a binder? Is this standard for all reality shows these days?"

"Brought it for transparency," she said, adjusting her mic as if she were testifying. "We are clearing the air, remember?"

Mac cleared his throat, his tone smooth but curious. "Wait. That says you and Troy Alexander got married six weeks ago. Didn't you two break up last season? I could have sworn there was a whole situation with that fitness trainer. Or was it the producer?"

Dani glanced toward the camera, too quick with her deflection. "Mac, let's not."

LaMya flipped to *Exhibit B*, screenshots cropped tight and highlighted in yellow. "That wasn't really a thing," she said. "That was work."

Mac tilted his head. "Work."

"Yes," she said, nodding too fast. "We were collaborating on something together. A brand… Joggers… You know, athleisure."

Mac's brow lifted slightly. "Joggers?"

"Yes. Joggers. For, uh…"

I couldn't help myself. "When's the launch for said joggers? September, spring, summer… or still pending script approval?"

Dani snorted behind her mug, trying to swallow her laughter.

LaMya blinked once, her smile thinning, but she recovered with a smooth page turn. *Exhibit C.* A photo. Then, from the binder pocket, she slid out a phone. Troy's phone.

"This," she said, unlocking it with practiced ease, "is where it gets good."

My breath caught. The matte case with the small scuff near the corner was familiar. It was the phone he'd said was for work. Then emergencies. Then me. It should not be here, and it should not be in her hand. She entered a passcode that unlocked it like she'd done it countless times before.

She scrolled, her eyes gleaming. "*Still can't believe you wore my hoodie and drank the last mango energy,*" she read aloud.

The monitor glowed with proof as the camera zoomed in behind her. There I was in a pic I remembered him taking in his bathroom, gloss on the counter, bonnet tied, wearing his favorite USC tee. His message flashed on screen, BB. Exactly where she belongs.

The comments flooded the live feed. Hearts. Flames. Popcorn. The binder became her stage, each plastic sleeve a new act. *Exhibit D. Miami receipts.*

"Our honeymoon," she announced, her voice bright. "Brief but beautiful. Miami, before the real trip, where it was just us and sunshine. Turks and Caicos. Private chef, infinity pool, the whole fantasy."

She tilted the phone toward the camera, showing a credit card receipt with my name listed as guest.

Her smile glinted. "It's giving sidepiece. Showing up to our first stop and calling it coincidence? Cute."

I recognized it immediately. The logo. The date. My throat went dry, that slow, sinking heat that starts in your chest and tries to climb. I'd covered scandals for years, but nothing prepared you for starring in one.

It was for the same trip he'd booked weeks before. The same one he said was a brand retreat. He told me to come after press wrapped, that it would be quiet and private, that he wanted to see me off the grid. I believed him. I believed every word.

He said he could not stay overnight because of meetings. He said he would circle back once things calmed down. I'd told myself he was tired, overworked, trying to figure things out. I told myself a lot.

But looking at that screen now, it clicked into place. Those dates were his honeymoon. And I was the layover between his vows and the woman he came home to.

Dani let out a low whistle. "Booked for the weekend after the marriage certificate was signed. Bellamy, you were not outside like you posted that week. You were inside with somebody's fresh-out-the-wrapper husband."

The live chat exploded and filled the control room with its own kind of heat.

LaMya beamed. "When I say my man, I mean it in every freshly inked, legally binding way. He's mine. So back off, you pathetic little thirstbot."

The insult landed rehearsed, like she'd practiced it in a mirror. I stayed still, spine locked, pulse climbing. Every excuse Troy ever gave went through my mind like a bad rerun.

Dani broke the silence. "Miami as a pit stop on the way to the honeymoon," she said, slow and steady. "That's creative. Makes you wonder how many Airbnbs a man can juggle while standing at the altar."

Mac set his mug down, his gaze moving from me to LaMya. "Wild how the man in the middle of all this is the only one who stayed off camera," he said, voice even. "The mess is his, but somehow the women are the ones bleeding for it."

Laughter rippled through the crew, but LaMya's smile tightened.

"Anyways… Bellamy, I guess your little situationship gave this show a bump," she finally said. "Can't knock the hustle. But don't think I won't circle back for repayment for the boost."

I met her gaze. "The show was thriving long before either of you decided attention was currency. But thanks for bringing your contract drama into our studio."

Karen's voice crackled in my earpiece. "Bellamy. Don't say another word."

I stopped listening. When I saw my mom's next message notification pop up, Keep your face calm. People believe what you show them, I flipped the phone over.

I exhaled slowly. "Funny thing about relevance," I said. "You can't fake it forever. Eventually the truth leaks out." My eyes followed the curve of her mouth. "Like expired lip filler."

The crew broke. Dani covered her mouth to hide her laugh. Mac muttered, "We are *live* live."

LaMya leaned back, pretending calm, but her jaw twitched once. Dani gave me that look that meant stop.

I smiled anyway. "You're right," I told her. "It probably did help the show. Whoever planned this must have forgotten I've been producing long enough to spot a setup before the cameras roll."

Her eyes narrowed, just slightly, the first crack in the performance. The crew shifted behind the glass, pretending not to listen but hanging on every word.

"But you made it personal. He told me it was over. Said the two of you were just for the cameras."

LaMya's tone softened, all sugar again. "Oh, I know what he told you. Men love testing out lines with a new sense of charm. Sound familiar? Like what your daddy told your mama back in the day before that little break of theirs turned into an outside baby."

The words hit the soft spot I never protected. For a beat, I couldn't tell if the heat in my chest was rage or shame. Probably both.

Karen's voice cut through the headset, tight and deliberate. "You've already said more than enough. Do *not* respond to that."

I almost listened. Almost. But I knew better than to mistake production notes for protection.

LaMya tilted her head. "Nothing to say? That's new."

There it was. The moment she expected me to fold.

I breathed once. Then again, slow and measured… For a beat I nearly believed I could hold it together. I stared at my phone, hearing one of the many voice notes from my mother in my head: *Do not let anyone play in your face. If they want a show, give them front row.*

The cup gave beneath my grip. The liquid moved before I did. One blink, and it was in the air, tracing a clean, perfect arc across the space between us.

It landed square in the center of her designer white jumpsuit. The collective gasp that followed was pure theater. The horrified crew froze, and the only sound left was the soft drip of smoothie sliding down LaMya's collarbone onto the floor like punctuation.

Karen's voice pierced my headset. "You are so fired!"

I lifted my gaze, my voice calm but quietly lethal. "As long as you're out here lying while cashing those *Glam City* checks, remember this. Recycling storylines might keep you trending, but copying legends will never make you iconic."

LaMya didn't move. She just sat there, drenched in shock and spiked oat milk, her expression frozen somewhere between disbelief and damage control. Beyond the glass, phones rose like a tide, every screen trained on us. There was no delay, no mercy, no room to take it back.

I met her eyes. "Now we're even. Debt resolved."

The studio burned behind me. Sugar, smoke, and the sound of my career catching fire.

I'd always said I wanted my moment. I just never meant as breaking news.

Dani arrived a few minutes later, still on the phone, voice velvet and volume measured. "No, leave the full segment," she said. "The rawness is what sells it. Just cut before the cup hits. Frame it as emotion under pressure."

She listened for a moment, her expression smooth and unreadable. "Yes, make sure the clip posts first. Everyone else can react to us. Don't let someone with a screengrab control the views for what's ours." Her eyes flicked toward me, soft but assessing. "We'll say she's resting and reflecting. That always plays well."

She ended the call, slid into the booth across from me, and gave a small, assessing smile. "Tequila?"

I nodded. The bartender set down two shots like he'd seen this movie before.

Dani raised hers. "To surviving another spin cycle."

I lifted mine. "Clearly to the spin."

The burn was clean, almost grounding. For a few seconds, neither of us spoke.

"You've been suspended," she said finally, like it was a scheduling update.

I could break down anybody else's story without blinking, but the second mine unraveled, I couldn't find the words for it. "You already know?"

"They pulled the team into an emergency meeting the minute you were escorted out. Karen couldn't even look me in the eye. It's temporary, at least on paper."

"So…" I kept my tone steady. "Is it really suspended, or fired?"

"Actually, HR is calling it administrative leave, but basically it all means the same thing. From what I heard, they're still deciding, but we already know Karen's out for blood."

"Figures."

She lifted her drink, tapping her nail against the glass like she was choosing her words.

"It's crazy… the network already asked if I could take the lead on your morning block this week. Just until they figure out the fallout." She smiled like it was nothing, like she didn't hear how that sounded. "You know how they get when the heat shifts."

"Right." I nodded once, keeping my face still. "Of course they did."

Dani studied me the way stylists study before and after photos, eyes curious but detached. "You really threw it."

"With conviction. You were obviously there and witnessed it."

Her mouth curved. "At least you hit the mark. I ducked, by the way, so I missed her reaction."

I was on the cusp of laughing, but it caught somewhere between pride and nausea. "Always thinking ahead."

"Somebody has to." She sipped her drink, eyes never leaving mine. "You do know this'll trend for days, right? The network's pretending they're shocked, but they've already clipped the footage for engagement."

"That tracks." They were counting ad dollars off the same mess they were pretending to be disgusted by. Nothing said corporate loyalty like using my mess for clicks while HR drafted my exit plan. Go figure. "That's who you were on the phone with, though, right? Helping to walk them through posting your good side?"

She smiled, but it was weak. "One of the interns working social media wasn't sure what to do… I just gave them some direction, since everyone else is running around trying to figure out what to do next."

Above the bar, the TV flipped from local news to sports

highlights. And there he was—Cole Howard.

He rose mid-play, sweat bright along his hairline, jaw tight with that carved-from-stone focus that made him the league's quiet storm. The shot left his hand clean, net only. He held the follow-through a second too long before pivoting on defense, like he was teaching the game patience. Six foot nine. Built like a magnificent structure. Shoulders you could lean on and still lose your balance. His skin glowed warm under the lights, rich brown and beautiful. That trimmed beard, that jawline, those eyes that measured everything and reacted to nothing. And I hated him for all of it.

Even through bar light static, he radiated control. He was a man who never had to raise his voice to remind people he was the center of gravity. I also hated that I noticed.

Something in his stillness jabbed at me, sharp and unwelcome. I didn't care why. I just wanted it gone.

Dani followed my gaze. "Oh, look. Your favorite scandal."

"Not mine. Just the one that paid the bills."

She laughed. "Come on. You practically broke the internet when his marriage fell apart. Laura Howard crying on daytime TV? His team threatening to sue? It was gold."

"I reported the facts."

"Sure. Facts that turned the Black love prototype into trending topic carnage. They were Steph and Ayesha until you hit upload. Then it was Ciara and Future before prayer."

On screen, Cole answered calmly, face carved from composure. The reporter kept poking, looking for a crack that didn't come. Something pulled tight in my chest. He didn't even flinch anymore. Maybe that was what surviving looked like when you'd run out of places to hide.

Dani noticed. "Don't tell me you're feeling sorry for him."

"I'm not."

"Good. Because while you're benched, he's back on top. Player of the Month. A whole redemption arc. You can't script that kind of symmetry." She said it like she was pitching it to the trades. "Full circle, babe."

"You say that like it's cute."

"Just poetic." Her smile glinted. "He's trending for a comeback. You're trending for a collapse. Feels… cosmic."

I gave her a long look. "You sound almost happy about that."

"I'm realistic. Some of us play chess. Some of us get played on camera."

That landed, and I tossed a few bills on the table while reaching for my bag. "Thanks for the pep talk."

"Don't do that," she said lightly. Her smile faltered. "Don't make me the bad guy. I'm just trying to make light of the situation. You think you're the only one catching heat?"

"I think you gave someone the match." A flicker crossed her face. I leaned back, taking my time. "One of the *Peach City* producers just hit me up before you got here. It's someone I've known since their first season. They mentioned the planning of today's little ambush was actually caught on film during LaMya's girls' trip earlier this month. And guess who happened to be her plus-one… and auditioning friend to the show… A bachelorette trip to Tulum sound familiar?"

Dani's face went perfectly still.

I let the pause stretch, my voice low. "You really thought it wouldn't circle back to me?"

"It wasn't like that," she said quickly, all soft denial and press-release tone. "It was supposed to be harmless. They asked about you, I answered. That's it."

"'Harmless,'" I repeated, tasting the word like something expired. "You call it harmless, but somehow LaMya ends up walking into the studio mic'ed for war. That doesn't happen by accident."

Her expression pinched. "I didn't know she'd pull that stunt. I just mentioned you two when we were filming, that's all. She was telling stories, I was laughing, it was content. I didn't think—"

"No," I cut in. "You didn't."

The words came out low, steady as I added, "You thought it was cute. You thought being seen with her made you look connected. You didn't stop to think who she'd weaponize it against."

Dani parted her lips, caught between defense and guilt. "You're overreacting. And if you're gonna be mad, start with the man who played you."

Her voice wavered at the end, thin and stretched, like she wasn't as sure as she wanted me to believe.

"I'm reacting," I said, leaning in, voice cool as glass. "Big difference. And trust me, everyone who deserves a hit is getting one, including the man who tried to make me content, whether it was on my set or hers. Don't think I don't know you've also been cozying up to Karen a lot more these days."

She looked away, and for a split second, I saw it, the calculation behind the calm, the moment she filed me under collateral damage. That was all the confirmation I needed.

Her phone buzzed against the table again, face down, the vibration slicing through what was left of our friendship.

"You'll land on your feet," she says finally, slipping her poise back on like lip gloss. "You always do. Just… keep your legs closed to married men, even if the marriage license appears to be scripted, then you never would've been in this little predicament in the first place."

She said it like a woman trying to hit something before it hit her back. I felt the sting she wanted, then it faded. She didn't get that part of me. I stood, slow and deliberate.

"You should save that line for *Peach City*," I said. "They love secondhand dialogue." I stared at her for a long, squirm-inducing beat. "You came here for the tea, not the hangover."

She shrugged, unbothered. "Can't it be both?"

That was it. The moment everything inside me settled. The math clicked. I stood, sliding cash onto the table. "Here's the thing, Dani. You're not my crisis team. You *are* the crisis."

Her eyes flashed, but she didn't argue. Her mouth tightened, and still she smiled, too polished to let the mask slip. "You'll call when you calm down."

It was cruel, but it rang with insecurity more than confidence.

"No," I said, turning toward the door. "I won't."

I smoothed my sleeve, giving her a look reserved for people who mistake proximity for loyalty.

"Enjoy your audition. You've been rehearsing long enough."

She was already reaching for her phone as I walked away.

Chapter 2

COLE

MORNINGS WERE THE ONLY TIME I TRUSTED MYSELF, before the chatter crept in, before the cameras twisted silence into a story, before practice stripped me down to nothing but memory and muscle.I learned the hard way that silence kept me standing, even if the world decided to turn it into something else.

It was just me then. The hush of this high rise I'd chosen to keep me above the noise below. The ache in my shoulders reminding me I was not twenty anymore. Stillness I couldn't seem to find anywhere else.

I moved barefoot across the hardwood, the cool pressing into my feet, grounding me in the moment. At six foot nine, I had never blended in. Not on the street. Not on the court. Not even in my own apartment building. Broad chest, heavy arms, legs built for a load I'd never asked to bear. People saw me and measured what I could do for them, not who I was when the lights were off. My jaw tightened before I caught it, an old habit that still answered to pressure before I did.

The bathroom mirror fogged from the shower, the edges blurred like even my reflection was not ready to come into focus. I wiped a streak clear with my hand. The taper was still clean, beard lined even, cut the way barbers liked to take credit for, though I knew it was just bone doing its job. My body still looked the part with shoulders squared, chest solid, arms and legs thick from seasons of wear. I could still pass for the man the league drafted, even if the years since had written their own story in the tightness of my knees and the heaviness behind my eyes. They had grown tired, those eyes. Set deep and steady, holding more than they ever said. I pulled on sweats and a hoodie, then glanced back at the mirror satisfied with the way I planned to step into the world.

The kitchen pulled me in the way it always did. I cracked two eggs into a bowl and hit them with salt and pepper before whisking. And yes, always before. I did not care what anyone online swore by. A splash of heavy cream followed and I whisked slow, letting the motion settle me. Cooking was the one place I did not rush. If the heat was too high, you scorched the edges before the center set. If you stopped stirring too long, it fell apart. You learned to move just enough to keep it together. Just enough to guide it toward what it was supposed to be.

The eggs hit the pan with a hiss, soft but grounding. I folded them from the edges toward the center, patient and careful, as if they would punish me for getting it wrong. My teammates would laugh if they saw me like this, treating breakfast like it was game film, but food did not lie. Pay attention and it rewarded you. Ignore it and you were left with scraps.

I plated the eggs, ate in silence, and rinsed the pan clean. The ritual did not erase the ache in my chest, but it gave it shape. Something solid before the day started chipping away at me.

The elevator mirrors caught me from every angle on the ride down. Hood up, jaw set hard, eyes fixed on the floor. I looked like a man expecting impact.

Daryl nodded from the concierge desk when I stepped into the lobby. He'd been on mornings and picking up the occasional night shift since I moved in, steady and dependable, without the need to be reminded that showing up counted. I nodded back, making a mental note to bring him something next week. Maybe sweet potato cheesecake if I could get the texture right.

Outside, San Antonio felt clean and crisp with fall air, every breath cutting through the fog in my chest. The streets were quiet, joggers pacing steady, a cyclist rounding the corner with head bent low. I shoved my hands into my pockets and started the few blocks toward Jawn, the city still soft with morning.

Jawn was hallowed in its own right. Nina had made it that way. The forest-green awning stretched wide above the entrance. Inside, the music always told the truth, the pastry case always emptied early, and the regulars guarded their corners like it mattered. Nina moved through it all with the ease of someone running a world built on trust.

She spotted me as soon as I stepped in, her grin already cutting through the morning. "You actually slept? What was it, three hours? Four?"

I shrugged and slid onto my usual stool. "Don't gas me."

She slid a cortado across the counter, almond milk, no sugar. Exactly the way I liked it. Jill Scott faded into Snoh Aalegra overhead, brass giving way to bass, comfort giving way to tension the way the best stories did.

For a while, I just sat in it. The chatter in the back. The hiss of steam from the espresso machine. Nina's easy movement behind the counter. It all folded into something that felt like sanctuary.

Habit won. I unlocked my phone and notifications immediately flooded the screen. Articles, mentions, reminders of the version of me the internet refused to let die. I swiped past them and opened the account that still felt like mine, the burner one under ChefSwishWhisk.

Last night's post filled the screen. Cast-iron skillet cornbread, honey butter spilling into the corners. Simple, clean, everything in its place.

Comments moved fast beneath it, arguments about sugar and strangers begging for recipes. Then her name appeared, calm in the middle of it all.

You expect me to scroll past this and stay virtuous?

A smile threatened, and I let half of it through. She always wrote like that, playful and quick, as if her sentences were balancing on a breath. She did not care where I played or what I had lost. She only cared about what I made.

I did not answer. Not yet. I scrolled back instead and found one of her older comments. *Nothing brings the past forward faster than a good meal.*

She was right. She usually was. And I still did not know if that made her risky or necessary.

The TVs above the bar flickered, pulling eyes upward. A morning show clip for *Wake Up, Let's Brew* rolled. The banner at the bottom screamed in red, *Radio Host Fired Live on Air.*

Then I spotted Bellamy Barnes. It wasn't the version I remembered, the one who could slice a man open with a clickbait and call it journalism. This version looked stripped down, human under the lights, wide-eyed but steady.

Her skin held warmth the cameras could not dim, deep brown and luminous even under the glare. Her features were small but certain, full lips pressed tight, lashes low, eyes piercing enough to cut through humiliation. She was beautiful, undeniably, with that quiet kind of beauty that did not ask for permission. And I noticed, like a man who was supposed to know better.

Even with her world unraveling, she did not fold. She stood square, mouth set, daring the room not to look away. Then I caught it, the flicker. That instant where she decided she would not give them the break they came for.

I knew that look because I'd worn it.

Nina glanced from the TV to me, eyes narrow over her mug. "That her? The jawn who let your business slip while the mic was still hot?"

"Yeah." The word landed clean.

At the window, a group of college girls laughed too loud. Nina cut them a look and the noise died instantly. She did not even raise her voice.

I stared into what was left of my cortado. "Karma's got a wicked crossover."

Nina did not blink. "You sure it is karma? Or the one woman you swore didn't matter still getting under your skin?"

I did not answer because she was not wrong. I'd noticed. Not just the scene playing out in the highlight clip, not just the mess on LaMya's clothes, but Bellamy herself. The way she lifted her chin against humiliation, the way she refused to shrink. The part of me that should have enjoyed it didn't. That part was the problem.

So I set the cup down harder than I mean to and let the silence close it out. On my way out, I held the door for a woman pushing a stroller. She thanked me without recognition, and I nodded.

The cameras never caught that. Not the small moments. Not the quiet ones. They only caught the glare, the clenched jaw, the still frame they could twist into proof of who they wanted me to be. No thanks to Bellamy Barnes.

That was who I was to them now. A threat mid-frame. Maybe I'd let it stick because it was easier than reminding people I was still human.

It was the fourth quarter with just under two minutes on the clock. The scoreboard glared down, unflinching, a reminder of how quickly everything could tilt. The crowd swelled in one relentless roar, pressing into my chest, into my lungs, into the worn seams of my body. I'd been on the floor more than thirty minutes, every cut dragging heavier than the last, every breath scraped raw, but I kept my eyes on the wing.

The guard crouched in front of me was young, spring still fresh in his legs. His hands twitched, too eager, his body leaning too close, as if crowding me would break me. He didn't understand that adrenaline left my game years ago. This was footwork now. Angles. The patience of a man who had already paid for his mistakes.

I lowered into him, took one sharp dribble, then dropped my shoulder and slipped past, the collision glancing off me like it never had a chance. The whistle shrilled.

At the line, the sounds of fanfare didn't vanish, but it thinned, enough for me to claim a small circle of air for myself. My chest expanded once, the breath controlled, the release steady. The ball rolled off my fingers, pure, clean. The first one landed. Then the second. I let them fall without flourish. No celebration, no grin at the bench. Just the execution I had clawed back to with every sleepless night and every headline that swore I was finished.

The arena exploded, but it felt distant, like applause at the end of a film I sat through without being in the cast.

The buzzer sounded, sealing the win. Teammates slapped my shoulders, coaches nodded, fans rose in a wave, but the weight in my chest remained. Victories didn't always loosen what you carried in. Sometimes they just marked time.

In the locker room the air hung heavy, a mix of liniment and sweat cooling too quickly on skin still pulsing from the game. My chest hadn't settled, not because of the minutes logged on the floor, but because of the reporters pressing closer, cameras already recording, microphones angled like weapons, waiting for me to slip. They circled the edges of the room as if it belonged to them, patient and certain, drawing the focus of players who only wanted to breathe before the next storm began.

I leaned back into my stall, the towel draped across my shoulders still damp, and lowered my eyes to my phone. A notification lit the screen, one new DM that made my mouth twitch against my will.

@BeautyIzHerName
I almost burned my kitchen down trying
to make peach cobbler. That feels like a sign. Right?

We'd found each other by accident months ago in a thread about men who owned Le Creuset, and what started as a few harmless jokes about seasoning cast iron turned into late-night exchanges about food, memory, and comfort you could only create in a kitchen. Somewhere between the pictures of Sunday dinners and arguments about internal temperatures for meat, she'd become the one person who never asked about basketball, never mentioned the trade, never tried to link my name to anything other than the dishes I put on a plate.

With her, I was not Cole Howard the trade, the divorce, the man the internet had turned into fodder. With her, I was only the guy behind the stove and what it meant when a meal felt like home. That was the appeal. She was mystery, levity, a part of my world that still belonged only to me.

I started typing, the phone balanced in my hand, every letter a small release.

@ChefSwishWhisk
You saying you almost set the place
on fire just for dessert?

The reply came fast enough to make me smile, quick and unguarded, like she'd been waiting for me.

@BeautyIzHerName
Reckless for cobbler seems on brand.

Don't judge me.

Before I could type again, a voice cut in.

"Cole."

The sound of my name pulled me back. Janelle, the team's publicist, stood closer than I realized, her voice pitched low so only I could hear.

"Not now," I answered, eyes still on the screen.

Her reply sliced cleaner. "You're going to want to shut this down. Now."

That made me lift my head. One of the beat writers had pushed in too close, his voice raised just enough to claim the room.

"Howard, any thoughts on that essay your ex wrote last year? Especially now that your name's making the rounds again?"

The question cut through the noise, designed to hit a bruise that never healed. Everyone remembered that piece, two thousand words in a glossy magazine, branded as a meditation on love and loss but really a manifesto designed to reframe her betrayal as mine. She painted herself as a woman abandoned, spinning long paragraphs about being married to a man too cold, too driven, too unreachable, while carefully leaving out the part where she had been the one stepping outside our vows.

She'd never used my name, but she didn't have to. The details were precise enough to hang me in public. We had once been the golden couple of the league. The example. The marriage that teams pointed to when they wanted proof that family and basketball could coexist at the highest level. She'd dismantled all of that in a single article, turning her betrayal into my failure and leaving me as the cautionary tale.

Once the piece hit its second page, my face was everywhere. Headlines. Think pieces. Podcasts debating how a man could fail his wife so completely. She turned her infidelity into my indictment.

It gutted me for months. Not because I cared about her words. I had already learned what they were worth. It was because the world swallowed them whole. Strangers nodded along like it was scripture. Fans debated my value off the court. Sponsors hesitated. And the version of me she created lingered longer than the truth ever could.

The reporter knew all of that. That was why he asked.

I did not blink. I did not shift. I gave them nothing, but the silence rippled outward, pressing into every corner of the room. Ronan's eyes found mine, steady, a captain's gaze, a reminder that someone in here still believed me even when the outside world didn't. The rookies stalled mid-motion, jerseys half on, sneakers untied, realizing this was bigger than basketball.

I breathed once, deep enough to keep the anger down, and keep my voice even. "Not today."

Janelle clapped her hands once, loud enough to make the walls cringe. "That's it. Any more goes through the press room."

The reporters filed out, too slow, dragging their cameras, still angling their heads like they expected me to break before the door closed, but I didn't.

When the door shut, I let my shoulders drop a fraction and looked down again at my phone. Her message was still there, steady on the screen, reminding me that not everything had to bleed.

I erased what I'd started and typed again.

@ChefSwishWhisk

Let me guess. You tried to multitask, huh?
Next time just hit me up before you light the stove...
or test out some random recipe you probably found on TikTok.

The pause stretched, then her reply arrived.

@BeautyIzHerName

Ouch. How did you guess the source?

@BeautyIzHerName

I'll take that as an offer to supervise when I do.
I might even share if you play your cards right.

This time the smile didn't fight me. It came easy, the first one I'd felt all night.

The taco spot Ronan picked sat a few blocks from Vantage Arena, tucked in a worn strip between a pawn shop and a cell phone store with bars on the windows. The air outside still carried traces of the game, that buzz of traffic and leftover adrenaline that followed us home whether we wanted it or not. You didn't find places like this online because nobody needed to review it. You came once, you came back.

We hit it after most home games when the win was good enough to celebrate but not loud enough for cameras. Cheap food. No press. No fans waiting with phones out. Just space to breathe.

Ronan ducked through the doorway first, tall enough to brush the frame. He held it open for the rookies, then for the two security guys trailing behind us. They peeled off to a booth near the door, quiet and alert, part of the furniture but always watching the exits. The smell of grilled meat, onions, and cilantro clung to the air thick as steam, and the jukebox played Tejano songs that sounded older than the paint on the walls.

Nico and Javon followed, still wired from the game. Both twenty-one and convinced the world belonged to them. The dynamic duo was all sneakers and confidence and had no clue how fast a spotlight can burn through a career. Nico grinned at the hostess like charm was his birthright. Javon trailed behind, hoodie up, mouthing lyrics to a song only he could hear. Their laughter hit the room first, big and careless. For a brief moment it practically felt good, being surrounded by something that light.

I took the corner seat, back to the wall out of habit. The server didn't bother with menus. Everyone here knew what they wanted before walking in. Plastic cups of horchata, a couple of bottled sodas, and four plastic tumblers of water loaded with ice cubes landed on the table. A tray of tacos followed right after, steaming and perfect.

"Coach saw that dunk?" Nico asked, reaching for a lime.

Ronan didn't look up. "He saw you forget the play before it."

Javon barked a laugh, grease shining on his fingers. "Coach already clipped that for film, bro."

Their energy rolled between them, loose and easy. I watched it from a distance that probably only existed in my head. I used to sound like that once, before every word I said could be turned into a rumors or a meme. Before a mistake could stretch into a month long conversation about who I was as a man.

I nearly smiled. Then Javon spoke again, his mouth full of taco. "Yo, that girl who threw the smoothie? You see that clip?"

Nico jumped in. "Yeah, yeah… Bellamy Barnes. She's the one who—" He stopped short, too late. His eyes flicked toward me.

The table went still. My fingers curled once against the edge before I made them still. Music drifted from the back, kids laughed at a booth nearby, and somewhere, a blender roared to life. Inside our corner, everything froze.

Ronan didn't lift his head. "Eat," he said.

They did. Quickly.

I took another slow bite, the silence thick enough to chew. *The one who threw the smoothie.* Like it was funny. Like she hadn't helped turn my life into a train wreck once upon a time. Her name scraped at something I had stopped trying to numb.

Ronan leaned back and said quietly, low enough for my ears only, "They're good kids."

"I know."

"They talk because they don't know," he said. "They don't know what it's like to lose everything in public and still have to show up like nothing cracked."

He was right, but that didn't mean I wanted to hear it. My ex wrote her version. Bellamy Barnes made sure everyone heard it. Different players, same game.

"You've been quiet for months. Not focused quiet… shut-in quiet." He didn't look at me when he said it. He never had to. "Open something up before it sets in."

I didn't argue. No point in it.

The conversation at the table picked back up in small bursts. Nico asked the waitress about the salsa. Javon swore he could taste the difference between the red and green just by smell. Ronan paid the check before I even noticed, a quiet move that meant he was giving me an exit.

Outside, the night pressed in thick and humid. The smell of carne asada drifted from the open door as we stepped out. Ronan's bodyguards flanked the entrance, giving us the illusion of privacy in a life that never really had it.

"She wrote her story," he said, voice low. "You don't have to keep living in it."

I didn't answer. There wasn't anything left to say. He clapped my shoulder once before walking off. The rookies were already laughing again by the time they reached their cars, their voices bouncing off the concrete until the doors shut and the sound vanished.

I stayed behind a moment longer. The reflection in the taco shop window caught my face and the glow of the streetlight behind me. For a second it looked like I was still sitting there at the table, still stuck in that moment. Then the glass shifted, and I was gone. Just the streetlight, the night air, and the quiet truth that no matter how far I moved, some stories found a way to follow.

Chapter 3

BELLAMY

IF THERE IS ANYTHING MORE HUMILIATING THAN BEING turned into a trending topic for all the wrong reasons in real time, it is what follows in the weeks after, when the noise fades, but the waiting starts. The calls. The meetings. The polite "we're still assessing" emails that sound like lullabies for your career. Everyone pretending it's still a conversation when the decision was made the moment Karen and Dani threw me under the bus live on air.

For weeks, it dragged. The public relations team wanted distance while legal wanted quiet and my agent wanted updates I didn't have. The network called it a "review period." I called it what it was. Purgatory with Wi-Fi.

When the paperwork finally came, it was all precision and pretense. Termination "for cause" tucked neatly between paragraphs about brand integrity and public trust and signed off with polite signatures. Phrases like "failure to uphold company values" that read like someone trying to sanitize a hit job.

My badge stopped working before the ink dried. The hired car service disappeared from the curb the next morning. IT folded my inbox into a polite goodbye faster than Kehlani could remix the song again and replaced it with a legal notice about preserving records, like I was evidence in my own crime scene.

By then, my agent had already softened her tone to something that sounded like regret. "It's the clause, Bellamy," she said, gentle like she was reading from a script. It wasn't personal, it was policy, but it still hit like betrayal.

The first week I kept waiting for someone to call. The second, I stopped checking my phone. By the third, I'd stopped believing I'd walk back into that studio. When the courier finally arrived with the thick, heavy, official envelope, I already knew what was inside. Every word leaned on urgency, like it had been rehearsed.

Return all property immediately.
Termination effective upon receipt.

And just like that, the silence became final.

The notice to vacate came next. Not thirty days. *Three.* Printed thin and taped eye level right on my door. Most of my neighbors walked by pretending not to see, but the woman down the hall didn't bother pretending at all.

Inside, the corporate apartment still looked the same, but it wasn't mine anymore. It felt like a set after closing night. Props left behind, spotlight off, and the audience had gone home. And outside, the industry had already moved on to its next scandal.

And right on cue, my parents decided I'd run out of time to dodge them after word spread quickly about my termination becoming official.

The names of my divorced-twice-from-each-other-but-still-somehow-in-sync parents flashed across the screen like a reunion alert for the last two surviving members of a nineties boy band.

They only teamed up for two reasons, when they thought I was spiraling or when they were flirting with the idea of round three. Judging by Mom's calm concern and Dad's slightly unhinged grin, I was praying to Black Jesus it was not the latter.

Their faces filled the screen side by side, perfectly framed like the opening shot of a sitcom no one asked to reboot.

On the left was my mom, Jacqueline Barnes. Elegant as ever, she was seated at her dining table in San Diego, delicately spooning acai and granola like she was in a soft-focus commercial for grace under pressure. Her skin glowed like self-care personified. Her ponytail was pulled so sleek it could anchor a yacht, and even her activewear looked expensive. Stud earrings caught the morning light just right. She was composed, centered, and the human embodiment of "I told you so."

On the right sat my father, *the* Terrence Barnes, in full contrast. He leaned back in a Nike tech fleece, grinning like a man who still got recognized in airports. A plate of pizza sat in front of him. His goatee was trimmed sharp, his bracelet caught the light, and I could already tell he was about to say something that would make Mom sigh.

It still blew my mind that they'd met on the set of one of his early music videos. One of the ones with rented drop tops, pastel furs, and a woman dramatically packing her bags in slow motion while fake rain poured down like heartbreak on cue. She was supposed to be an extra. He was supposed to show up on time. Neither did what they were told. By the end of the week they were writing songs together and rewriting each other's lives.

Now, decades later, they were the most coordinated divorced couple I knew. Still finishing each other's sentences and still united when it came to managing me like a lifelong group project.

"Belle, sweetheart, you can always come home," Mom said, voice dripping with concern and motherly authority. But despite decades of perfecting her vocal cadence, the Carolina roots still slipped through. Thick, rich, and impossible to miss.

I suppressed a sigh and caught my reflection in the corner of the screen. Today I looked like life hit rewind and forgot to press play again. Hoodie slipping, hair undecided, and peach cobbler cooling in the skillet in front of me while I eat around the burned edges. It wasn't glamorous, but right now, survival rarely was.

I rolled my neck and rubbed my shoulder. "Mom, I'm not twelve. I don't need to come home."

The last time I did, I'd left with a migraine, a suitcase full of Daddy's old tour merch, and zero interest in repeating the experience. Mom called it a cleansing ritual, insisting the shirts had to be the hell up outta there. Her words, not mine. Whatever Dad did to trigger that purge, I knew better than to ask.

"You don't have to do this alone," she said, spooning up another bite of antioxidant righteousness while dissecting my life between mouthfuls.

Before Mom could launch into her usual speech about how home was a "safe space," the other half of the screen lit up with my dad, mid-blow on a slice of pizza. His voice barreled through the speaker, full of that over-the-top energy he always brought. "Babygirl, forget your mom's house. You need to stay with me. Guest room's already set up, just waiting on you."

I nearly snorted. "Guest room? You mean the futon in your home office that's buried under crates of vinyl?"

Dad still had that bad-boy appeal that made him a legend in the nineties and a headache for the industry. That swagger hadn't dimmed, even if his career had, long before TikTok unearthed his catalog and gave it new life. His bone structure and captivating bedroom eyes were the same ones that had left women fainting at his concerts, unless they were busy tossing Victoria's Secret thongs on stage. He always acted like he was one phone call away from a comeback tour, especially now that influencers kept tagging him in old clips like they were trying to resurrect the menace he used to be.

"Terrence, she's not staying there," Mom snapped, her tone

flat and final. "Especially not on that damn Black Friday futon you bought ten years ago."

"It's a top-tier futon, Jackie. And if I recall, you didn't have a single complaint when we broke that motherf—"

"Terrence," Mom warned, tone flat enough to kill a signal.

I didn't need to see it to know he was grinning. And I could already hear my therapist calculating the next round of copays.

Let's get one thing straight: money and fame don't live in the same tax bracket. My sibling and I had learned early how to smile through conversations that made it sound like my dad had yacht money sitting in the bank. Truth was, he was more "comfortable suburb" rich with royalty checks still coming in but not Scrooge McDuck diving into gold coins. Think somewhere between Martha Stewart fresh out and stirring mashed potatoes with Snoop rebuilding her empire and that *White Chicks* moment when the Vandergeld sisters realize they're "MC Hammer broke."

Fame never really left our family; it just switched lanes. Daddy still got name-dropped at brunch spots he hadn't visited in years. My aunt treated boundaries like gossip, and my cousins turned every gathering into a family reunion special nobody filmed. But people who believed popularity equaled wealth always assumed we were rolling in it.

My mother, on the other hand, had a presence that settled a room just by how she walked into it. After the last divorce, when they finally admitted that the second marriage had been born out of surviving her breast cancer together more than true compatibility, she'd traded Atlanta humidity for West Coast calm and moved to San Diego. She said the weather made her joints kinder and her patience longer.

Daddy, meanwhile, "retreated to Birmingham for creative clarity," which was adorable and only half true. He wanted cheaper rent, sweeter tea, and the casual recognition of getting stopped in aisle five like it was still 1998. He'd FaceTime me from the cereal row so strangers could say, "Your daddy's a legend," and I'd roll my eyes while grinning because we both knew he lived for that.

"Belle needs peace," he said, gesturing toward the screen like this was a debate. "Real peace. Not one of your cleanses or some damn goat yoga on a canoe."

I pinched the bridge of my nose, tension already blooming at my temples. This was exactly what I'd expected. I sent a quick SOS text to my sibling, hoping they'd come through with just the excuse I needed to break free.

"Oh, grow up, Terrence. I asked you to try paddleboard yoga once. Once, Terrence. And only because it was my birthday." Mom sighed and looked straight at me, carefully avoiding Dad's exaggerated eye roll. "Sweetie, I know you're overwhelmed, but running to your father's won't fix anything. What you need is a plan."

Did I mention my mama once took a life-coaching course? Never finished it, but that didn't stop her from tossing around her half-earned wisdom like she had letters after her name.

I sank deeper into the couch cushions, the weight of the day pressing into my spine. For a week, I'd avoided packing, knowing the boot was inevitable while mourning the life I'd built in this sterile corporate apartment. Now, with two days left, I was scrambling to get it all into storage and pretend I had next steps. Each box felt heavier than it should, like I was packing away every regret alongside my air fryer and old bodycon dresses that deep down I knew I'd never wear again.

How had I let this happen? Worse, how had I let *him* happen?

Troy had mastered the choreography of manipulation. Every conversation had a purpose; every touch carried subtext. I used to think that meant we understood each other. What it really meant was that he knew how to make his version of the story feel like the truth. Once I recognized the pattern it was too late. I'd already memorized my part as the girlfriend who mistook performance for partnership.

My laptop chimed again from the cluttered coffee table with another round of unread alerts flashing across the screen. The gossip sites hadn't missed a beat, and neither had Threads. Every post picked at the scab, twisting the narrative until even I'd started to question it. I knew what had happened, but there was still that voice, low and mean, asking if I'd brought this on myself.

Dad's voice cut through, pulling me back to the room. "Bellamy, I'm serious. I know a lawyer. We'll sue. Shut this whole thing down. Make 'em pay for dragging your name."

Sue? I blinked, realizing I'd missed the last few minutes of his rant. Leave it to my father to think the solution to a PR stunt was suing the entire internet.

Mom rolled her eyes with the patience of someone who'd survived this cycle more than once. "Terrence, she doesn't need a lawyer. What she needs is a new direction. A fresh start. And that's here, with me, in San Diego."

Her voice smoothed into the background, calm and clipped, as I wrapped another picture frame in packing paper. Around me, the apartment had already started to feel like it belonged to someone else. The framed snapshots of my old radio crew, the celebrities I'd interviewed, the glass plaques I used to display like armor bubble-wrapped, sealed, and stuffed into boxes labeled "Misc." Even the apartment itself, once a flex, now felt like a stage after closing night. It was giving empty, echoing, and drop-the-curtain over.

Outside the window, Atlanta stretched wide, pretending not to notice the fall. This city used to be my empire. My playground. Now, it was a cage. The weight of it all pressed down on me, and I couldn't stop wondering how I'd gone from morning radio's rising star to… this.

I pressed a strip of tape across a box marked "Trash" filled with Troy's things, briefly considering dropping it all on his doorstep tomorrow. It would be petty, deliciously so. But I hesitated, picturing him catching me in the act unwashed, underdressed, and nowhere near the woman I used to be. If I was going to let go, it needed to look effortless, not desperate.

Mom's voice returned to the foreground, steady and coaxing. "Bellamy, do you really have to move out so quickly? Can't we extend it another month?"

"No, legally they don't have to."

On screen, her face was a careful composition of concern and restraint. A look only mothers perfected. "Take a breath. Come home for a little while, then. I insist."

Mom was not one to make suggestions. She made declarations dressed as concern. I tried to keep my tone neutral when I responded, "Mom, I'm fine. Really."

Dad leaned closer, his face filling the screen with that familiar, unwavering warmth. "Babygirl, let your old man step in. Guest room's ready. I even got a new grill set up—"

"Terrence," Mom snapped, cutting clean through his pitch. "Belle doesn't need barbecue. She needs an action plan."

I reached for the tangled cords of my portable studio, the same ones I used to pack for gigs, live remotes, and last-minute bookings. Every mic and crumpled show rundown felt heavier now. Like proof of a life I'd built with my bare hands, slipping through them anyway.

Just as I started winding the cables, Dad's voice cut in loud, animated, and clearly not talking to me. He was staring at the second phone in his lap, the one he changed numbers on more often than his passwords. The one he swore was for "business," even though the whole family knew better. TJ and I called it the Bat Phone. Mom called it his ho hotline.

"Jackie, our daughter is a *mee-mee*!"

The hell? I froze, a power cord sliding from my fingers. "A what now?"

Dad's face filled the screen, flushed and wild-eyed. "A *mee-mee*, Bellamy! People are laughing at you on the internet! They're making these little… clips! Your face is all over them!"

On Mom's side of the screen, she was sipping from her favorite mug, eyes closed like she was praying for strength. Not the heartfelt silent prayer Shanice would sing about, and it was definitely not giving Johnny Gill energy.

"Terrence, it's called a meme. And Bellamy is not one. You're being dramatic."

"No, Jackie, I'm not!" Dad shouted, waving his phone like evidence in a courtroom. "These little videos are everywhere! On the 'Gram! On the TikToks!"

"The TikToks," I repeated under my breath, trying not to laugh.

"And Facebook! Let me check my Pinterest," he added, like that sealed it. "Bellamy is going viral for all the wrong reasons. She's a *mee-mee* now!"

Mom didn't even open her eyes. "Whatever you say, Teddy Riley."

"It's not funny, Jackie!" he barked. "This is serious. People think they can just tarnish our daughter's name with these… internet shenanigans!"

"Shenanigans," Mom echoed, dry as sandpaper. "Terrence, go smoke a blunt or something and calm down. Bellamy will be fine."

"I don't need no damned weed. I need to save my daughter's reputation!"

"Dad, relax," I said, keeping my voice steady and just thankful she hadn't recommended an edible, because my nerves couldn't deal with my dad high off a gummy right now. "It's just a few of them. They'll be forgotten by Thursday."

"That's what they said about who bit Beyoncé," he muttered darkly, disappearing from the screen.

Mom and I locked eyes and both lost it.

"Jackie!" he bellowed from somewhere off screen. "This isn't funny! Our daughter is getting dragged through the mud, and you're laughing? We need a press conference. We need Gayle!"

Mom exhaled slowly and set her mug down with a controlled thud. "Terrence, do you hear yourself? You're talking about viral clips, not a federal indictment. The last thing Bellamy needs is you storming the gates like some Nino Brown vigilante. You're going to make it worse."

He reappeared in the frame with megachurch-bishop-level intensity. "You don't see Beyoncé getting turned into a one of these clips, do you? No! Because she's managed properly!"

"Dad, stop," I said, grabbing another box of old show promos. "Beyoncé has been memed a thousand times. This isn't a scandal. It's just the internet doing what it does."

"It's character assassination!" he boomed, fingers flying across his phone. "These little internet gremlins think it's funny to mock my babygirl. Well, I'm not laughing. And neither should you!"

My phone buzzed with three, maybe four new messages from the family group chat. Dad was dropping links like we were on a press tour.

"Terrence, stop flooding the chat," Mom snapped. "No one wants to see this mess."

"This is serious!" he insisted, ignoring her completely. "We'll call a press conference. Set the record straight. I still have connections. The Barnes name means something. We'll fix it."

"Dad," I sighed, tossing a stack of old headshots into a box, "you can't sue the internet. This isn't a legal battle. It's a cycle. Let it go."

"Babygirl, don't worry," he said, his voice softening. "Daddy's got you. I'll handle this."

Mom pinched the bridge of her nose like she was resisting the urge to log off life.

But, of course, "enough" wasn't in Dad's vocabulary. All I knew was if this was what nineties R&B felt like, I wanted no part of it.

My phone buzzed with a new text from TJ as I watched the two people who'd taught me everything I never wanted to know about the flip side of love go at it again.

TJ: Tag me in before you lose your shit.

I hung up before either of them could drag me into another round. The quiet that followed was a little shaky but a step toward me reclaiming my peace, even when I knew my parents meant well. Then I did the only sensible thing and called TJ. My lifeline in this mess.

Their angled cheekbones and flawless skin filled the screen, backlit by the soft glow of the San Antonio skyline. TJ was lounging on their high-rise balcony, wineglass in hand, every inch the picture of curated calm.

"Girl, you good?" they asked, one brow lifting with surgical precision, concern and judgment wrapped in one familiar look.

I groaned and sank deeper into the cushions. "Define good. I just hung up on Mom and Dad."

TJ blinked, then burst out laughing. "Oh no. You know they're about to call me next."

"Sorry, not sorry. I hit my limit."

"I don't blame you." They set their glass down and leaned closer. "Tag team Terrence and Mama Jackie is too much for one person.

Dad's been blowing me up all morning asking if I know anyone who can scrub posts from the internet. Let me guess, he wants you to sue the world while Mom's plotting a rebrand?"

I sighed. "That about sums it up. Mom wants me to move back home, like proximity to her Vitamix is going to resolve a crisis. And Dad's ready to start issuing press releases. He was five minutes away from calling the NAACP."

"Classic." TJ tilted their head, already forming that familiar don't-make-me-say-it look. "You already know what I'm about to suggest."

"Yes, and I'm not sure I want to hear it."

"You're going to hear it anyway." They folded one leg beneath them, face softening. "Come stay here. Take the job. Be the nanny my spoiled fur babies deserve. Evan and I have three trips lined up, and I need someone I trust. I mean, the Chateau takes good care of my babies when we board them, but they'll be so much happier sleeping in their own custom orthopedic beds."

TJ (Terrence Jr., technically) was my older sister by six months. Same dad, different moms. Yes, you heard that right. I know you're doing the math.

TJ's mother had her sights set on a future with an R&B star. A baby, she figured, would seal the deal. When that didn't happen, my mom stepped in and raised TJ like her own. There were no halves, no steps, just TJ. The one who always knew how to drag me with love and show up when I couldn't stand on my own.

Back when we were kids, TJ was still figuring out who they were, especially in the shadows of being Dad's namesake. Mom took it all in stride. No dramatic sit-downs or ultimatums, just steady love while TJ found the courage to live out loud.

I also had to credit Dad for trying. Even when he always joked, stumbled, and asked awkward questions. But he showed up. Clumsy or not, our daddy loved hard.

"TJ…" I drew the word out for effect, knowing deep down that our family was messy and too involved, but it was ours. And it was real.

"Don't start," they said, pointing a manicured finger at the screen. Their polish gleamed like it was just cured under a salon-grade LED lamp, and I instinctively tucked my chipped nails out of view. "This is a win-win. Free rent. A change of scenery. Three adorable dogs who already think you're a celebrity."

"Adorable?" I scoffed at the thought of her demonic corgi brigade. "Last time I visited, MiMi chewed through my Marc Jacobs bag, RihRih barked at her own reflection until the sun came up, and Nippy buried a treat in my tampon box. TSA was hella confused."

"They're spirited," TJ said, smiling. "And expressive."

"Spirited is one word. In need of deliverance is another."

"But seriously, Belle. Get out of Atlanta. Stop swimming in the madness around you and reminders of that little stank who will catch these hands on sight along with her lying-ass prop of a man-child. Give yourself room to breathe. No parents. No trolls. Just quiet."

I hesitated, eyeing the cluttered mess around me. "Running away isn't really my style."

"This isn't running. It's regrouping. And it comes with corgis. I'll even convince Evan to book something this week for him and I to get away on an extended vacay just so you have some me time."

I laughed in spite of myself. "How thoughtful of you."

"It's what I do best."

"Mmhmmm." I considered the options as my phone alerted me of our parents trying to reconnect me back to their call. "A trial run as a dog nanny?"

"Auntie-in-residence slash soul reboot. You just might fuck

around and like it here enough to stay longer."

"Highly unlikely," I muttered, but the words felt lighter than they had before.

TJ leaned forward, their voice warm. "You are allowed to hit pause, sis. You don't have to perform being okay. Not here."

I glanced around at all that was left of the life I'd built in Atlanta, refusing to let myself cry, but I couldn't help it. I felt a few tears slip while reconciling how much the apartment around me felt hollow now. All the snapshots of the life I used to live were packed away into boxes labeled like evidence. I wanted to believe there was still something ahead that felt like mine, but I wouldn't know or even find it if I was holed up and suffocating in a gilded cage.

I nodded. "Okay. I'll come to San Antonio."

TJ lit up. "You won't regret it. MiMi, Nippy, and RihRih are going to think Christmas came early."

I smiled. It was faint, but real. After days of heaviness, the thought of being somewhere else, even for a moment, felt like relief.

I should've been asleep, in a deep, responsible slumber that people with steady lives and intact reputations fell into without a fight. But sleep hadn't found me in weeks. Instead, I was cocooned beneath a blanket, phone in hand, scrolling through feeds I'd sworn I'd ignore. My thumb moved without asking my permission, and I told myself it was just a way to pass time until my brain shut off. Except I knew better. I was waiting for *him*. I needed him to make my world feel bright again. I was even tempted to tell him about the season I had just so he could pour into me his usual sage wisdom, but that meant explaining all the parts of me I wasn't ready for him to know just yet.

And then it appeared as if he'd heard the whispers of my mind. A new reel from ChefSwishWhisk.

The instant I tapped, Jill Scott's "So Gone (What My Mind Says)" unfurled through the speaker, her voice a rich, velvety current that didn't just fill a room, it filled a chest cavity, pressing against the places you forgot were tender. The music settled me, but the video undid me.

And it all started with his hands. Large, sure, warm-toned hands that moved with an ease that came from knowing exactly what they were doing. He wasn't rushing, not here. His motions were deliberate, practiced, almost intimate. His fingertips skimmed across a bundle of rosemary before he stripped the leaves clean, his knife following in neat, controlled strokes… each tap on the cutting board slipping into Jill's rhythm so perfectly it felt intentional… like the song was written to score him.

I knew this was just cooking, but my body read it like something else entirely. Like the most decadent erotica one could experience without batteries or a walk of shame involved.

Oil poured into the pan in a thin, gleaming stream that caught the light before lamb chops met the heat with a sizzle so deep and lush it felt just shy of indecent. He pressed them down gently, making sure every inch met the heat, and I felt my breath catch. Hunger, I told myself. Pure hunger. But the warmth pooling under this blanket argued otherwise.

The camera slid closer, and that was when he dropped a few pats of butter into the skillet. It melted into gold, bubbling and hissing while he tipped the pan and bathed the chops in slow, steady strokes. His wrist flexed, forearm tightening, the movement precise and sensual in equal measure. It was unfair, how much he made of this simple act. Unfair and yet so deliciously addictive.

He rarely added captions, because he didn't need to. The reel spoke for itself. The music, the cinematic light, the quiet confidence in every motion. Together, they created something that felt less like a recipe and more like a story. And against my better judgment, I wanted to be inside it.

I shifted beneath the blanket, suddenly overheated, craving the forgotten hunk of support cobbler in my fridge just to have something to put in my mouth while I thought about him. Jill's voice dipped low, sultry and certain, curling around the sound of sizzling and sauce thickening until the air felt heavy with suggestion.

It was only food. I reminded myself of that fact like it would save me. Only food. Only a man's hands cooking said food. But when I closed my eyes, I didn't see ingredients. I saw steam rising, sauce rolling, fingers steady, deliberate, skilled… working on me.

I turned my phone face down on the nightstand like that could cut the spell, then dragged the blanket over my head, heart thudding louder than it had any right to. Sleep should come. Sleep needed to come. Because if it didn't, I was going to start wondering what it would feel like to let a stranger feed me. And if I started wondering that, I didn't know that I'd be able to stop.

The wheels on my carry-on groaned across the floor at Hartsfield-Jackson, loud enough to draw stares I did not need. I told myself it was the acoustics, that everyone's luggage sounded like this when dragged for miles across linoleum. Then I caught two women near the Hudson shop sneaking glances over their phones, and I knew better.

"That's her," one whispered. Not loud, but not soft enough either.

I kept my sunglasses in place. Not for style. As armor. The tint gave me distance, a thin layer between their curiosity and my face. My hand tightened around the suitcase handle, nails tapping against the worn grip. *Keep walking. Do not give them more than this.*

A boy in a soccer jersey slowed as he passed, his phone tilted toward me like he wanted proof I still existed. I lifted my chin and let the overhead lights catch the edge of my shades, offering the same polite, untouchable smile my father used after his own stints with drama. The one that said, *You do not know me well enough to break me, but in the meantime, you can kiss my entire Black ass.*

It had always worked before. This morning it felt thinner, like paper holding back a flood.

When I reached my gate, the suitcase handle had carved a dent across my palm. I found a seat by the far window, watched planes crawl across the tarmac, and breathed through the knot in my chest.

A teenage girl hovered nearby, pink hoodie bright against the rows of gray chairs. She hesitated, then blurted, "Um, aren't you the girl who threw—"

I slid my sunglasses to the top of my head and met her eyes. "Here's a travel tip. Stay hydrated before you speak to strangers."

Her friend burst into nervous laughter. I joined the boarding line before she could finish the question. My smile stayed fixed until the plane lifted off. Then it finally cracked.

Hours later, San Antonio greeted me with a sunset the color of ripe peaches, low and wide against the wing. I leaned around one of my seatmates toward the window, trying to believe it meant something, perhaps maybe even a chance to start over.

At baggage claim, I did not see TJ first. I heard them.

"Bell Bell!"

Their voice cut through the carousel announcements and rolling suitcases. Heads turned, but they did not care. They never did. Boots clattered against tile, followed by a flash of patterned silk trailing behind them. Sunglasses covered half their face. Their cropped hair framed it with precision. They moved like they owned the space, laughter following close behind.

They reached me in a swirl of Black Orchid. "You made it," they said, pulling me into their arms before I could set down my bag.

I did not move. I let the weight of their hold sink in. TJ hugged like they had been waiting for me to stop pretending. Her arms locked around me, a solid and certain embrace that says *I got you* without a single word. My chin fell into the curve of their shoulder like muscle memory. After weeks of tightening up, I didn't brace for the hit. TJ always saw straight through me, knew every messy piece, and still claimed me loud.

When they finally stepped back, their hands stayed on my arms. "Do you know how many times I refreshed your flight status?"

I smiled, the first real one in days. "Twice?"

"Thirty-seven. Evan threatened to cancel the trip if I didn't stop checking."

The warmth of their grip lingered.

"Take it in," TJ said softly. "You did it. You got out. That's the hardest part."

I looked around as the carousel whirred, a toddler shrieked, and a man in a cowboy hat cursed about his missing luggage. The sounds folded together, unremarkable but alive, proof that life kept moving whether I caught up or not.

TJ squeezed my arm once more, their smile turning sharp again, protective and proud. "Enough before we cry these lashes off. We have three small divas waiting to meet you."

She pressed a heavy set of keys into my palm. Then came the leashes… three of them.

MiMi, RihRih, and Nippy came barreling from behind TJ like a glittered stampede with opinions. MiMi barked as if defending choreography, RihRih wagged her entire body, and Nippy was already barking at a rolling suitcase that had somehow offended her.

"You're handing me three dependents in baggage claim?" I

asked.

"Dependents? Please. These are the daughters of your new life."

One blink and the leashes were a knot around my ankles. MiMi was barking orders, RihRih vanished under the rope barrier, and Nippy charged a luggage cart like it had disrespected the family name.

"This feels like a setup," I said. "Why are you telling me this now? Here?"

TJ ignored the question and pulled a glitter-covered spiral notebook from their bag. Across the front, in thick marker, it read, *The Gospel According to the Girls.*

I raised an eyebrow. "The gospel?"

"Chapter one," they said, flipping it open. "MiMi steals socks, never a pair, always one, like performance art. Chapter two, Nippy barks at shadows. Don't reason with her. You will lose. Chapter three, RihRih eats throw pillows. Protect them or start budgeting for replacements."

I laughed despite myself, clutching the notebook as the dogs pulled me in three directions at once. "You're serious."

"One thousand percent. I have about an hour before boarding. Evan is already texting in all caps."

"Boarding to where?"

TJ's grin told me this was about to be outrageous. "Call it an extended work trip for Evan. A few weeks between Morocco, Paris, and Lisbon. He is touring potential properties. I am there to make sure he doesn't buy a castle just because it photographs well."

"So you are leaving me with three dogs, a bedazzled manual, and your keys."

"Exactly. Remember, reset, not rescue." They kissed my cheek, scarf fluttering as they backed toward the escalator. "You've got this,

Bell Bell. And remember, the girls respond best to affirmations."

"I'll try not to get us all evicted before you land," I muttered, juggling leashes and luggage.

She called out one last time, voice bright above the crowd. "San Antonio loves you already."

The dogs tugged again, and I laughed, the sound surprising even me. "All right, team. Let's make an entrance."

Wrangling three leashes, a carry-on, three suitcases, and a backpack onto a luggage cart left me sweating through my hoodie. The sliding doors opened to the evening air, cool and unhurried, steady, and patient in a way Atlanta never was.

Then my phone buzzed with a text from TJ: Row P4. Don't laugh.

I followed the signs into the parking garage, cart squeaking, dogs weaving around my ankles like it was a relay race. A car chirped when I pressed the unlock button. A turquoise Beetle waited under a flickering light, its paint chipped, bumper dented, and personality unbothered.

Of course.

The license plate, slightly crooked, read BVGURL. I groaned. "Naturally."

Loading the car felt like punishment for every bad decision I'd ever made. I wrestled three suitcases into the Beetle, each one a test of physics and faith, before wedging the dogs in wherever they fit. When I finally slammed the last door shut, I leaned against the car, breathless and sweating, surrounded by fur, luggage, and the faint rattle of my dignity.

I shut the door and leaned against the car, sweat prickling at my hairline. Three dogs. Three suitcases. One nervous system on its last leg.

Welcome to San Antonio.

The DMs

You've been quiet. Thought the great
peach cobbler experiment finished you.

Please. I buried that disaster beneath
two Hefty bags and a prayer. May it rest.

Still holding a vigil for those peaches.

Dramatic. Anyway, while you sit there
pouring one out for the homies, I've moved on.
Pickles with potato chips.

That's not a snack. That's emotional turbulence.

Bruh I'm PMSing. Consider it hormonal triage.

Then I respect the effort.
No judgment from this side of the screen.

Good. I don't need another man with
opinions about what I eat.

Never that. I just think it's wild
how you make questionable choices
sound like recipes worth trying.

I'll take that as a compliment.

@ChefSwishWhisk
It was. You type like you mean it.
Even when it's absurd.

@BeautyIzHerName
Look at you being emotionally aware.
You say that like you know me.

@ChefSwishWhisk
I know your words. They don't hesitate.

@BeautyIzHerName
Or maybe I just text fast.

@ChefSwishWhisk
Nah. Fast reads different. Yours
sound like you already argued
with yourself, won, then hit send.

@BeautyIzHerName
That's oddly specific.

@ChefSwishWhisk
Comes with observation.
I read people for a living.

@BeautyIzHerName
So you're a therapist now?

@ChefSwishWhisk
Closer to a referee. Different kind of crisis
management.

@BeautyIzHerName
Hmmm. You sound too calm for that.

@ChefSwishWhisk
Calm is practice. Doesn't mean peace.

@BeautyIzHerName
That was deep for a man who
lights candles for peaches.

@ChefSwishWhisk
I contain multitudes.

@BeautyIzHerName
I see that. What's the vibe tonight?

@ChefSwishWhisk
Hotel room. Game on mute. Thinking too loud.

@BeautyIzHerName
That sounds lonely.

@ChefSwishWhisk
Sometimes quiet just needs a witness.

@ChefSwishWhisk
It's strange how easy it is to tell the truth to
someone who doesn't expect anything from you.

@BeautyIzHerName
That's almost poetic. You sure you're not a therapist?

@ChefSwishWhisk
Depends on the day.

@BeautyIzHerName
What kind of game?

@ChefSwishWhisk
Stanford versus South Carolina. Women's side.

@BeautyIzHerName
You really watch women's hoops?

@ChefSwishWhisk
Always. They play like the game still means
something.

@BeautyIzHerName
That's kind of beautiful. Most men only
care when there's a highlight reel.

@ChefSwishWhisk
Maybe I just like watching people
who love what they do.

@BeautyIzHerName
So you're sentimental.

@ChefSwishWhisk
Observant. Big difference.

@BeautyIzHerName
Depends who's watching.

@ChefSwishWhisk
Habit. I like players who don't hesitate. Drive,
finish, let the moment go.

@BeautyIzHerName
Conviction again.

@ChefSwishWhisk
You noticed.

@BeautyIzHerName
You keep circling it like it's personal.

@ChefSwishWhisk
Maybe it is. Maybe I just respect people who mean
what they say.

@BeautyIzHerName
That's rare.

@ChefSwishWhisk
It shouldn't be. But people perform too much.

@BeautyIzHerName
And you don't?

@ChefSwishWhisk
I try not to. Some performances
just pay better than others.

@BeautyIzHerName
Fair point.

@ChefSwishWhisk
What about you? You perform?

@BeautyIzHerName
I think we all do. Some of us just learned to smile
through it better than others.

@ChefSwishWhisk
You sound like someone who's had to.

@BeautyIzHerName
Maybe. Or maybe I just like to win arguments.

@ChefSwishWhisk
So we agree. Conviction.

@BeautyIzHerName
You're obsessed with that word.

@ChefSwishWhisk
Only because you wear it well.

@BeautyIzHerName
Now you're flirting.

@ChefSwishWhisk
I'm cooking.

@BeautyIzHerName
Cooking what, exactly?

@ChefSwishWhisk
Patience. Maybe curiosity.

@BeautyIzHerName
You sound like trouble.

@ChefSwishWhisk
Only when invited.

@BeautyIzHerName
(Typing… then deleting.)

@ChefSwishWhisk
I'll pretend that was a goodnight.

@BeautyIzHerName
Pretend better. Goodnight, Chef.

@ChefSwishWhisk
Nite, Beauty.

Chapter 4

COLE

I PULLED INTO MY USUAL SPOT IN THE LOWER GARAGE.
The Storm had handled business tonight. No drama, no overtime,
just a clean win that settled right in my bones and offered just enough
sweat to remind me I still had it. My body liked games like that.

The guys hit Los Hermanos after, but I only stopped long
enough to grab my order and a few laughs before heading out. The
engine clicked off, leaving me with quiet that hits different when
you've been surrounded by movement all night. I grabbed the paper
sack of tacos riding shotgun, slung my duffel over my shoulder, and
headed for the private entrance to the residential floors. The scanner
blinked green when I tapped my fob, the glass doors sliding open to
the smaller lobby reserved for tenants.

That was when I saw them.

Three of TJ and Evan's dogs were skidding across the marble,
leashes tangled, barking like they had something to prove. Then I
heard her. Low, firm, a voice that cut clean through the commotion
without needing to get loud. "I told you, TJ cleared everything. Evan
too. Check the list again."

Bellamy Barnes, of all people. My hand flexed once at my side
before I made it stop. I'd learned a long time ago what giving myself

away looked like.

The name landed before the full picture did. Daryl looked like he already regretted covering tonight, shoulders sagging like he was ready to retire mid-shift. She stood there, chin lifted, arms crossed, surrounded by enough luggage to make it clear she wasn't visiting. She was moving in.

"You need proper confirmation, Ms....?" Daryl squinted at the ID she shoved across the desk.

"Barnes," she said, clipped. "Bellamy Barnes. I'm sure you know my sister's dogs already. You just confirmed TJ and Evan live here. Who even makes up a name like that?"

That was when TJ's text clicked into place. The one she sent earlier that morning before shootaround. Hey, it's TJ from across the hall in 34A. Heads up, my sister's flying in to watch our fur babies while we're gone. Look out if you can. Appreciate it!

I'd skimmed TJ's text earlier without giving it much thought. They'd mentioned a sister before, but I hadn't connected the dots to her. That's usually how I move, keeping things surface, no follow-ups, no chance of getting tangled in something that doesn't concern me.

Then I found myself skimming *her*.

Her eyes caught me first. Keen. Steady. Focused in a way that said she'd seen worse and walked away anyway. The light in the lobby brushed her skin, bringing out a deep bronze that looked alive, sunlit in spite of the harsh overhead glare. A few braids had slipped from the knot at her neck, grazing her shoulders each time she moved. She wasn't smiling, but she didn't need to. Calm lived in her face, born from knowing exactly who she was even when the world forgot to act like it. Her posture did the rest. Shoulders back, chin high, still standing like nothing life threw at her had ever taken her balance.

She also was thick in all the right places, soft where it counted, built like real life and not a filter. Full up top, a trim waist, hips that could make a man forget his manners. My pulse jumped before I could stop it. She looked irritated, and I should've left it at that, but something about her held steady, like she didn't need to prove a thing. I told myself it was nothing, but my body had already decided otherwise.

I should've kept walking. Could've let Daryl handle it and watched her wear down his patience. But there was something in her voice, low, sure, and edged with someone who'd run out of options that stopped me. I told myself it was neighborly instinct. The truth sat heavier than that.

"She's with TJ."

She turned at the sound of my voice, recognition flashing before she caught it. Daryl nodded and finally handed over the tablet for her to sign.

"I didn't need your help," she said, eyes steady, pride intact.

"Didn't look like you had it handled," I answered.

Her mouth tightened, maybe to keep from snapping. Then one of the dogs lunged at a shadow, the leashes jerked, and her purse hit the floor, the contents scattering. Lip balm, charger cord, sunglasses, and a handful of tampons rolled across the marble like someone upstairs was testing her patience.

Before she could move, one of the dogs went for one, nose down and curious. I reached out fast, catching it just in time. "Hey," I said, pulling it away, slipping it from his mouth and sliding it back into her bag. "That's not a fetch toy, trust me."

She froze, then sighed, a small, incredulous laugh catching in her throat. "Of course. Because why not?"

Daryl suddenly found the lobby monitor very interesting. I crouched before she could, keeping my voice low. "Hey," I said. "It's fine." I gathered what I could, careful and steady, making sure not to turn it into a scene.

When I looked up, she was watching me carefully, her face softer than before.

"You're unusually calm for this moment," she said.

"Travel's rough enough," I said. "Happens to half the world, nothing to hide."

Something in her shoulders eased. "Add 'menstrual while flying' to my list of today's greatest hits."

"Sounds like you deserve a drink," I said. "And some sleep."

She gave a small nod, a gesture people use when they're too tired to say thank you but still mean it. Her voice dropped, quieter now. "Thanks."

"Anytime," I said, and meant it more than I should have.

She steadied herself and finally met my eyes.

"So this is your moment, huh? The perfect setup for payback."

I raised a brow. "Payback?"

"You could've left me there picking up my life off the floor," she said, her voice dry but edged. "I probably deserve it, considering the way I—" She stopped herself, chewing the rest of the sentence. "Let's just say I wouldn't have blamed you."

"Didn't cross my mind," I said.

Her gaze flicked up, keen and searching. "You expect me to believe that?"

"I don't expect anything," I said. "Just didn't feel like watching you struggle."

Something in her expression loosened for half a second before she caught it, like she realized she'd let me see her tired. She looked away, pulling the dogs close.

"Guess I'll add that to today's surprises," she said, more to the floor than to me.

I nodded toward the elevator. "You coming, or are we waiting for round two?"

She pressed the button, jaw set. "You can stop playing hero now."

"Good," I said. "I'm not built for capes."

She moved toward the elevators, pressing the button with more force than necessary. Nothing happened.

"It won't move without a fob," I told her, stepping beside her but leaving space between us.

Her eyes flicked toward me, guarded but curious. "Of course it doesn't."

I held the fob to the sensor, the light blinking green as the doors slid open. She guided her dogs and luggage inside, whispering encouragements that sounded like part pep talk and part warning. One suitcase caught on the threshold, and she wrestled it through, determined not to ask for help.

I followed her in, hitting the button for the thirty-fourth floor. The doors closed, sealing us in with the shuffle of paws and the quiet whir of the lift. For a moment, neither of us spoke. Then one of the leashes tightened around her ankle, and she stumbled. Instinct had me reaching out. My hand found her elbow.

She steadied but didn't pull away this time. "You're persistent," she said.

"Just observant."

She tilted her head slightly, studying me now. "You're not what I expected."

"What did you expect?"

"A man who'd laugh," she said, teasing, although I knew she was also testing.

"Guess you caught me on a better night."

Her gaze lingered a moment too long before she looked away. The elevator continued upward, the silence dense but not hostile.

When the doors opened on thirty-four, I held them for her.

She guided the dogs out first, then the luggage.

"Welcome to San Antonio, Bellamy," I said. "Hope you're a better neighbor than you are at taking help."

That sparked the full glare again, but there was something behind it now, something curious, maybe even amused. She stepped into TJ's apartment and closed the door behind her, final as a period.

I stood in the hall longer than I meant to, tacos cooling in my hand, wondering how someone running on empty could still feel like a full room.

Inside, the condo looked exactly as I'd left it. Everything lined up, quiet, predictable. Most nights, that steadiness worked for me. Tonight it felt staged, as if even the walls were waiting for something I had not decided to say.

I set the bag on the counter, kicked off my sneakers, and leaned on the island. The city lights reached in through the glass, blinking slow, but my head was still in the lobby. Her voice. The dogs. The way she squared her shoulders like she had been fighting her whole life and was not about to take another round from a concierge.

I took a long drink of water, hoping it would shake loose whatever had me replaying the moment. It didn't. The quiet pressed in harder. Through the door, I thought I heard faint movement, a jingle of collars, the soft scrape of paws, maybe even her voice coaxing the dogs to calm down. I told myself I was imagining it. The thought still made me smile.

TJ's text from this morning ran through my mind again. I had glanced at it between drills, never connected the name, never thought that sister would be Bellamy Barnes. Now she was here. Across the hall.

The tacos still smelled good, but I was not hungry. All I could see was her, eyes sharp even when tired, mouth set like she would rather bite through pride than ask for help. It was too much and not enough all at once.

I told myself to leave it. She had made it clear she did not need help. I had seen that pride before, usually in the mirror after a bad season. The smart play was to walk away, finish dinner, and mind my own business. But pride did not cook, and she had not eaten. The smell of the tacos turned heavy again. Before I could stop myself, I was knocking.

My body moved before my brain did. The door opened halfway, soft light spilling out. One of the corgis barked once, quick and curious. She looked at me like she was deciding whether to shut the door or ask what I wanted. Her braids had slipped loose from the ponytail she wore earlier, a few strands framing her face and pulling all the bite out of her glare.

"What?" she asked, wary but too tired to pretend she wasn't curious.

I held up the bag. "Dinner."

She blinked. "From where?"

"Los Hermanos. Small spot near the arena. It's a hidden gem. I have brisket and adobo chicken. Trust me, their tortillas ruin all others."

Her eyes dropped to the bag, then back to me. "Why?"

I started to say I'd ordered too much, but that wasn't true. "Because you look like you had a day where no one should have to think about food."

She studied me, trying to find the catch. "So this is your idea of a truce?"

"For now."

Her mouth twitched, the start of something just shy of playful. She reached for the bag, careful not to brush my hand.

"Thanks," she said quietly, like the word cost her something.

"Don't mention it."

I started to turn, then stopped. "You really didn't know I lived here?"

She met my eyes, steady and unguarded. "No. I didn't."

Silence stretched between us. Up close, she looked even more undone than she had downstairs, but something about her refused to wilt. Her shoulders stayed squared, her skin caught the light, and a faint trace of vanilla hung between us.

She nodded once and stepped back, closing the door without another word.

I stood there longer than I meant to, tacos gone, her name still turning over in my head. She looked too worn out to keep sparring, yet somehow she left me feeling like I had already lost the first round.

Inside, the condo waited. Still, precise, everything where it belonged. Most nights, that steadiness worked. Tonight it felt too neat, as if even the walls were holding their breath.

The team flight was at eight. Three cities on the West Coast. I hadn't touched the suitcase in my closet. But all I could see was her standing there, eyes steady even when everything else in her life looked like it was falling apart.

I told myself it didn't matter. She was just a neighbor. A complicated one. My body didn't buy it.

I leaned against the counter, waiting for the tension in my shoulders to fade, but it only sharpened. The game had left my body sore in a way that should've felt satisfying. A win was supposed to fix everything, or at least silence it for a few hours. But my head refused to rest. The only thing that ever helped was putting my hands to work.

The fridge opened softly, and cold air hit my face. I stared inside until the decision found me. Butter I'd tucked behind the eggs, heavy cream waiting in the back, and a neat row of eggs lined up like soldiers. I then reached for the pantry door. A bar of dark chocolate waited behind the spices. The sight of it sparked a recipe I hadn't made in years. One of comfort, decadent, unnecessary, and exactly what I needed.

I set everything out on the counter, dropped the needle on a record, and let Amy Winehouse's *Frank* drift through the room. Her voice filled the space the way light fills a crack, quiet but impossible to ignore.

The camera came next, out of habit more than plan. The lens was positioned to stay close to my hands, never higher. I had learned the hard way what happens when people get too much of your face and not enough of your truth. I set the shot and started filming.

Soon the whisk scraped against the bowl, steady as breath. My shoulders eased, but my jaw didn't. Chocolate softened over the flame, the cream easing in after, sugar dissolving grain by grain until the air turned warm and sweet. My hands moved without thought, steady and certain. This was the only kind of focus I trusted, focus that made time loosen its grip.

Once the last ramekin met the counter, the room felt settled. Amy's voice rose through the record, smooth and jagged all at once, and something in me went still enough to listen.

I cracked the first one open, let the spoon sink through the thin shell until the center spilled molten across the plate. Steam rose lazy and soft, curling like it had somewhere to be.

Later, when I trimmed the footage, I dropped Amy's "You Sent Me Flying" under it. The track built in soft, smoky layers, filling the spaces I left quiet. Sugar falling into the bowl. The slow fold of batter. The crack that opened like punctuation. Every cut followed her phrasing, the music doing what language couldn't. Turning silence into something that felt alive.

For a moment, it didn't look like my life at all. Just hands, control, and a man who still knew how to make something worth keeping.

Post.

The likes came fast. They always did. People wanted me to drop a playlist, the recipe, the behind-the-scenes I'd never give. I set the phone down before I could get pulled in. Tonight wasn't about them. It was about building something steady when everything else refused to stay still.

The quiet settled in again, leaving me face to face with myself. Most days I leaned into it. Other days, it leaned back. People called it calm, but really it was me avoiding the parts I didn't know how to say out loud. That marriage taught me how fast you get rewritten when you stop speaking for yourself. I let too much go unsaid, thinking love would bridge the distance. Instead, silence only made it louder.

Then the phone buzzed again.

@BeautyIzHerName
Molten chocolate at this hour? Dangerous.

I exhaled through a laugh I hadn't meant to let out.

@ChefSwishWhisk
Better than sitting in the dark pretending I'm not awake.

@BeautyIzHerName
Can't turn your head off either?

@ChefSwishWhisk
Something like that.

@BeautyIzHerName
That's vague. You always this mysterious?

@ChefSwishWhisk
Only when I should be packing for an early flight.

@BeautyIzHerName
Work trip or escape plan?

@ChefSwishWhisk
Work trip. Same schedule, different skyline.

@BeautyIzHerName
You make it sound like you're hauling freight.

@ChefSwishWhisk

Sometimes it feels that way. Airports, hotel beds,
the same view from different windows.

@ChefSwishWhisk
Not the kind that fixes anything.

@BeautyIzHerName
But you still go.

@ChefSwishWhisk
Comes with the job. The miles just make it easier to think.

@BeautyIzHerName
You could think at home.

@ChefSwishWhisk
Tried that. Still working on it.

@BeautyIzHerName
You ever figure out what you're running from?

@ChefSwishWhisk
Not yet. But I'm getting closer.

@BeautyIzHerName
That sounds like progress.

@ChefSwishWhisk
Or exhaustion. Hard to tell the difference some nights.

@BeautyIzHerName
Then sleep. Let the world wait a minute.

@ChefSwishWhisk
Only if you do the same.

@BeautyIzHerName
No promises.

@ChefSwishWhisk
Maybe. You ever do something that stopped
making sense but still made you feel like yourself?

@BeautyIzHerName
You make that sound noble.

@ChefSwishWhisk
I make it sound real.

@BeautyIzHerName
I'll give you that. For what it's worth,
your insomnia looks delicious.

@ChefSwishWhisk
And dangerous, remember?

@BeautyIzHerName
Only if you're sharing.

The corner of my mouth lifted before I could stop it.

@ChefSwishWhisk
Careful. Midnight talk like that
makes people do reckless things.

@BeautyIzHerName
What kind of things?

@ChefSwishWhisk
Depends on who's listening.

The typing bubble flickered, vanished and then came back.

@BeautyIzHerName
Goodnight, Chef.

@ChefSwishWhisk
Night, Beauty.

The record kept spinning even after the side I was listening to ended, leaving the soft crackle of vinyl filling the space. I should've turned it off. I should've finished packing. But instead, I stood there, spoon in hand, thinking about how the woman across the hall had shut her door on me like I was the last thing she wanted and how the woman in my DMs had just left me wanting more.

Chapter 5

BELLAMY

A DRAMATIC, INDIGNANT YIP AT THE EDGE OF THE BED made me bolt upright, heart punching through my chest like I had missed a final exam I didn't know I was signed up for. The room was still dark, a little slice of moonlight sneaking through gauzy curtains, but I didn't need light to know who the culprits were.

The corgis.

Three pairs of eyes glowed at me like they had staged a coup and I was late to the surrender ceremony. You know the meme where Prince is giving judging vibes? It really doesn't matter which one you pick, just know I woke up to the canine version of it.

MiMi, the ringleader, barked once, crisp and authoritative, then pawed at the duvet like she was peeling me out of bed herself. Nippy stalked back and forth by the door, nails clicking on the hardwood, huffing like an unpaid landlord. RihRih, the diva, sighed so dramatically that if she'd had a fainting couch, she would've collapsed onto it.

I groaned and pulled the blanket over my head. "Five more minutes."

MiMi barked again. Short, clipped, and final.

"Fine," I muttered, throwing the covers back. "Congratulations.

70

You win."

This was not how I had imagined my glamorous fresh start in San Antonio. My first official morning as the corgi-wrangler slash dog-au-pair slash woman-in-hiding began with a canine mutiny before dawn.

The guest bedroom TJ said I could stay in for however long I needed to get back on my feet was obscene. A portrait of the three of them hung directly across from the bed, painted like they were royal heirs. RihRih wore pearls, Nippy had a crown tilted just so, and MiMi glared down at me in full tiara. The artist had captured their personalities too well, which meant that even in the middle of the night, I felt judged by oil paint.

"This is how horror movies start," I told them, fumbling for my phone on the nightstand. "The dog painting comes alive, and the single woman dies first."

Nippy barked like she agreed. Or maybe she just wanted me to hurry up.

I dragged myself out of bed, tripping over the hem of TJ's oversized silk kaftan, which I'd borrowed last night to sleep in after taking a peek inside her closet before swapping it for my sweats, and shuffled toward the pile of leashes hung by the door.

It took me a good five minutes to get everybody clipped in. Once we hit the lobby, the concierge looked at me like he still thought our run-in late last night was all my fault. He didn't say anything, but the faint arch of his brow said, *Really? At this hour?*

I gave him a brittle smile, as if this pompous bootleg Geoffrey wasn't familiar with these damn dogs already. Yet still today was a new day, so I attempted small talk. "Don't suppose you want to trade places?"

He didn't answer, which was fair. I wouldn't have taken the offer either.

The sliding doors to the outside slid open, and cool morning air brushed against my face with a light breeze that carried the faintest trace of water nearby, reminding me TJ often bragged about living on the Riverwalk.

"Slow down," I hissed as their little stubby legs carried us down the sidewalk. "We are not in the Iditarod."

They didn't care. They sniffed, pulled, darted, barked at a passing jogger, tangled me into knots so tight I nearly toppled over. If anyone passing by recorded this for social media, I'd trend again, and not in a good way.

When we made it back upstairs, the concierge had that fake polite look people wear when they're trying not to laugh. He was enjoying every second of my humiliation. I caught the twitch at his mouth and narrowed my eyes just enough to make him look away.

Inside the condo, I unclipped the dogs and stood still. The corgis scattered in three different directions, tiny blurs of fur and entitlement. MiMi climbed onto the couch, RihRih trotted toward the kitchen, and Nippy jumped onto the rug, rolled once, and let out a satisfied sigh.

The condo itself was stunning. High ceilings, floor-to-ceiling windows, and furniture that I knew cost a grip, and some of it likely required a passport to enter the country. Every piece felt deliberate, from the emerald velvet chairs to the perfectly arranged art books stacked on the coffee table. It was modern and curated. A place that whispered calm and control. TJ and Evan's fingerprints were everywhere.

Without them, though, it didn't feel like home. It felt like I was squatting inside someone else's dream life.

I toed off my shoes and stared out at the skyline, trying to convince myself this was temporary. That I could use this time to breathe, regroup, figure things out. My stomach disagreed, letting out a growl that made MiMi's ears perk. I was starving. Not snack hungry, but real hungry. I wanted a real meal. Pancakes that soaked up syrup like they had a purpose. Eggs cooked in butter. Bacon that snapped when you bit it. Freshly brewed coffee that hit like a sermon with an altar call after "Maybe God Is Tryin' to Tell You Somethin'."

I opened the refrigerator with hope and closed it with disappointment. Sea-moss gel, oat milk, and chia pudding. The fridge equivalent of small talk. Polite, but offering nothing real. Mason jars labeled for MiMi, Nippy, and RihRih filled the fridge, each packed with salmon and quinoa, poached chicken and pumpkin, or turkey with barley. Even the dogs had a meal plan.

"I see how it is," I muttered, glaring at RihRih as she sniffed the baseboards. "Y'all win."

Thirty minutes later, I was freshly showered and back in sneakers, hair tied up, and walking out the door. The corgis stayed behind, sprawled across the sectional. I needed space and food, preferably in that order.

The streets stretched ahead, slow and awake. Vendors were setting up their stalls, the air fragrant. Somewhere nearby, someone flipped breakfast tacos on a griddle, and the smell made my stomach twist with envy.

Then I saw it. Four bold letters above a brick storefront. *Jawn.* Philly slang, right here in the middle of Texas. I stopped short, squinting just to be sure I wasn't imagining it.

Inside, the café buzzed quietly in a way that showed people were happy but not trying too hard to show it. Sunlight poured through the front windows, catching on the glass jars and record sleeves that lined the walls. A stack of vinyl sat beside a turntable, including Philadelphia's neo-soul legacy soundtrack featuring Erykah Badu, Jill Scott, and The Roots. The music playing was an old Bilal track, low and perfect, bringing out that "if you know, you know" vibe.

The place was packed in a way that felt good. People working solo and in clusters on laptops, a pair of aunties playing cards near the window, and a couple sharing a cinnamon roll big enough to reside in added to the vibes. The smell alone could cure a bad mood.

Behind the counter, a woman about my age worked the griddle. She had curls piled on top of her head and wore a faded De La Soul hoodie. When her hazel eyes fell to my sneakers, she smiled like she had found a secret handshake.

"Hold on," she said, voice smooth but teasing. "Are those jawns the Rust Pink Jordan 1s?"

I looked down and smiled despite myself. "Graduation gift. My dad said they were proof I took the long way but still crossed the stage."

Her grin widened. "Your dad? Terrence Barnes been setting trends since satin shirts and matching sets were a movement. Prints on prints, leather in July, and it always worked. Half these stylists owe him royalties."

The way she said my father's name hit different. Like she knew the Barnes who still got invited to cookouts, not the one people whispered about online.

"You favor him," she said, flipping a pancake with one hand like she'd been born behind a griddle. "Same smile, same expressive eyes, same 'I know something you don't' energy."

"Loaded trait," I said.

"Or good genes," she countered. "Depends who's asking."

"Don't get too impressed. I'm temporary," I said. "Holding down the fort for my sibling."

Her grin curved slow. "Housesitting or dog-sitting? MiMi, Nippy, and RihRih, right?"

I blinked. "How do you know that?"

She nodded toward the cooler behind the counter. "I make their meals twice a week. TJ treats those dogs like heirs. Poached chicken, quinoa, pumpkin purée. The girls eat cleaner than most folks in this city."

A real laugh slipped out, light and unexpected. "This the same TJ who used to eat Froot Loops with orange juice?"

"We all evolve, right?" She slid me a mug of freshly poured coffee and offered her hand across the counter. "I'm Nina."

"Bellamy."

"I know." Her smile softened, and after weeks of tension, it didn't feel loaded. "You deserve breakfast to remember."

Before I could answer, she poured batter onto the griddle, the scent of butter filling the air. A few minutes later, she set a plate in front of me. Buttermilk pancakes dusted with powdered sugar, scrambled eggs that looked too good to be an accident, and a side of thick-cut bacon that glistened in the light.

"One order of welcome to the neighborhood," she said.

The first bite nearly made my eyes close. Soft pancakes, real butter, just enough sweetness to remind me what joy tastes like.

"This should come with a warning," I said around a mouthful.

"Good kind or bad kind?"

"The kind that might make me believe in mornings again."

Nina grinned, satisfied. "Then you'll fit right in. Welcome to Jawn, Bellamy."

I smiled into my coffee. Something in me eased in a way it hadn't since I landed. Maybe this city wasn't home yet. But it was trying.

The condo had finally gone still. Four days in, and I was proud to report all three corgis were still breathing and accounted for. A victory I didn't take lightly.

It should have felt peaceful by now. Instead, the quiet settled thick in the corners, reminding me I was the only human left to fill it. I sank deeper into the couch, remote in hand, flipping through channels without really seeing anything. Scrolling that's less about finding something to watch and more about avoiding whatever's waiting when the screen goes black.

My fingers betrayed me next, instinct taking the wheel. One second I was flipping channels, the next I was scrolling social media out of reflex, chasing distraction like it was oxygen. Somewhere between boredom and curiosity, I typed in *Cole Howard*. If curiosity killed the cat, boredom must've written the obituary.

The search lit up with links of stats, trade recaps, and a few think pieces dressed as concern. One headline caught me. *Cole Howard's Silent Comeback.*

I told myself not to click. Then did it anyway. The article framed it as "rebuilding his image," like redemption could be managed with PR and distance. I closed it before the guilt had time to register.

The phone buzzed with TJ's name. Naturally, FaceTime. Texting was too small for their personality.

I debated ignoring it. The dogs were finally asleep, and if I so much as whispered, they'd take it as a signal to start their second act. But the second buzz rolled in, and I could already picture TJ's face if I didn't pick up, followed by a barrage of texts that would not let me live in peace.

I swiped.

"There she is," TJ sang, as if I had been hiding for weeks instead of hours. Oversized sunglasses swallowed half their face, a silk scarf tied like they had just stepped off a Paris runway. The backdrop stretched wide, ocean for days, sunlight catching on the waves like it was showing off just for them.

Evan leaned into the frame with a smile that made you forgive him for TJ's antics. "About time. We were about to call international rescue."

"You wouldn't dare." I pulled the blanket higher around my shoulders.

"Don't test me," TJ said, sliding their sunglasses down just enough to deliver judgment with a side of glare like the church mother of Fashion Week. "You forget, I know your weaknesses."

"And exploit them," I muttered.

They grinned like I'd paid them a compliment. "Exactly. Now, give us the rundown. How's my household holding up?"

"Your dogs are fine," I said.

Evan chuckled and adjusted the phone so the light hit them both. "And how are *you* doing? Settling in okay?"

I hesitated before answering. The truth felt heavy, but I wasn't about to hand it to them raw. I said finally, "It's too quiet. Even with your little rugrats afoot."

Evan's gaze softened, like he'd heard the unsaid part anyway. "Quiet can be good. Give it time." He tapped at his phone, and a second later mine buzzed. "I just sent you some links. A couple restaurants, a gallery, a bookstore we stumbled into recently. Nothing heavy. Just places to check out if you feel like it."

"You made me an itinerary?"

"Not an itinerary," Evan said, steady. "Simple options. I'll email that, since it's more involved. Speaking of, we finally got our full vacation schedule together. I'll send that over, too."

TJ rolled their eyes so hard I almost heard it. "Don't let him bore you with his recommendations and don't dare get jealous of our extended trek around Europe. What you really need to know is that your sibling looks flawless in vacation light. I mean, tell me I don't look like a sponsored post right now."

"You absolutely do," I said.

"Exactly." They preened, tilting the screen to catch another angle of sun. Then, with a dramatic pause that meant nothing good was coming, TJ said, "Speaking of looking good… Cole Howard… How's that going?"

The blanket slipped from my shoulders. "Excuse me?"

Evan groaned. "Here we go."

"You knew?" I said, sitting upright.

"Knew what?" TJ asked innocently, sunglasses back in place like a shield.

"That he lives here. Across the hall. You couldn't have dropped that little fact before I boarded my flight?"

TJ pursed their lips, pretending to think. "I mean… Technically, I didn't think about it until the day of, but honestly, would it have changed anything? You'd still be there babysitting my girls."

"You could have warned me."

"Warn you?" Their hand hit their chest. "About what? The rent? The humidity? The fact that my neighbors have too much disposable income?"

"You know what I mean."

TJ sighed dramatically. "What am I, your talent scout? You think I keep a spreadsheet of my neighbors for reference?"

"Yes."

They grinned. "Fine. Maybe I do. For safety reasons."

I gave them a look. "Safety?"

"Of course. Knowing who's likely to call security versus who's likely to help you hide the body. Mrs. Patel, nosy but her samosas are the business. The dentist couple in 33C, friendly until April fifteenth. The guy with the Peloton upstairs ain't nothing but a motivational threat. I had to repent after asking God to take him out instead of Mr. Big."

I wheezed so loud the dogs thought it was their cue to harmonize. "You're sick."

"The Lord knows my heart," TJ said smoothly, "and my noise tolerance."

I shook my head, still smiling. "All right, then what's Cole's category?"

TJ didn't miss a beat. "Tall. Brooding. Probably owns too many gray sweats. Grocery-bag forearms. Keeps to himself, which is refreshing, considering most of the city would trip over their own dignity for a selfie."

I raised a brow. "Cole Howard keeps to himself?"

They grinned. "Retired from drama, apparently. Plays ball. The man is peace personified."

"Then I'll keep it peaceful and mind my business."

TJ tilted their head. "You say that like you're not already curious."

"I'm not."

They smirked. "That's cute. Denial looks good on you. Just so you know, he's got a spare set of keys to our place in case you ever need to do your underserved hot pocket a favor and conveniently get locked out or something. You're welcome."

"Goodbye, TJ."

TJ shrugged, all smugness and no shame. "In all seriousness, though, Cole's a solid neighbor. Better than the overzealous political couple who lived there before him. Polite. Quiet. Smells good. You could do worse."

"This isn't an apartment mixer."

"Could be," they said, unbothered.

Evan cut in, the voice of reason. "Don't listen to her. TJ can't help herself. Just focus on settling in. As for 34B, Cole's just... there."

"Exactly," TJ echoed. "Just there. Across the hall. In case you ever need some sugar."

I buried my face in my hands. "You're insufferable."

"True," they said cheerfully, "but I'm also never wrong."

Then I added, "I think he's out of town anyway. Apparently, the Storm is playing a bunch of away games at the moment."

"Sounds like you miss him."

"Sounds like you got jokes."

Their laughter rang out, spilling through the speakers until I couldn't help laughing too, even as I shook my head. That was the thing about TJ, who was impossible, relentless, messy as hell—but sometimes the only thing keeping you from drowning. Evan steadied it, as always, anchoring their shenanigans with warmth and reminders that the world wasn't closing in. Together, they made me feel less like I'd been dropped into a city I didn't ask for.

The call ended with TJ blowing kisses big enough to knock their sunglasses sideways and Evan's wave lasting just a beat longer, like he wanted me to feel it through the screen. When it cut to black, the room felt emptier, but not in the same hollow way as before.

I glanced at the email Evan had sent with their full itinerary of flights and hotel stays. Three and a half additional weeks. The dogs were mine, the condo was mine, the silence was mine. It sank in then that no one was coming back to fill it.

The quiet pressed in, heavier than any of it. I'd tried to outrun the humiliation, the fallout, the mess I'd made, but all of it was waiting for me in the stillness. And for the first time since everything blew up, I didn't have anywhere left to hide from it.

The DMs

@BeautyIzHerName
Ever have one of those nights where someone just... needles you? Not loud or rude. Just enough to stick with you.

@ChefSwishWhisk
Depends who's holding the needle.

@BeautyIzHerName
Someone entirely too sure of themselves.

@ChefSwishWhisk
Sounds personal.

@BeautyIzHerName
I wish it wasn't. Some people walk in, throw off your balance, then act like it's your fault for noticing.

@ChefSwishWhisk
So you met your match.

@BeautyIzHerName
More like a spark I didn't ask for.

@ChefSwishWhisk
Sparks start fires.

@BeautyIzHerName
Only if you stand too close.

@ChefSwishWhisk
You sound like someone who hasn't stepped back yet.

@BeautyIzHerName
Maybe. What's it to you?

@ChefSwishWhisk
Just noticing you're still bothered.

@BeautyIzHerName
I don't usually open up like this. I guess it feels
safe in here... safer than it does out there.

@ChefSwishWhisk
He got under your skin.

@BeautyIzHerName
Didn't say it was a he.

@ChefSwishWhisk
You didn't have to.

@BeautyIzHerName
How did you know, then?

@ChefSwishWhisk
Observation. Needling's an underrated skill.

@BeautyIzHerName
Or a weapon.

@ChefSwishWhisk
Depends who's holding it.

@BeautyIzHerName
You sound like someone who
likes watching people burn.

@ChefSwishWhisk
Maybe I just notice who doesn't wince.

@ChefSwishWhisk
Doesn't mean they didn't take the hit.

@BeautyIzHerName
I regrouped. Retired before I caught a charge.

@ChefSwishWhisk
Smart move. Pride's expensive.

@BeautyIzHerName
Don't make me block you.

@ChefSwishWhisk
Please. You'd miss me by sunrise.

@BeautyIzHerName
Bold assumption.

@ChefSwishWhisk
True one.

@BeautyIzHerName
You're impossible.

@ChefSwishWhisk
Persistent. There's a difference.

@BeautyIzHerName
You're not subtle either.

@ChefSwishWhisk
Never learned how to be. I just notice things.

@BeautyIzHerName
Like what.

@ChefSwishWhisk
How people get quiet when they care too much.

@BeautyIzHerName
That's deep for a man who probably matches
his aprons with his socks.

@ChefSwishWhisk
Should I be insulted?

@BeautyIzHerName
You always talk like this?

@ChefSwishWhisk
Only when people stay up to listen.

@BeautyIzHerName
You're dangerously close to smooth.

@ChefSwishWhisk
Close but not there yet.

@BeautyIzHerName
Don't test me.

@ChefSwishWhisk
Too late. You're smiling.

@BeautyIzHerName
I'm annoyed.

@ChefSwishWhisk
Same thing if it keeps you typing.

@BeautyIzHerName
Fine. Distract me. What's on the plate?

@ChefSwishWhisk
Roasted chicken with lemon garlic and thyme.

@BeautyIzHerName
That's not a snack. That's Sunday dinner.

@ChefSwishWhisk
Cooking's cheaper than therapy.

@BeautyIzHerName
For real. I just spent an hour watching
food reels I'll never make.

@ChefSwishWhisk
Reels are propaganda. They promise peace
in thirty seconds and convince people
they can sell sourdough.

@BeautyIzHerName
You're saying this to the woman who made peach
cobbler jerky last week.

@ChefSwishWhisk
CobblerGate. My favorite cautionary tale.

@BeautyIzHerName
It had potential.

@ChefSwishWhisk
It had trauma.

@BeautyIzHerName
You're relentless.

@ChefSwishWhisk
Someone's got to keep you grounded.

@BeautyIzHerName
I'm humble enough.

@ChefSwishWhisk
Nah. You're confident. Whole different thing.

@BeautyIzHerName
Confident? Not tonight.

@ChefSwishWhisk
Could've fooled me. You text like someone
who believes her own punctuation.

@BeautyIzHerName
That's oddly poetic for midnight.

@ChefSwishWhisk
Blame the thyme.

@BeautyIzHerName
You're bold.

@ChefSwishWhisk
Hungry people are.

@BeautyIzHerName
You're really eating that right now, aren't you?

@ChefSwishWhisk
What's your snack rotation tonight?

@BeautyIzHerName
Oreos with almond butter. Don't judge.

@ChefSwishWhisk
I wasn't.

@BeautyIzHerName
You paused too long.

@ChefSwishWhisk
Had to picture it first.

@BeautyIzHerName
It's art.

@ChefSwishWhisk
It's suspicious.

@BeautyIzHerName
You're judging.

@ChefSwishWhisk
Observing.

@BeautyIzHerName
Still dangerous.

@ChefSwishWhisk
Only if you send proof.

@BeautyIzHerName
You're a mess.

@ChefSwishWhisk
You keep saying that like it's a bad thing.

@BeautyIzHerName
Maybe it is.

@ChefSwishWhisk
And yet here you are.

@BeautyIzHerName
Insomnia pact.

@ChefSwishWhisk
Standing agreement.

@BeautyIzHerName
Careful. That sounds like a promise.

@ChefSwishWhisk
Only the ones I can keep.

@BeautyIzHerName
You're not bad at this.

@ChefSwishWhisk
I work well under pressure.

@BeautyIzHerName
Don't ruin it.

@ChefSwishWhisk
Too late.

@BeautyIzHerName
Goodnight, Chef.

@ChefSwishWhisk
Night, Beauty. Try not to dream
about cobbler jerky.

@BeautyIzHerName
Tragic. You just had to ruin it.

@ChefSwishWhisk
Fine. Let the night take it from here.

@BeautyIzHerName
I'll try.

Chapter 6

COLE

THE LOCKER ROOM SETTLED INTO THAT POSTGAME QUIET that pretended to be peace. It wasn't. It was the sound of frustration and the weight of a loss nobody wanted to claim. Sweat, tape, and disappointment hung in the air. We'd dropped two of three on the road, and this one cut deeper.

In the second half, I'd gone up for a rebound harder than I needed to. Clean enough to avoid a whistle, but I felt the force of it in my wrist when I came down. A crack in my composure that only I would notice. My control thinned more than I liked.

Denver had been a grind. Tonight, worse.

People swore I was unshakeable. What they didn't see was the work it took to stay upright. Some days silence was armor. Other days it was just a habit I couldn't break.

I peeled the tape from my fingers, letting the sting keep me present.

I packed fast. No small talk. Just the thud of my duffel zipping shut and the hiss of the showers in the background. The sooner we got back to San Antonio, the better. Two days off enough time to disappear to quiet the noise. To forget that my last shot had rimmed out when it mattered most.

I slung the bag over my shoulder, ready to vanish into the team bus, but our GM Devin McMillan's voice stopped me. He was standing near the exit with Coach Parker, both wearing expressions that meant this wasn't about stats.

"Cole," McMillan called. "Got a minute?"

I nodded, though every muscle said to keep walking.

He opened with that management smile. "Good to see the media buzz dying down. Publicity team says things are trending in the right direction."

Coach didn't bother pretending. "We brought you here because we believed you were ready to move forward. We need your head here. Not in the past."

It landed clean. Not cruel, just clear. But it still hit. Were they watching to see if I'd unravel again? Waiting for proof that the last year wasn't a fluke? They talked about focus like it was a switch. Like what happened could be shut off.

If they knew the truth, they'd understand there was no switch. There was only the moment your life collapsed in real time.

Hours after the championship parade, confetti still in my hair, champagne drying on my shirt, the city roaring our names, I'd stepped out of the club to look for my wife. Her location pinged a few blocks away. One of the team shuttles sat parked in the alley, door cracked, bass low, windows fogged. I thought she'd ducked away to take a call. Get air.

Inside, the light was dim, blue from a strip running along the ceiling. The air thick with sweat, Baccarat Rouge, and the distinct scent of something I didn't want to recognize. I took one step up, then another, and saw them.

She was on him. My wife naked, straddling my best friend, whose pants were pooled around his ankles. The man who'd shared my dorm room, stood beside me at my wedding, later stood in the same locker room as my assistant coach when his own career was derailed by injury. Her hands pressed to his shoulders, his face buried against her neck; they were moving together like they'd practiced it a hundred times before. Every sound scraped. Every breath hurt. There was no misunderstanding, no distance left to hide behind. It was betrayal, raw and deliberate, and it hit hard enough to leave me standing there, waiting for the world to tilt back into place when it never did.

They didn't even see me at first. The sound of her voice hit before the silence did. The floor shifted. My chest went tight. Stillness before something breaks.

I didn't yell. Didn't ask why. I just swung. One clean hit. Broke his jaw and the myth that we were ever anyone's dream couple, the reigning ambassadors for Relationship Goals offering proof that such a marriage could exist in pro sports.

McMillan cleared his throat, bringing me back. "What Parker means is, we believe in you. These last games are a blip. We just need to keep the story moving forward."

They'd dressed the spin up as a narrative, clean and marketable, but it was never mine.

I was up for a new contract that season, one with commas big enough to make executives nervous and bonuses that would make an owner sweat. Then came the punch. Reggie stayed. I couldn't. The team called it a culture reset, but everyone knew what it was. A chance to cut costs and wash their hands while keeping the story neat. Never mind the years I gave them or the championship I helped bring home. In the end, I was a liability with a highlight reel.

The front office had the nerve to call me in a week later, suits lined up like a jury, asking me to issue a public apology to help "protect the brand." Not the player. Not the man. The brand. I sat there listening to people who never picked up a ball talk about image like it was oxygen, and all I could think about was how fast loyalty turns to PR when the numbers don't fit the narrative. Ten minutes in, I'd had enough. By the time I left, half the conference room table was on its side, a chair missing a wheel, another through the glass wall, and security trailing me out while the same men who used to call me family couldn't even look me in the eye. Knowing damn well if it were them in my position, they'd have done worse.

And Bellamy… maybe she didn't start the fire, but she sure fanned it. She turned my worst moment into morning-show content, her voice giving gossip a microphone. Every rumor that followed, every think piece that bloomed from it, traced back to her. It was the perfect soil for the team to grow their own version of events, one that kept their image spotless and left me holding the mess.

Now she was here. A reminder I don't need, showing up in thoughts I couldn't quiet. A voice that slipped in when I was alone. A smirk that stayed long after she was gone.

I gave them both a curt nod. "Understood."

Parker was already halfway down the corridor when McMillan softened. "Get some rest. We'll regroup at practice."

I just shouldered my bag and headed for the bus. When we eventually were wheels up, my body was finished but my mind wouldn't quit. Then my phone lit up.

@BeautyIzHerName

Still thinking about those smoky
bourbon-maple BBQ wings. You sure I won't burn
the kitchen down trying them?

A grin tugged at the corner of my mouth. The first genuine one in days.

@ChefSwishWhisk

If you can't handle a little heat,
maybe you're not ready for my recipes.

Her reply popped up before I could lock my phone.

@BeautyIzHerName
Wow, the ego. Bold for someone
I've never even seen actually cook.

A low laugh slipped out.

@ChefSwishWhisk
Touché. But don't let my confidence
scare you off. Trust the process, Beauty.
You'll be a master soon enough.

This space was the only part of my life that still felt untouched. No public mess. No expectations. Just banter and quiet between the lines. It was playful and easy, a reminder that I could still talk to someone without every word being turned into content.

We fell into sync like always, with her asking how to save a broken roux, me explaining every step in too much detail. She admitted she'd used the wrong pan. I called it a rookie move. She threatened to revoke my kitchen privileges. Each exchange untangled something tight inside me. For a while, I stopped replaying the missed shot and the look Coach gave me afterward.

As the plane dipped toward San Antonio, my mind finally felt like it was back in my own hands. I stretched, shoulders sore, thumbs still resting on the phone screen.

@BeautyIzHerName
I'm gonna get this roux right next time.
Then you'll owe me wings. Fair is fair.

I paused before typing back.

@ChefSwishWhisk
Deal. Just don't burn your kitchen down before I get there.

The send light blinked. I hit it and let myself believe, just for a moment, that maybe the worst was behind me.

The engines settled beneath the cabin, a steady vibration

through the floor. I leaned back and watched the city lights scatter until they dissolved completely.

As I reached my door, the hallway was still and lit low. I punched in the access code, ready for a shower and a few hours of real sleep. The keypad beeped once, then movement pulled my attention left.

Bellamy's door opened across the hall.

She stepped out before I could reach the handle, hair loose now, the braids gone, damp strands pulled into a low bun. Slate-blue leggings clung to her hips, a cropped jacket unzipped just enough to show the sports bra beneath. My gaze trailed lower before I could stop it. Curves that didn't ask for attention but got it anyway. She moved like her body knew exactly what it was doing, and for a second I forgot why I was standing here.

Bellamy was holding a cake container, condensation fogging the edges of the lid. A thin draft spilled from her apartment, trailing the smell of burnt flour and oil. A scent that hangs after a recipe goes sideways for just a second too long.

"Full disclosure," she said with a small smile, "I was going to make you dinner too. TJ said the team usually heads back right after the last away game, so I figured I'd catch you before you disappeared again."

I raised a brow. "And?"

Her grin widened. "Let's just say the dinner didn't make it. This cake was the only survivor."

I nodded toward the container. "You baked me a cake?"

"Don't make it weird," she said, stepping closer. "I caught the game. You looked like you could use a pick-me-up, and food seemed better than a pep talk you didn't ask for."

Her mouth lifted, not quite a full smile, more a careful test of how close she could get before I flinched. There was fatigue behind her eyes, softened by something steady, bordering on patient. When she looked at me, it was direct, without apology, like she was trying to say more than she wanted to admit.

I just about smiled. "What kind of cake?"

"Pecan praline," she said with a shrug, her voice low and a little playful. "My grandmother's recipe. I even followed directions this time."

The words came easy, but the look she gave me wasn't casual. There was a flicker in her eyes, something slow and sure that pulled me in before I could look away. Her fingers shifted against the lid, her nails tapping once against the plastic, a small, unintentional rhythm that felt more intimate than it should.

I took her in fully now. She was flushed from the heat of her apartment oven, a sheen of sweat along her collarbone, a soft curl escaping her bun. The slate-blue fabric clung to her curves in all the ways my attention didn't need to notice. I adjusted the strap on my duffel, grounding myself with the weight of it.

"You want to come in?" I heard myself ask before I could think better of it.

She blinked, surprised. "I don't want to intrude—"

"You're already standing here holding dessert," I said, pushing the door open wider. "It'd be rude not to share."

She laughed quietly and stepped inside just in time for three corgis to rocket through her open door.

"Guys! No!" she groaned as they scattered like they owned the place. One hopped on the couch. Another sniffed the corner of the coffee table. The third spun in happy circles on the hardwood.

"This is not how I planned this," she muttered.

"It's fine," I said, fighting a grin. "They make better guests than most people I know."

She shot me a side glance. "Rough trip?"

"You could say that."

We moved to the kitchen. She set the container on the counter and lifted the lid. The caramel glaze caught the light, thick and glossy, pecans nestled like they belonged there. The smell of butter and brown sugar filled the air, warm and familiar. My stomach growled before I could hide it.

"Looks good," I said, reaching for a knife. "You sure you made this?"

She huffed a small laugh. "Cute."

I cut a piece and took a bite. Sweet, nutty, a little crunchy at the edges. "All right," I said around a mouthful. "You weren't lying. It's solid."

"I figured everyone could use something sweet after this week," she said quietly.

I nodded, still chewing. "Appreciate it."

She studied the cake for a beat, then said, "My grandmother taught me how to make it. She'd stir everything by hand, never measured a thing, just said she knew by feel. I used to sit at her kitchen table and watch her scold anybody who tried to taste the glaze before it cooled."

"She sounds like a force," I said.

"She was," Bellamy said, voice softening. "This is my dad's favorite. I wanted to get it right… for her, for him. Felt like it was important to keep a piece of her alive."

I nodded again, slower this time. The story pressed heavier than I'd expected, maybe because it felt like something she hadn't planned to share.

She glanced at the dogs. "They've claimed your couch."

"Guess you'll have to bring cake more often."

She smiled. "We'll see."

She rounded them up, calling each by name. The smallest

one stalled, looking back like it was losing its favorite spot. At the doorway, she paused, hand braced on the frame. "Can I ask you something?"

"Sure."

"How do you do it? Keep showing up after a loss. After all of it. How do you walk back out there like it didn't crack something open?"

The question settled clean and quiet. I looked at the cake, then at her.

"You don't," I said finally. "You just learn to carry it better."

Her expression softened. She nodded once. "Goodnight, Cole."

"Goodnight, Bellamy."

The door closed, and the apartment exhaled around me. I looked down at the cake, still warm under the glaze. It wasn't not just dessert. It was a shift. A small truce. A reminder that maybe not everything good had to be earned through pain.

The quiet finally felt like something I could live with.

A Tribe Called Quest played low through Jawn's speakers, the bass steady enough to settle a room without taking it over. The scent of espresso and brown sugar drifted from behind the counter, chasing the bite of roasted beans and something sweet baking in the back. Morning light pushed through the windows, soft and forgiving.

This place always hit the reset button for me. It's quiet without trying to be. A spot that makes you forget what time it is.

I slid onto my usual stool. Nina clocked me before I even spoke. Gold hoops, apron tied high, and an expression like she already knew what I came for.

"Look who decided to touch grass," she said, wiping her hands on her apron. "What's this, a coffee run or ingredient recon for your little secret account?"

"Need caffeine before I run film with the team," I said, setting my phone down and giving her a look. "You also talk too much."

"Occupational hazard," she said, sliding a mug my way. "Try this. New roast from that Black-owned spot in Houston I told you about. Deep caramel notes with a subtle hint of citrus. You'll like it."

I took a sip. "Not bad."

"Not bad?" she repeated, laughing. "High praise from Mister I Cure Heartbreak with Marinades. I think I'm going to start carrying it. Anyway, I got something for you." She ducked under the counter and came back with a small jar. "Fermented chili paste. My cousin brought it back from Thailand. Figure it might be cameo-worthy."

I twisted the lid open and caught the smoky, sharp tang. "Oh that joint's alive. You might be right."

"I usually am." She winked.

Before I could answer, the bell over the door rang. Bellamy walked in like she owned the light that followed her. Gray sweats with a matching unzipped jacket over a black sports bra and her hair slicked into a low ponytail. Her makeup-free face naturally caught the morning glow and made the room take notice.

She spotted Nina first as she made her way toward us. "TJ said you've got the girls' meals ready?"

"Right here." Nina reached into a small cooler on the counter and pulled out a mason jar with layered ingredients for Bellamy to see. "Salmon, turkey, chicken, and a few bottles of that absurd Norwegian water they treat like it's imported from heaven."

Bellamy laughed. "They eat better than I do."

"You and me both," Nina said.

I glanced over. "Water from Norway for dogs. I can't even be mad. That's luxury."

Bellamy looked up at me, a small scowl forming. "Don't start."

"Wouldn't dream of it, Bella."

The scowl deepened. "Don't call me that."

Before I could respond, Nina stepped out from behind the espresso machine, drying her hands. "You two already know each other?"

"Neighbors," I said, keeping my tone easy. I caught the quick spark in her eyes and knew what it meant. Nina's wheels were already turning, and once that happened, there was no slowing her down.

She grinned. "Of course you are. San Antonio's small. You'll be running into each other everywhere. So are y'all flirting or fighting? Hard to tell."

Bellamy shook her head, sliding her card across the counter. "Just trying to get my order and leave before somebody writes about it."

"Coffee?" Nina asked.

"Please," Bellamy said. "And your grits with the works. I'm on a mission to taste everything on your menu, but right now those grits have a hold on me."

Nina moved toward the kitchen, leaving us in a quiet that filled itself. Bellamy hopped onto a stool and scrolled through her phone. I watched the steam rise from her cup when Nina set it down, and a steaming bowl of what looked like Philly's-South-Street-meets-the-Bayou grits. They were thick enough to hold a spoon upright, piled with blackened chicken, roasted peppers and onions, and the secret Cajun sauce she still refused to give me the recipe for. A slow cheese pull followed, indecent in all the best ways.

When Bellamy finally looked over, her tone was light but edged. "You always here this early?"

"Some mornings," I said. "Helps me think."

She muttered, "Figures."

Nina soon returned and leaned her hip against the counter, eyes gleaming with that look that always meant trouble.

"All right, Bellamy," she said. "Tomorrow night, you're coming with me to the Storm game. Courtside seats. You're my plus-one."

Bellamy didn't even glance up from her phone. "Hard pass."

"Not a request," Nina said, flipping her towel over her shoulder. "Cole's getting us the tickets."

I raised a brow. "I am?"

She gave me that innocent smile that never once meant innocent. "Don't act brand new. You're the plug."

Bellamy finally looked up, skeptical. "You're the plug?"

I shrugged. "Apparently."

"Then I definitely shouldn't go," she said, stirring her grits like that settled it. "I'm fine sitting at home."

"Didn't sound like an RSVP," Nina said, setting a biscuit next to Bellamy's bowl of grits. "You need a night out."

"For what?" Bellamy asked dryly.

"People," Nina said, giving Bellamy that look that always came before a scheme. "Real ones. Conversation that talks back. You've been here a week, and the only souls you've connected with have four stubby legs and snack demands. It's time to let somebody taller than two feet say hi."

Bellamy smirked. "They listen."

"Uh huh," Nina said. "Storm game tomorrow, and that's all I'm gonna say about that."

I leaned back on my stool, pretending to sound annoyed but too entertained to sell it. "You're bold for volunteering me when you don't even have the seats yet."

She smirked. "You'll make it happen. You always do. You like pretending you're not a soft, mushy giant."

"Soft? Mushy?" I repeated. "You're lucky I don't revoke your access to my ticket stash."

"Try it," she said, already smiling like she knew I wouldn't.

She continued to grin, unfazed. "And I figure I should use my perks before some lucky somebody comes along and gets first dibs."

I narrowed my eyes. "That supposed to mean something?"

"It means I'm not waiting to find out," she said, already smiling like she'd won.

Bellamy shook her head, the corner of her mouth tugging up. "This feels like a setup."

"That's because it is," I said, and let the words hang there, practically daring Nina to call my bluff.

"Only if you call fun a setup," she said. "Come on. Sit courtside and be cute with me."

"I'm not dressing up for a game," Bellamy said, but her tone was losing its edge.

"Good," Nina said. "Because it's better when you're dressing up for yourself. Six o'clock."

I pushed my cup aside and stood, pulling a few bills from my wallet. "I'm leaving before she starts picking outfits for both of you."

"Bye, Cole," Nina called, too sweet. "And text me once my seats are confirmed and ready at VIP."

Bellamy didn't look up, but a small smile caught at her mouth.

Tomorrow's game just got a lot more complicated.

It was after eleven. The condo was night quiet except for the syrupy bassline of Mariah Carey's "Honey" floating through the kitchen on loop for inspiration. Not loud. Just enough to garner inspiration for today's special guest ingredient. I let it run while I prepped. Low volume, high vibe.

I'd already set the tripod. Camera framed, angle locked. It wouldn't catch my face. Never did. ChefSwishWhisk was hands, technique, precision. Just food and feel.

I rubbed seasoning into a thick pork chop, the surface glossy under my fingers. Black pepper, sea salt, a brush of maple glaze. The air shifted as it hit the pan, offering up a clean sound. Heat doing what it did best.

The butter started to brown, and I whisked together honey, mustard, and a little apple cider vinegar until the glaze turned the color of late sunlight. It slid over the meat like lacquer. Steam curled at my wrist, carrying a scent that settled deep. Warm, savory, and sweet enough to remember.

Carrots roasted in the oven until the edges turned crisp and dark. I finished them with lemon zest and a drizzle of olive oil. Everything found its place on a black plate, arranged without hesitation. The pork angled. The carrots pressed close. The glaze streaked across the edge with just enough restraint.

The edit was quick. Trim, sync, post. Water ran in the sink as I rinsed the bowl, the last swirl circling the drain. My phone buzzed before the sink finished, offering up a few fire emojis and a message from a food blogger who kept hounding me for a collab. Then hers.

@BeautyIzHerName
Now who told you to cook like somebody's husband?

A smile started before I could stop it. Another message appeared.

@BeautyIzHerName
Okay, two things. I don't even know
what you used on that pork. And are you free tomorrow
for me to fly in so you can teach me, or nah?

I leaned against the counter, watching the light move across the floor. Her timing never missed. She had a way of showing up just when everything else quieted. I let the moment stretch, then typed.

@ChefSwishWhisk
Technically you're supposed to ask for the recipe,
not invite yourself to the kitchen.

Her reply appeared before my hand left the counter.

@BeautyIzHerName
You're avoiding the question.
So is that a yes or are you gatekeeping?

I shook my head, smiling into the stillness.

@ChefSwishWhisk
If you're serious, I'll make extra. Just promise
not to set your place on fire again.

A few seconds passed. Then her final message arrived.

@BeautyIzHerName
Try me.

I read it twice. The music kept playing, smooth and unbothered, while the scent of honey and heat lingered in the air. I stayed there, phone still in my hand, knowing exactly what I should do next. And not doing it.

I woke on the couch to barking. Not one bark, but a full chorus from across the hall. For what I pay to live here, the walls shouldn't let me know how many dogs my neighbor owns.

The throw blanket had slipped halfway off, and my neck ached from sleeping crooked. Early light pushed weakly through the blinds, just enough to trace over the glass coffee table littered with notes from last night's film review. The barking kept going, nails tapping against wood, tags jingling, a little too lively for this early.

Then came her voice. Low, patient in that way patience gets when it's about to run out. She wasn't yelling, but she didn't need to. Every sound in her tone said she'd already lost the argument with the dogs and was trying to save face.

I rubbed a hand across my face, reached for my notebook, and wrote the first thing that came to mind.

Some of us still sleep at this hour. Respectfully. - 34B.

The hallway was cool against my bare chest. I crouched, slid the note under her door, knocked once, and turned back toward my apartment. When I looked over my shoulder, the edge of the paper that still peeked from beneath her door vanished fast. It made me laugh, a real one, like the ones that sneak up before coffee.

I'd barely made it to the bathroom when I heard a soft knock at my door. A yellow sticky clung to the center when I opened it.

Respectfully, they are adjusting. Try earplugs. -34A.

I peeled it off and set it on the fridge, smiling before I could stop myself. I told myself that would be the end of it.

It wasn't.

The coffee machine hissed to life. Rain began tapping against the window, a thin, steady sound that made the apartment feel smaller. I poured a second cup into a travel mug and wrote a new note.

Since we're both awake. I'll save you a trip in the rain. Just don't tell Nina. - 34B.

I left it outside her door and came back to the couch. The dogs quieted right away. Ten minutes later, another knock. A fresh sticky waited when I opened the door.

Truce accepted. Coffee's good. You're still on thin ice. - 34A.

I laughed, shook my head, and decided this was already the best morning of the week.

Fifteen minutes later, I heard a faint shuffle outside. When I opened the door again, a small brown paper bag sat just outside my threshold. Inside were two warm cheddar biscuits wrapped in foil and a note folded on top.

For your efforts. And your aim. We can't have fans throwing tomatoes on the court tonight. You're welcome. - 34A.

The biscuits were soft, buttery, and still steaming. I ate one over the sink, grinning like a fool at the way she'd managed to feed my ego and my appetite in one move. Maybe it was the salt or the butter. Or maybe I just hadn't traded this kind of smart talk with anyone in too long.

I went to the closet and pulled out a black alternate jersey from the stash I kept for charity events, tags still attached, the number twenty-four stitched bright across the front. I slid it into a paper bag and wrote across the top with a thick black marker.

Here's something you can wear proudly tonight, Bella. - 34B.

I added my cell number beneath it, using careful, deliberate handwriting. *In case you have any issues at the arena tonight, you can reach me.*

I set it outside her door, knocked once, and headed for a shower.

When I opened the door again, the bag was gone. A pink sticky waited in its place.

Respectfully, I don't do team colors. But I'll still show up. - 34A. (And it's BELLAMY. In case you forget, it rhymes with frenemy.)

I pressed that one on the fridge beside the yellow note, the two lined up like a scoreboard I couldn't stop checking.

The dogs barked again, only once, as if to sign off. I leaned back against the counter, coffee cooling in my hand, watching the rain streak down the glass. Somewhere across the hall, she was moving around, probably still barefoot, probably still fighting the morning.

For a building this expensive, the walls were too thin. But for once, I didn't mind what came through them.

Chapter 7

BELLAMY

NINA: DOWNSTAIRS AT THE BAR HOLDING A SPOT FOR US.

I knew better than to keep her waiting. Nina waiting was an act of grace the world didn't deserve twice.

The hotel bar glowed under warm brass fixtures, the light low enough to flatter but not so dim you couldn't tell who was watching. A deejay in the corner eased through Kaytranada and Cleo Sol, bass steady enough to feel like a heartbeat while a small crowd circled the bar, trading laughs and glances.

Nina was already posted up at the bar, a glass of something fruity and sparkling in her hand. She wore high-waisted cream trousers that skimmed her hips, a cropped black corset top under a slouchy linen blazer, and a pair of sleek black Sambas. Her look sat right at that intersection of effortless and intentional, with every detail chill until you realized it wasn't.

I slid onto the stool beside her. "You said casual. You didn't mention editorial casual."

She gave a slow smile, eyes flicking toward my reflection in the mirror behind the bar. "And you didn't mention you were showing up like a soft launch for somebody's high-end brand."

I glanced down, pretending offense. "Please. This is jeans and a top."

"Those jeans are tailored, and that top has structure." Her gaze was knowing. "Don't play coy."

I smirked. "Fine. Maybe I'm one glass of wine away from pitching this look for a brand partnership."

She laughed softly. "You've got jokes."

The jeans were dark indigo, hemmed just above my ankle. The white wrap top dipped low enough to flirt with scandal but stopped just short, and my boxy leather jacket balanced the line between chill and effort. My freshly braided hair was stitched back into a low bun, hoops catching the light just right.

I flagged the bartender. "White wine, please."

Nina chuckled. When the bartender set my glass down, she tapped hers against it. "Here's to new chapters and bad decisions smart enough to stay off camera."

I smiled at that, even if it stung a little. "Still too soon."

"Exactly why I said it." She took a sip, her eyes softening. "Tonight's not about timelines or chatter. It's about breathing again, that's all. I just want to see you healed and whole. Don't hand anybody power that makes you forget you deserve joy. Every bit of it."

"Easier said than done when people keep looking at me like they're trying to remember where they know me from."

She turned slightly, her voice low but firm. "Then let them. Recognition isn't ownership. They can look all they want... you're not their entertainment anymore."

Something loosened in my chest. I was learning fast that Nina had a way of speaking like she was defusing a bomb with the same effort as someone painting their nails.

"Fine," I said before finishing my drink. "But if anyone tells me everything happens for a reason, I'm out."

Nina laughed knowingly. "Then I better keep you close,

because people love preaching when they don't know the half."

The ride share arrived half an hour later. The driver had on old-school Donell Jones playing soft and low. Nina climbed in first, reapplying lip gloss in the darkened window.

"You sure about this?" I asked, buckling my seatbelt.

"Positive. I want to witness the Storm win tonight, and you need to stop hiding."

"I'm not hiding."

"You're in Texas," she said, arching a brow. "That's witness protection with better food."

I couldn't help but laugh. "You're not wrong. And honestly, if the witness protection menu includes brisket and sweet tea, sign me up."

She turned toward me, her voice gentler now. "I got you. You don't have to prove a thing tonight. Just show up."

"Yeah, except showing up apparently is in courtside seats at a game against one of the hottest teams right now. Sounds like a recipe for disaster."

"Or a hot topic you finally control."

The car merged into traffic, city lights sliding across her face like gold ribbons. For a second, I envied her ease.

When we reached the arena, the street outside pulsed with energy. Fans in jerseys filled the sidewalks, vendors shouted over each other selling snacks and souvenirs, and the air smelled like rain and excitement.

Inside, the shift hit fast under the controlled madness of lights, cameras, and cheers. Nina led us through the entrance reserved for players' families and suite holders like she'd been doing it for years. A few heads turned as we passed. One woman whispered my name like she was testing it, eyes dropping to her phone. The sound slid under my skin, a familiar tightening in my chest.

Nina caught it before I could react. "Don't start," she murmured.

"They can look, but they don't get access."

"I just—"

"Don't finish that sentence," she said. "You look good, you smell expensive, and you're with me. That's all they need to know."

I exhaled, letting her confidence settle over me like armor.

The seats were impossibly close. You could hear the sneakers squeak against the polished wood, the sound of players calling out rotations, the swish of a perfect shot during warmups. Nina was already in conversation with a photographer two rows over, and I was left watching the court.

Then Cole jogged out of the tunnel.

The sound from the crowd swelled, but everything else in me went still.

He looked different here. Bigger, somehow, and more grounded. Whatever weight he carried off the court didn't follow him under the lights. I wondered then what it must feel like to move through the noise with that kind of composure, to have the world watch you in motion and assume you were fine.

The game started fast. The Storm played like a team shaking off something heavy, sharper and leaner than they'd been on the road. Every pass hit clean, every dunk drew the crowd higher until the whole arena felt charged.

Nina was locked in from the opening tip, calm and collected until Ronan Edwards came into view. The shift was small but impossible to miss. Her shoulders straightened, her hand drifted to her hair, and she glanced at her phone like it had suddenly become fascinating.

"Subtle," I said.

"Don't start," she muttered.

"Who is he?"

"Ronan Edwards. Team captain. And before you ask, he's a

problem."

"Looks like the kind of problem that tips well."

Her side-eye was quick but not loaded. "He's also persistent. Keeps finding reasons to show up at Jawn, but somehow his orders only get complicated when I'm behind the counter."

"Maybe he likes the coffee," I said, though I already knew better.

"He stays doing the most and he also likes a challenge," she replied. Then, after a beat, "And I don't mix business with… *that*."

The pause after that told its own story.

I turned back to the court, trying to mask my grin. Cole was back in, moving like precision given form. Nothing wasted and every cut clean. The arena lights caught the sheen of sweat on his arms, and I hated that I noticed. He hit a jumper, landed light, and glanced toward the sideline just long enough for my breath to catch like I'd been caught doing something I shouldn't.

When the final buzzer hit, the Storm won by eight. Nina threw both arms up, whooping loud enough to draw a camera our way. I ducked before the jumbotron could catch me.

"See?" she said, bumping my shoulder. "Home wins cure everything."

"Pretty sure that's not medical advice."

"Neither is overpriced arena wine," she said.

"And yet here we are. Thriving on bad science and good shoes."

"Close enough. Come on. I want to say hi to the guys before they head out."

Ronan spotted us first, grin already spreading as he lightly jogged toward us inside the tunnel. He'd traded his uniform for a slate suit that fit too well to be accidental, the top buttons of his dress shirt undone just enough to make Nina forget her sentence halfway through. A diamond-laden chain caught the light at his collarbone, his game-day edge tempered into something disarmingly charming.

"Thought I heard that laugh," he said, voice smooth enough to belong on a playlist. "My girl Nina sitting all cute front row. You trying to throw me off?"

She smirked, crossing her arms. "You didn't need my help for that. Those free throws spoke for themselves."

He laughed, full and unbothered. "Guess you'll have to come to the next one."

I bit the inside of my cheek to keep from smiling too hard. I might've teased them if my attention hadn't shifted.

Cole came up behind him, dressed in a fitted black cashmere sweater and charcoal trousers that did things to the definition of casual. The gold at his wrist caught the tunnel lights, a quiet kind of flex that didn't need attention to work. His gaze found mine, steady and unreadable, before a small crease formed at the corner of his mouth, offering equal parts acknowledgment and warning.

"Bella. Didn't think you'd actually show," he said.

"I said I'd be here," I replied. "Shockingly, I keep my word."

Nina's smirk curved slow. "If tension was cardio, you two would be Olympic ready."

Ronan laughed under his breath and stepped closer. "Hey, Nina, let me holler at you for a minute."

They moved a few feet away, his hand grazing her lower back as they talked. I also noticed that she didn't pull away.

Cole's attention drifted back to me. "You all right? Looked like you nearly got taken out when Brooks went for that rebound."

I nodded, still smiling at the memory. "He definitely came in hot. Thought Nina was about to swing her purse at him."

He shrugged, casual. "He got a little too sloppy for my liking.

I had to clean it up on the next play."

I turned my head toward him.

"Consider it a reminder to keep his rebounds and his balance in check."

"That was on purpose?"

"Call it accountability." His tone stayed mild, but the corner of his mouth gave him away.

I tried to look unimpressed and failed. "That's petty."

"Effective, though."

"What happened to your 'no capes' manifesto?"

"So you'd rather end up with a broken nose because dude's got hands like butter?"

Before I could respond, Ronan and Nina returned. She looked a little too pleased with herself.

"We're starving," she said. "You two are coming with us."

Cole lifted a brow. "Are we?"

"Yup."

Nina gave him a once-over, her smile sharpening. "And since when do you dress like that after a game? Don't tell me you ironed for nothing."

Ronan laughed. "Yeah, man, postgame fit looking real intentional."

Cole didn't balk. "Didn't realize there was a dress code to adhere to."

"I have a fridge full of leftovers," I offered weakly.

"And my guys already have the truck warming up," Ronan added, like that settled it. "Come on. You can't say no to Loretta's Table with good people."

Cole gave him a look that said he was at least considering it. "You sure about the good part?"

Nina waved him off. "Don't start. Bellamy, he's driving you.

Ronan wants to finish a conversation with me."

Ronan grinned. "Meaning, I'm kidnapping your girl."

"Borrowing," I corrected him.

He laughed. "We'll see."

Cole gestured toward the exit. "Guess that's our cue."

I hesitated just long enough for Nina to arch a brow. *Go,* she mouthed.

So I did.

Outside, rain slicked the pavement, and the waiting SUV idled under the overhang. A black Range Rover Autobiography, polished to mirror gloss, lights low, engine purring quiet and steady. One of the arena staff handed him the fob with a quick nod.

"Appreciate it," Cole said, taking it before opening the passenger door for me. The gesture was casual, deliberate, practiced in a way that didn't need to draw attention. "After you."

"Chivalry still exists?" I asked, arching a brow.

"Depends on the company."

The interior smelled faintly of leather and cedar. I slid in to where a butter-soft heated seat awaited me. Rain traced down the windows while Cole settled into the driver's seat, adjusting nothing, like the car was already calibrated for him.

"Nice game," I said, watching the lights blur outside.

"Thanks."

"You looked… focused."

He glanced over. "You were watching that close?"

"Hard not to. You were everywhere."

A small, humorless sound left him. "Guess our GM will sleep better tonight."

"Does he ever?"

His smile was faint, more habit than joy. "Depends on the direction of my stats."

That brought out a laugh I didn't mean to give.

Then the quiet crept back in, thicker this time. I could have left it there. I should have. But the question pressed until it found air.

"Do you still hate me?"

His hand flexed once on the steering wheel. "You don't ease into things, do you?"

"I figured we're past pretending."

He didn't answer right away. The traffic lights washed red across his face, then green, before he spoke. "I don't hate you. I hated how it happened. What you said. Hearing someone I'd never met turn my life into a rumor mill before I'd even figured out how to explain it to myself."

"That's fair," I said quietly. "You came for me too, though."

His mouth curved in something close to a smirk. "Yeah. I did."

"I still remember the interview. 'Radio host playing dress-up as a journalist when she's really just a gossip influencer who lucked into a mic.' You said I was proof that charisma sells better than credibility."

The words hit harder than I expected, even now. He didn't blink, but his grip on the steering wheel tightened.

"My dad heard it live," I said. "Called me five minutes after it aired, swearing if he ever ran into you, it would be on sight."

A ghost of a smile flickered across his mouth. "Guessing I deserve that one."

"You did," I admitted. "But it still cut deeper than it should have."

"I was angry," he said after a long pause. "Didn't stop it from feeling true at the time."

"Maybe not," I said quietly. "But it wasn't fair either."

He turned his head slightly, eyes catching the green glow of the traffic light. "You sure you want fair from me now?"

"No," I said. "I just want honest."

The car filled with the soft patter of rain against the glass. I let it settle before I spoke.

"When everything happened with your ex, the call came through almost immediately. Someone close to her wanted to steer the story and knew exactly who to call. They came to me because I had the mic and the audience that believed I told women's truths, even when it got messy. They played it like concern, said they hated seeing another woman dragged into a man's mistake. They left out the cheating, but what they gave me still checked out. The assistant was in the hospital, and a short video clip that confirmed something happened hit my inbox. I never aired it, but I bought the rights in case I needed to prove the source was real."

I paused, watching the rain streak down the windshield. "Looking back, I can see what they were doing. They didn't need a journalist. They needed someone people already trusted to make the story sound like justice." I exhaled slowly and turned slightly toward him. "Cole, what happened was huge. The story moved fast, too fast. We went live before the sports networks, before the national outlets, before anyone had the full picture. I wanted the win, and I won't pretend otherwise. But when the truth finally came out and I saw how deep the lies ran, I buried that video and made sure no one could ever touch it. Some stories didn't need an audience, but I did try to unspin it.

"A publicist Laura tried to hire reached out in the middle of it all. Said they couldn't believe the lengths she was willing to go just because she had the money. I pitched a follow-up, a correction, something that told the truth. My producer shut it down before I finished the sentence. Said it was old news. Said the scandal had already done its job."

His jaw tightened again, though not at me this time. "And you let it go?"

"I tried not to," I said. "But Karen would've made me the

next segment, which she eventually did anyway. And by then, you'd already decided what kind of person I was."

His eyes flicked toward me, steady now, studying my face longer than before. "And what kind is that?"

"The kind you don't forgive."

He didn't argue. Something in his expression shifted, like he finally noticed the space between anger and regret. The silence that followed wasn't pointed this time. Just full. Heavy with what both of us could've done differently.

He exhaled, eyes fixed on the road. "For what it's worth, those cracks in my marriage were there long before you talked about them. You didn't break anything that wasn't already falling apart."

"That doesn't make me feel better."

"Wasn't supposed to," he said quietly. "But hearing you now… It doesn't change what happened, just how it sounds in my head."

I turned toward him. "Why?"

He didn't look away from the road, just let a hint of a smile ghost his mouth. "You sound like you mean it."

The rest of the drive held steady silence, broken only by the low thrum of the rain and the turn signal. When he finally spoke again, his voice was calm, even.

"Dinner's still on the table."

I looked over, unsure if he meant it literally or as a peace offering. "You sure that's a good idea?"

"Probably not. But I'm still hungry."

That got a small laugh out of me, soft and real this time.

We pulled up to Loretta's Table, tucked behind a row of wet oak trees, the sign glowing soft and gold under the rain. The valet jogged forward with an umbrella, but Cole rolled his window down and lifted a hand. "Give us a minute."

The valet nodded and stepped back under the awning. For a

moment, neither of us spoke. I traced the edge of my seatbelt with my fingers just to keep from fidgeting.

"Cole," I said quietly, "I'm sorry."

His jaw went rigid again, but he didn't turn right away.

"I should've asked more questions," I continued. "I should've waited. I wanted the win so bad that I didn't stop to think who it cost. You didn't deserve that. None of it."

He stared through the glass, the rain reflecting light over his face. "You think that fixes it?"

"No," I said. "But it's true."

That hit somewhere deeper than I meant it to. He sat back, closing his eyes briefly before he spoke. "People think rebuilding starts when you get the apology. But it starts when you stop needing it."

"That something you figured out or something you're still learning?"

"Both."

The silence that followed wasn't brittle anymore. It felt quieter, almost level. He turned the engine off and let the rain take over the sound.

"Come on," he said finally. "Food's waiting."

Inside, Loretta's Table glowed with soft light and low jazz. Cole gave his name to the hostess, who nodded and led us to a table in the back where Nina and Ronan were already seated. The staff greeted him with easy familiarity, which he returned with polite nods that said not tonight.

When we sat, he unfolded his napkin and leaned back. "You like Southern food?"

"Do I look like I don't?"

That drew a small, genuine smile. "Then you're in the right place."

He ordered grilled redfish, collard greens, and cornbread without looking at the menu. I asked for red-wine-braised short ribs over parmesan mashed potatoes, my appetite finally catching up to the night.

When the plates arrived, the air between us finally eased. Whatever weight was left had softened into something peaceful, close to easy. He looked over at me. "You good?"

"Getting there," I said.

"Same."

By the time the waiter brought the second round of drinks, the restaurant had loosened around us. A woman from the next table jumped up to sing Anita Baker with the live band like she couldn't help herself, and before long, all four of us were doubled over in laughter.

Nina was in the middle of a story about one of her employees when Ronan lifted his glass and tapped it twice with his fork, loud enough to turn a few heads in our direction.

Cole groaned under his breath. "Here we go."

I followed his line of sight and spotted Ronan with that spark in his eye, like he was about to turn dinner into a bit. Nina saw it too and started laughing.

He grinned, already too pleased with himself. "I can't help it. The spirit moved me."

I narrowed my eyes. "Should I be nervous?"

He turned toward me like it was his cue in a play nobody else had auditioned for.

"Not at all. You should be honored. Because tonight"—he dragged it out for full drama, milking the pause—"we are gathered here to celebrate." Ronan stood, glass raised, tapping his fork once against the rim, grin wide. "To celebrate… your *diii-vooorrrrce.*"

He sang it just like Taye Diggs in *Brown Sugar*, slow, dramatic, and entirely too proud of himself, stretching it like a note he'd been waiting his whole life to hit.

The table erupted. Nina hollered, someone a few tables over shouted, "Amen," and I dropped my face into my hands.

"A divorce from what?" I managed, fighting a smile. "I've never even been married."

"From the bullshit, Shorty." He waited for the laughter to fade before raising his glass higher. "To Bellamy. For standing tall when they tried to make her fall for sport." He took a slow sip, eyes still on me. "They pulled a stunt meant to humiliate you and ended up showing their own cards. Happens every time a woman won't stay small."

Nina groaned. "Here you go again."

He smirked. "Tell me I'm lying."

I shook my head, still smiling. "You're not."

"Didn't think so." He leaned back, grin easy but knowing. "And come on now. Ray Charles was blind, for real cheating in every zip code, and even he could see the truth for what it was. Anybody with eyes or ears knew you weren't the problem. That punk-ass coward and his fool's gold of a rent-a-housewife were."

Nina was wiping tears, breathless. "You're going to hell."

"Front row," Ronan said. "But we'll look good on the way."

"Now why you takin' us along for the ride?" she shot back, laughing.

That sent another ripple through the table. I shook my head, cheeks warm. "Y'all are hilarious."

He clinked his glass against mine. "To what didn't break us. And to letting the whole world know they played the wrong one."

"You're stupid for that," I said, laughter still catching in my throat. "But I appreciate you for it."

Ronan pressed a hand to his chest, the teasing gone from his face for once. "We got you, sis."

Something in his tone hit deeper than I expected. My smile

lingered, smaller now but real.

Nina lifted her glass. "To Bellamy. The reboot."

I raised mine, voice a little steadier. "To the reboot."

Cole lifted his last, eyes steady on me before he broke contact to toast with the rest.

The laughter returned, softer now, and for once I let it. No bracing, no pretending. Just laughter, real and unguarded.

When the dessert plates were cleared, the restaurant had softened into something quieter. The jazz trio had packed up, leaving a single pianist trailing notes that felt like an exhale at the end of the night. Outside, rain dotted the tall windows in slow, steady lines.

Nina was laughing again at something Ronan had said, one hand on his arm, her posture more open now. Whatever had been circling between them at the arena had found its landing here.

Cole caught the waiter's attention, settling the check before I could reach for my card.

"You didn't have to do that," I said.

"I did," he replied, tone even. "You're my guest."

"I thought I was Nina's guest."

"She passed you off," he said, the corner of his mouth turning up. "I accepted the trade."

I shook my head, smiling before I meant to. "You really think everything's a game."

"Only the ones worth playing."

When we stepped outside, the air was damp but warm. Streetlights stretched across the slick pavement, gold cutting through the dark. Ronan was already steering Nina toward the valet station, his jacket draped over her shoulders like it had always belonged there.

"You're taking Bellamy, right?" he called over, grinning.

Cole glanced at me. "We live in the same building. Might as well share the ride. You good with that?" he asked, voice easy but eyes expectant.

"It's fine," I said, even though it didn't sound nearly as casual as I wanted it to.

Once we were settled inside his Range Rover, the city moved past in a wash of wet lights and soft reflection. For a while, neither of us spoke. The silence wasn't strained, just thick enough to hold all the words we'd already said tonight.

"You're quiet," he said after a few blocks.

"So are you."

"I'm pacing myself."

"For what?"

His eyes slid toward me, amused. "You tell me."

I tried not to smile and failed. "Fine. I'm just taking in the evening. The food. The company."

"Glad to know I made the list."

"You didn't," I said, but the way he looked at me made it sound like I was lying.

He laughed, low and genuine. It filled the space between us, steady and unforced. Something about the way the rain pressed against the windows pulled honesty out of me.

I said quietly, mentally tracing the condensation on my glass, "People always assume women like me want attention. That we need it. But I spent years learning how to perform being unbothered just so no one could see when I was breaking. It's exhausting, pretending to be fine so no one thinks they won."

Cole turned toward me, not quick but deliberate. "You don't owe anyone *fine*."

I laughed softly. "Tell that to every mic I ever sat behind."

He shook his head, the faintest curve of a smile tugging at his mouth. "That's the thing. They only ever hear your voice. They don't listen to it."

That landed. I looked his way, caught off guard by the accuracy of it.

"And you?" I asked. "People listen to you?"

"They watch," he said. "But they only see what they want. The shots, the rumors, the stats. Nobody asks if I even like the game some days."

Something about that truth cracked open the air between us.

"Then I'll ask," I said. "Do you?"

His answer came after a breath. "I like who I am when it's just me and the ball. The rest of it? I survive."

I nodded slowly. "Maybe that's what we have in common."

He studied me then, eyes steady, searching. "What's that?"

"We both had to build peace out of survival."

He didn't smile. He didn't look away. "Maybe we could stop doing it alone."

That was the shift. Quiet and simple. A line that pulled the distance between us into something neither of us pretended not to feel anymore. When we pulled into the garage, the rain had slowed to a light drizzle. He parked in his reserved spot, leaving the engine running while Anderson .Paak played through the speakers.

"Thanks for the ride," I said.

"Thanks for coming out. I wasn't sure you would."

"Neither was I."

Something shifted in his expression. An understanding, maybe, or just relief. "Feels like we started to clear the air tonight."

"First step," I said quietly.

He nodded once, as if that was enough for now. When I reached for the handle, he moved first, unbuckling and opening his door.

"Not necessary," I said quickly.

"Wasn't trying to impress you."

"Good," I said, stepping out. "You'd have to try harder."

That drew out a small grin as he fell into step beside me. The elevator wasn't far, and the quiet between us carried all the way to the lobby.

Daryl was behind the front desk, pretending to read something on a monitor. His smirk caught me before he could hide it, that knowing look of someone who had seen more than he'd admit. A grin you caught from a concierge who'd seen every kind of story unfold in the same lobby.

When my eyes met his, he straightened fast, suddenly serious. "Evening, Ms. Barnes. Mr. Howard."

"Evening, Daryl," Cole said smoothly, pressing the elevator button.

The car arrived almost immediately. We stepped in together, the mirrored walls catching the glow from the lobby lights. I could see our reflections side by side. His calm. Mine pretending.

When the doors opened onto our floor, we both hesitated.

"Night, Bella," he said, pausing outside our doors.

"*Bell-a-MEE*. Night, Cole."

He waited until I stepped across the threshold before disappearing into his place across the hall. For a moment, I stood there, leaning against my own door, listening to the quiet settle back in except for the soft snores of the dogs curled up in their respective beds.

It felt heavier than silence. Something closer to possibility.

<h1>Chapter 8</h1>

<h2>COLE</h2>

BY THE TIME THE RAIN BURNED OFF, THE CITY HAD THAT Friday morning glow that was subdued but awake, like it was remembering how to breathe. I hadn't planned to leave my apartment, but then I heard her door open.

Bellamy stepped into the hallway, leash handles looped in one hand, dressed for comfort but managing to make it look intentional. TJ's dogs bounced around her ankles, pure enthusiasm in triplicate.

"Morning," I said.

She looked up, surprised but not bothered. "Hey. Didn't think you were an early riser."

"I'm not. Just bad at sleeping in."

"Join the club," she said, crouching to untangle the leashes. "I'm heading to the Riverwalk before it gets crowded. The girls need to burn off energy before they unionize."

I didn't think about it. "Mind company?"

She paused, sliding her sunglasses into place. "It's a long walk."

"I've got long legs."

That brought out a laugh she didn't try to hide. "Fine. But if you slow me down, I'm texting Ronan and telling him you couldn't keep up."

"Fair warning."

The elevator ride stayed quiet except for the dogs' soft panting. Outside, the air smelled clean and new, rain lifting off the concrete in faint threads of steam. The city stretched wide and slow, storefronts flickering awake as we headed down the cobblestone steps toward the river, water glinting under early light.

She walked with purpose. I matched it. Every so often she glanced over, not to check on me, but because silence between us wasn't empty anymore.

"You ever come down here?" she asked.

"When I first got traded. Thought if I kept moving, I could outrun my own reputation."

"Did it work?"

"Not even close."

She smiled, small but real. "It never does. I tried the same thing with blackout curtains and delivery apps."

We made it half a block before passing Jawn.

"Coffee?" I asked.

Bellamy hesitated, the dogs already sniffing the planters near the window. "I shouldn't."

"You should," I said, pushing open the door. "Stay here. I'll grab something to go."

She didn't argue. I ordered two coffees and a couple of breakfast sandwiches because no one should try walking three dogs on an empty stomach. When I came back out, she was kneeling, whispering something to one of the corgis like they were in negotiation.

"You bribing them?" I asked, handing her the coffee.

"They respond better to democracy," she said, taking the cup. "Thank you."

"Apparently Nina told her staff she'll be in late this morning."

She smiled behind the lid. "Hmmm. You should reach out to your boy and see if he knows the reason why."

We laughed and started toward the Riverwalk again, paper cups in hand, the city opening around us. The dogs tugged forward, leading us through a few more turns. By the time we circled back, the city was fully awake.

"Guess this counts as our third truce," she said.

"Guess it does."

Her hand brushed mine when she adjusted the leashes. It might have been nothing, but it didn't feel like nothing. The elevator opened, and the dogs charged out as if they owned the floor. We followed. The air felt thick with something that hadn't figured out what to call itself yet.

She lingered by her door, the corgis orbiting her. I stopped at mine, a few feet away. "You want to come in? Or I could… for a bit."

She tilted her head, reading me the way she probably used to read an audience, catching everything I didn't say. "Would that be about the company or about not wanting to be alone?"

I didn't blink. "Maybe I'm tired of pretending I don't want both."

Her mouth parted like she might answer—

"Surprise!"

We both turned.

A man filled TJ's doorway, arms open, grin ready. "Well damn, babygirl. I drive twelve hours and this is what I pull up on?"

Bellamy froze. "Daddy?"

"That's what my license says." He stepped out fully, grin easy, eyes sharp. "You forget how to answer a phone, or that thing just for decoration now?"

"I meant to call you back."

"Mm-hmm." His gaze slid to me, slow and thorough, taking in height, build, proximity. "And who's this? Security?"

"Neighbor," Bellamy said, quick. "Cole Howard."

He fixed me with a look that could have been an invitation or a verdict.

"I saw that interview. Had me ready to see if Suge's number is still working," he said. He let the sentence hang between us with a warm, quiet bite and did not break eye contact. "Lucky for you, son, the Lord told me to sit that one out, and I listened."

I kept my tone light and respectful. "Glad He had my back."

Bellamy groaned. "Daddy."

He cut his eyes at her. "Hush. You think I don't know who he is? You play for the Storm."

"Yes, sir."

"Y'all lost that game in Denver."

"Two points."

He nodded, slow and deliberate. "Could've gone either way. Didn't, though."

"Daddy, please."

He ignored her. "So you live across the hall?"

"Right across." I nodded toward my door.

He smiled without softening. "That's convenient."

"Daddy."

He turned back to her, still watching me out of the corner of his eye. "I'm just saying, babygirl. You sure you're walking dogs or walking into trouble? 'Cause that hard head of yours still hasn't learned to keep you out of it."

She shot him a look cold enough to crack glass. "Do you mind?"

"Not at all." He crouched to greet the dogs, who immediately betrayed her and mobbed him. "Even they know their granddaddy."

I tried to keep a straight face. "Big fan of your music, Mr. Barnes."

He rose, brushing invisible lint from his sleeve. "Of course you are."

"Daddy."

"What? Man's got taste." He finally smiled. "Nice meeting

you, Cole."

"Likewise, sir."

Bellamy herded him toward her apartment. "Come on, before you start interrogating the whole floor."

"Wouldn't need to if folks weren't standing in hallways like they don't have business of their own," he said, throwing one more look my way.

"Catch you later, Cole," Bellamy said, her tone light but her eyes softer than she meant them to be.

I watched her door close, the sound of her laugh blending with his deep voice on the other side. Then it was just me and the quiet. I stood there another beat, the scent of her perfume lingering, her laughter still in the air. I unlocked my door and stepped inside.

Across the hall, her father's voice carried faintly, the sound of a man who still filled rooms without trying. Bellamy's laugh followed, lighter now.

I found myself smiling. Then it hit, the truth sitting plain in my chest. She was under my skin.

And I wasn't sure I wanted that to change.

Game day was always a slow burn. Especially with an afternoon tipoff.

I woke up earlier than I wanted to. This time it wasn't from nerves. The condo was still dim, morning light barely touching the floorboards. Bellamy's dad showing up yesterday had played in my mind longer than I wanted it to. The way he looked at me. Knowing, silent, and unimpressed. Like he'd seen everything he needed in three seconds. And maybe he had.

Still, I wasn't spiraling. Not today. I had time to kill before I headed out, that quiet space between waking up and locking in was mine.

I padded into the kitchen and pulled open the fridge. I already knew what I was making. Cinnamon brioche French toast, whipped mascarpone, spiced berries. Something indulgent but still clean. Sweet but not cloying. A little extra.

Something that said I was still thinking about her.

A low vinyl crackle cut through the silence as I cued up the record player. I skipped the obvious cuts and landed on Tamia's "So Into You." Midtempo, warm, sensual. It was flirtation wrapped in harmony. Fit the mood. Fit the memory.

Keeping the camera trained on my hands, I sliced thick pieces of brioche, then whisked the eggs with oat milk and a touch of nutmeg. The pan sizzled when the first slice hit. Lighting was soft, natural. I layered the mascarpone with vanilla bean and lemon zest, mixed it smooth, then built the plate like it was a canvas.

I finished the reel with a slow pour of warm maple syrup over the top. No voiceover, just visuals and Tamia's hook syncing up with the drizzle.

I uploaded it to ChefSwishWhisk with a simple caption. *Mood. Slow mornings and sweet cravings.*

The likes rolled in fast, usual mix of fire emojis and fork and knife reactions. Even a few brands reaching out wanting to pitch deals with me, not knowing I automatically declined all offers mentally to preserve my sanctuary.

I made it to the arena a little after nine. Trainers set up their stations, the low whir of the cold tubs drifting down the hall. Nico was already on a table, groaning through a hamstring stretch while one of the trainers laughed at him. I nodded as I passed and headed to my spot. By the time I dropped my bag, Chuck was waving me over.

"Let's get those knees right," he said.

I climbed onto the table and let him guide my leg through a series of slow extensions. Movement that kept me from feeling ninety-five in the fourth quarter. He switched to working the other side, thumbs finding every place that liked to tighten on game days.

"You slept?" he asked.

"A little."

He gave me a look that said he didn't buy a word of it. I smirked, but he wasn't wrong.

Chuck finished the last pass and strapped heat packs around both knees. "Ten minutes, then mobility."

I settled back, letting the warmth sink in. My phone buzzed from the stool beside the table. I reached for it, already expecting a team update or a message from the staff.

Not even close.

@BeautyIzHerName
That French toast looks criminal.
What time's brunch?

A smile pulled at the corner of my mouth. She was early and quick, as always.

@ChefSwishWhisk
Kitchen closes at noon. You might make it
if you don't stop to flirt.

Her reply came fast.

@BeautyIzHerName
Who says I'm flirting?
Maybe I just appreciate good plating.

@ChefSwishWhisk
Then you're welcome.
Aesthetics are part of the experience.

Nico raised a brow at me from across the court. "Something funny?"

I shook my head and pocketed the phone, but I could still feel the grin tugging at my mouth.

It wasn't just the banter. It was her. She got under my skin in a way I couldn't quite explain. There was no name or face attached to what we had, but it was real enough to feel like something I looked forward to. Something I protected.

I liked the way she saw things, called me out without being abrasive, made room for a different kind of connection. There was nothing performative between us. No cameras. No opinions. Just this thread we kept pulling.

And yeah, maybe I did think about her too much when I was on the road, when I couldn't sleep, when Bellamy crossed my mind and I was not ready to admit how often that'd been happening too.

But Beauty felt simpler. Lighter. Like I got to be someone unburdened by everything else. Still, that ease was shifting. I felt it every time she messaged me. We were heading somewhere.

And I wasn't sure what happened when we got there.

Chapter 9

BELLAMY

SATURDAY ARRIVED SUN-WARMED AND EASY, MAKING you believe in soft starts. It was just past noon and Daddy and I were at Jawn's, because that was what Terrence Barnes did. He showed up uninvited, disrupted the peace, then fed you until you forgot why you were mad.

He didn't ask permission to visit, didn't ask if I had plans, just showed up, and now we were here for a round of nourishment as if he hadn't just driven through the night on a whim.

"This the spot?" Dad asked, pulling off his sunglasses. He was in a denim button-up, black jeans, and sneakers with a resale value that could fund a semester. Even trying to be incognito, he drew attention. The silver in his goatee caught the light.

"This is the spot," I said, reaching to hold the door open for him.

He stopped short, giving me that familiar side-eye. "Now what kind of men you been dealing with that got you out here opening doors?"

I blinked.

"You know good and damn well I didn't raise you to hold a door for me… or any other ninja with a working arm."

Before I could argue, he waved me off and opened the door himself with a flourish, muttering something about how this generation was getting entirely too casual with the basics.

Nina saw us before we reached the counter, eyes narrowing with a grin as she wiped her hands on a towel and headed our way.

"Hold up," she said, grinning. "Is that *the* Terrence Barnes who just entered my establishment?"

Dad spread his arms wide. "That depends. This the famous Nina my girls are always talking about?"

"Depends on what's coming out of their mouth," she shot back, already stepping into a warm, two-armed hug.

"Bellamy swore up and down this was the place we needed to come to. Said you could throw down, which, judging by the smells and the welcome, might've been the most accurate thing she's ever said."

Nina laughed, a dimple showing. "She finally brought you around. TJ's been raving about you for years to the point where it started to sound like a myth. It's nice to finally say I've personally come face to face with the legend. You have no idea what an honor this is."

Dad leaned back, hands over his heart like he was touched, faux humility in full effect. "Myth. Legend. Taxpayer. I answer to all three."

"Any family of TJ and Bellamy's…" Nina said, motioning us toward a table near a small stage. "You're getting the VIP treatment today. Sit tight, and I'll send over something that'll make you rethink every other brunch you've had."

Jawn's was a whole vibe on the weekend, with all of the conversations, laughter, forks clinking against plates, and the way the deejay dipped into old-school soul. Maxwell, Mary, a little Raphael Saadiq. Dad nodded along, already relaxing into the space.

When the game popped onto one of the overhead TVs, he looked up. "No Lakers today?"

Nina set down our menus. "Only Philly, San Antone, and HBCU teams get screen time here. House rule."

A paasserby called out on reflex, "Go Birds!" A quick burst of laughter followed, then the room settled again.

"Fair enough," he said, easing into his seat like he'd done this a thousand times. Like he belonged here.

A moment later, the shift changed. First it was low murmurs and barely concealed stares. Then one woman nudged her friend and gestured subtly in our direction. Nina noticed and leaned in.

"You want me to redirect the attention?" she asked, casual but ready.

Dad shook his head, eyes still on the menu. "Nah, let 'em look. I'm retired, not extinct."

He didn't hesitate when a guest walked over a few moments later with shaky hands and a napkin, signing it without a pause. Dad flashed that signature smile and took the picture. It was autopilot at this point.

And I watched, like I always did. Not just how he handled people, but the machinery beneath the charm. He was warm because he was practiced. Present because he knew how to perform it. He'd taught me that trick. How to show up on empty, how to let people feel close while never giving them the part that cost you something.

Then Cole flashed across the screen cutting through the paint, calm and controlled. The camera lingered long enough for me to notice the sweat at his brow, the flex in his shoulders. I tried not to appear like I was looking and failed miserably.

Dad sipped his sweet tea, waited a beat. Then he shifted in his seat, angling toward me with that slow, deliberate focus I hadn't seen in years. It was the look he used to give me when I came home late with some weak excuse, the one that made me crack before I even sat down. There was no judgment in it. Just knowing. Like he was flipping through pages I hadn't meant to leave out.

"That the one from yesterday?"

I nodded, and in that second, I was sixteen again, sitting across from him at the kitchen table with a tear in my favorite jeans and my heart too full to explain.

He didn't rib me. Didn't raise an eyebrow. Just watched, and somehow it still got through.

"You liked him before you realized you liked him."

I glanced down, then back up. "Maybe."

He let the truth breathe between us. Didn't push it, didn't pack it with advice. Just left it right where it landed.

Nina swung back by to chat, arms folded, eyes dancing. We talked about TJ, the local artists showcase she was pulling together at Jawn, and whether the corgis had emotionally recovered from being away from their true parent. I smiled, I nodded, I participated, but I could still feel Dad watching me. Not hovering. Just seeing.

Eventually, he leaned forward and folded his hands like we were about to negotiate terms, like he was about to deliver news I wouldn't want to hear but needed to sit with anyway.

"You know I didn't just show up to meet up with you for brunch."

I waited, bracing.

"I needed to lay eyes on you. Make sure my babygirl's really okay."

He said it plain, but there was weight tucked in the softness, like he was reminding me who I'd always be to him. TJ might be all Mommy's heart, her ride-or-die partner for life, but I was Dad's shadow through and through. His mirror. His softness in a world that demanded steel.

TJ may have been the first to call him Dad, especially after their mother walked, but I was the first little girl to show him what that word had to mean. The one who cracked him open with tea parties and temper tantrums. The one who made him reckon with gentleness.

I wasn't his firstborn, but I was his first glimpse into a love that folds instead of fights. The one he used to carry on his shoulders, calling me his backup plan if singing never panned out. The one with a mouth too quick, a heart too loud, and a will that matched his pound for pound. I didn't ask to be his soft spot. But I became it anyway. And now, he watched me like I was still that girl with scraped knees and big questions, waiting to be told the world was safe. I saw it in the way he looked at me now, both worried and proud. And completely, undeniably mine.

"I'm good."

He let the lie settle between us like a too-full cup, just on the edge of spilling. Didn't challenge it. Just watched me with that quiet patience that used to feel like pressure when I was younger. Now it felt like grace.

"You don't let people in easy," he said. "Even when you want to. Especially when you do."

I pressed my lips together, staring down at the condensation sliding down my glass.

"I know where that came from."

That pulled my eyes back to his.

"I gave you a version of love that could disappear," he said, voice small. "One that showed up big and then pulled back when life got loud. I made it feel like you had to perform just to keep it. And I hate that you learned to guard your heart by pretending it wasn't ever asking for anything."

The words cut through me, settling deep because they'd been

waiting too long to be said.

He reached across the table, palm up, offering something without making it a demand. I slid my hand into his. That part never changed.

"You've already been through the fire," he said, nodding slightly toward the TV, where Cole stood still and centered. "And I don't trust easily when it comes to men around you. You know that."

I nodded. I did know.

"But there's something about this one," he added. "Something in the way you looked at him without realizing it. Something in how you're not trying so hard to hide it."

He let the pause sit between us, then softened.

"If he's different… don't run. Not just because it's unfamiliar. Just be sure he's showing you who he is, not who he thinks you want."

I swallowed hard, my throat tight. That was all I had.

Cole was still on the screen. Poised. Silent. Like he wasn't just comfortable in his skin, but accountable to it.

And that was when I let myself wonder what it would feel like to stop guarding the exits.

That evening, we were on one of the riverboats drifting down the Riverwalk, lights flickering off the water like the city was in on something sacred. After his nap, Dad had made chicken and dumplings, rich and light at once, comfort in a bowl that filled the house and your chest. The taste still lingered warm as we traded the kitchen light for the river. Tourists chattered nearby, but their voices faded under the steady roar of the motor and the faint echo of a saxophone somewhere down the bend. It was a night made for confession, where the sky held back its stars just long enough to listen.

Dad was beside me, arm draped around my shoulders as I tucked my head against his chest, his cologne laced with river breeze and time. He was scanning the horizon like it owed him an answer. Or an apology.

"This place always reminds me of how your mom used to look at water," he said eventually. "Said it made her feel like things were still possible. Even when we weren't."

I didn't answer right away, just watched the reflections ripple across the water. "Y'all had a lot of restarts."

"Too many," he admitted. "Thought love meant always coming back. Even when you had no business doing so."

"You loved her."

"Still do. Doesn't mean I always knew how to do right by her." His voice hit like a line from a song I'd never stopped knowing the words to. It looped quietly, lodged in memory worn, unresolved, and too close to the truth.

"You ever wonder how you could write all those songs about love… real love… and still be the reason someone lost their faith in it?"

His head turned slow. Like the words needed time to register.

I regretted it the second it was out there. Not because it wasn't true. But because I hadn't meant to say it out loud. Hadn't meant to bleed in front of him like that.

"That what happened to you?" he asked, his voice now raspy barely above the hush of the river.

I shrugged, throat tight, the boat's movement giving me something to focus on that wasn't the heat rising behind my eyes. "Some of it."

He exhaled, slow and heavy, like his ribcage had to uncage something first. "I was a fool, babygirl. I hurt your mother. And I gave you too many examples of love with strings attached. Grand gestures with empty follow-through. Love that looked good in a chorus but hollowed out in a bridge. Even performs when the lights are on, but disappears when the curtain drops. Shit, now I see it probably even taught you to shrink just enough to be loved in return."

I nodded, jaw clenched, staring out at the lights strung above the walkway. They all started to blur.

He glanced upward, at the stars inching their way into the night. "Your mom wanted something rooted. I kept arriving like a season. Showing up warm and leaving cold. Always promising to return."

The boat glided past a mural, lit soft and golden, of two brown-skinned girls holding hands beneath lantern-strung cypress branches, their silhouettes mirrored in the water like a memory still in motion.

"I used to think if I could sing about it enough, I could become it," he said, more to himself now. "Turns out knowing how to say the right words don't mean you've earned the right to live them."

I didn't speak. I didn't move. I just let him sit in the truth for once.

Then he looked at me. Really looked. Like he was measuring the damage and the grace in the same breath.

"You always were the one who held me to the highest standard," he said. "Even when you didn't say it. You watched me too closely not to be changed by what you saw."

"You're my daddy." My voice cracked on the last word. "How could I not?"

He nodded, eyes glassy. "You deserved better from us. From *me*. And I can't undo what that taught you. But I need you to know, because I see that uncertainty wavering in your eyes sometimes… you were never hard to love. Not even once."

The words moved something soft inside me. Not a break, just a quiet shift.

He squeezed my hand. "You don't have to prove you're worth

keeping. Not to anybody. Not even to yourself."

We drifted under a stone archway, the lights above casting halos on the water.

My dad looked out across it. "Let that man show up for you the way I should've shown up for your mom. Don't punish him for our lessons. Let him earn you in real time." He paused, thumb brushing the back of my hand. "I've done a lot wrong, Bellamy, but I know love when I see it… and I see it trying to find you."

I didn't respond. I just breathed. Let the silence fill the space between forgiveness and forward.

And I wondered if maybe this was what healing sounded like. Low and honest, floating on a river that finally knew where it was going.

The DMs

@ChefSwishWhisk

Ever have someone say something you already knew, but the way it landed made your back straighten like you'd been caught slouching?

@BeautyIzHerName

Sounds uncomfortable. And maybe necessary.

@ChefSwishWhisk

Both. I walked away feeling seen and slightly called out.

@BeautyIzHerName

That's the best kind of call-out. One that doesn't humiliate you, just removes your excuses.

@ChefSwishWhisk

Exactly. Left me wondering if I've been hiding behind the wrong ones.

@BeautyIzHerName

Or overusing them. I'm guilty of that. Tonight I said something sharp to someone I care about. The truth, but sharper than I meant. It felt good in the moment. Still feels heavy now.

@ChefSwishWhisk

Heavy isn't always wrong.

@BeautyIzHerName

No, but it lingers. I keep replaying their face.

@ChefSwishWhisk

Would silence have been better?

@BeautyIzHerName
That's the question. I don't know.

@ChefSwishWhisk
My opinion, silence usually rots. Truth stings but at least it breathes.

@BeautyIzHerName
You say that like you've lived it.

@ChefSwishWhisk
I have. The words I swallowed when I shouldn't have, that's the weight I still carry.

@BeautyIzHerName
That's annoyingly persuasive.

@ChefSwishWhisk
Take it as a compliment.

@BeautyIzHerName
I don't like compliments. They're slippery.

@ChefSwishWhisk
Then take it as agreement.

@BeautyIzHerName
Better. So what now? You try harder tomorrow.
I try softer.

@ChefSwishWhisk
Sounds like a plan.

@BeautyIzHerName
A fragile one, but a plan.

@ChefSwishWhisk
Fragile things can still hold.

@BeautyIzHerName
There you go again. You make honesty sound
less like a risk and more like a posture.

@ChefSwishWhisk
Maybe that's what it is. Stand how you
want to be seen.

@BeautyIzHerName
If I stand like that, someone might
notice the cracks.

@ChefSwishWhisk
Maybe that's the point.

@BeautyIzHerName
You're dangerous.

@ChefSwishWhisk
Only on good nights.

@BeautyIzHerName
Tonight counts.

@ChefSwishWhisk
Then let's leave it here. With both of us
straighter than we were an hour ago.

@BeautyIzHerName
I'll allow it. Goodnight, Chef.

@ChefSwishWhisk
Night, Beauty.

@BeautyIzHerName
Wait, before you disappear.

@ChefSwishWhisk
I'm here.

@BeautyIzHerName
You didn't answer the obvious.
What if you stand straighter and someone pushes
instead of steadying?

@ChefSwishWhisk
Then bend, not break.

@BeautyIzHerName
That's too smooth.

@ChefSwishWhisk
You asked.

@BeautyIzHerName
Fine. But if I wake up tomorrow sore from trying
this new posture thing, I'm blaming you.

@ChefSwishWhisk
Blame accepted. I'll even write the doctor's note.

@BeautyIzHerName
Make sure your handwriting's illegible.

@ChefSwishWhisk
Naturally. All the best signatures are.

@BeautyIzHerName
You're something else.

@ChefSwishWhisk
But still here.

@BeautyIzHerName
And that's why it feels lighter now. Goodnight for
real.

@ChefSwishWhisk
Goodnight. Stand tall, Beauty.

Chapter 10

COLE

THE SAUNA HEAT PRESSED IN SLOW AND STEADY, WORKING its way through the tightness in my shoulders until the ache eased into something manageable. I sat there, counting breaths, letting the quiet do its job. No phone calls, no trainers, nothing I had to answer to. Just space.

I'd skipped the team facility today, claiming a recovery day. The truth was simpler. I wanted to be left alone. There were too many voices in my ear lately about the next away series, about optics, about keeping a low profile. Everyone had advice and none of it made the silence in my head any quieter.

Through the fogged glass of the sauna door, a flash of movement cut across the gym floor. At first, I ignored it. Then she came into focus. Bellamy.

Her hair was pulled back, her sweatshirt loose enough to hang off one shoulder, and the rest of her was all quiet intention. She dropped her duffel, paired a small speaker to her phone, and let Biggie roll through the room. The bass hit, and she started stretching like she was warming up for a show only she was invited to.

I could've looked away. Should've. But the more I watched, the harder that became. Shit, the harder *I* started to become. She wasn't performing. She was somewhere else entirely, grinning at her reflection, mouthing lyrics, swaying like no one could see her. There was an ease to it. An ease you couldn't fake.

Then she moved to the weight machines and all that confidence vanished. She squinted at the settings like they were written in code, chose a weight that would humble her immediately, and grabbed the bar wrong enough to make me flinch. I lasted thirty seconds before standing.

The sauna door hissed when I opened it, steam curling out into the cooler air.

"Bellamy," I called out.

She didn't hear me, focused on the bar, teeth clamped down a little.

"Bellamy," I said again, louder.

She jumped, spinning around. "Shit, Cole! You can't just sneak up on people."

"I wasn't sneaking. I was saving you from a pulled shoulder."

Her eyes narrowed. "You were watching me?"

"Observing… for safety reasons." I gestured toward the sauna. "Do you want help, or do I let the injury run its course?"

Her hands landed on her hips. "Fine. Enlighten me, Coach."

"Hands a little wider. Keep your chest up when you pull. And breathe through the motion," I said, adjusting the seat height.

She mirrored me, careful this time, lips pressed together in focus, and I fought like hell at the thought of prying those pretty little things open with my tongue. "Like this?"

"Closer," I said. "Don't rush the movement. You're trying to lift the whole thing like you're mad at it."

"I *am* mad at it," she said through her teeth, pulling again.

"Thought so."

Her shoulders rolled back. "You always this helpful, or are you just looking for an excuse to critique me?"

"Depends. How much do you charge for attitude?"

That provoked a laugh she tried not to let out. "You're unbelievable."

"Accurate."

She took a step back, catching her breath, then pointed at me. "If I wake up tomorrow and can't move, I'm sending you the physical therapy bill."

"I'll forward it to management," I said. "Fourth truce, by the way."

"Fourth?"

"Lobby. Tacos. Riverwalk. This."

"You're keeping count?" she asked, eyebrows raised.

"Of course. It's called accountability."

"Right. Well, if you're counting the lobby then you forgot coffee delivery, so technically five," she said, smiling despite herself. "And here I thought you just liked to argue."

"I do," I said, "but I like being right more."

Her laugh came easier this time, softer, without its usual edge. The sound lingered even as she reached for her water bottle. "You always work out here?" she asked.

"Lately," I said. "Fewer cameras posted up outside the training facility, no questions, and the sauna doesn't tell anyone what I look like half naked."

She grinned. "So it's about vanity."

"Self-preservation," I corrected her. "Vanity's expensive. Peace is cheaper."

Her mouth curved, amusement flickering at the edges. "Oh-kay, then, Drake with the 2016 inspirational thirst trap caption."

"I'm evolving," I said.

She twisted her water bottle cap back on and tipped her head, smiling. "Easy there, player. Last time I let a man with quotable lines get too close, I almost needed a lawyer. And ain't nobody got time to battle you like they're Kendrick Lamar."

We stood there a beat too long, the air thick with humor giving way to something else.

She broke it first. "My dad's still in town. I needed a break from him taking every call on speakerphone."

I laughed. "That sounds trusting."

"No, it's loud as hell," she replied. "But yeah, he's happy to be here."

I nodded, studying her instead of answering right away. "You good? I mean, really good? After everything that went down on the show. I know what Ronan said the other night, but something in your eyes said it still feels raw even when you laughed it off."

Her gaze flickered, not defensive but careful. "Define good."

"Still standing," I said. "Still yourself."

She considered that, then nodded once. "Working on it."

"Looks like progress from here."

Her mouth tilted. "That your expert assessment?"

"Unofficial," I said. "Strictly observation. No clipboard, no billable hours."

She laughed, soft but genuine, the sound landing in the space between us and easing something I hadn't realized was tense.

"Appreciate the rescue, doc."

"Anytime," I said. "Rates go up if you ignore instructions, though."

She shook her head, smiling into her water bottle. "You're a mess."

"Am I now," I said, turning toward the sauna before I gave away that I didn't really want to leave.

Before I made it two steps, she caught my wrist. Just a tug. Light, certain, enough to stop me.

When I turned back, her eyes met mine, steady and unwavering.

Whatever joke was forming on my tongue died there.

"Bellamy," I started, but her hand slid higher, fingers curling just above my elbow. The air between us shifted as she pulled me down to the bench beside her.

"You talk too much," she said.

Then she kissed me.

It felt like a dare. Soft at first, almost exploratory, until her lips parted and heat spilled between us. Her mouth moved with intention, slow and deep, tasting of mint and something else sweet. Every breath we shared blurred the line between reaction and choice.

I met her halfway, angling closer, letting instinct take over where words had failed. Her tongue slid against mine, teasing, testing, until the rhythm found itself. She made a small sound low in her throat, a murmur that sent a pulse straight through me.

My hand found the curve of her waist, the slip of skin where her top had ridden up. She leaned in, chasing the contact, tugging at the tail of my shirt, her breath uneven against my cheek when we finally broke apart before diving back in.

The kiss deepened. No rush. Just a pull that felt inevitable.

She tasted like everything I'd been trying not to want. And when her hand flattened against my chest, steadying herself or maybe testing how far this could go, it didn't feel like a question either of us was ready to answer.

The bench creaked beneath us as she shifted closer, thighs brushing mine, her weight tipping into me until thought scattered and only touch remained. The air thickened, every movement a conversation neither of us had planned to start.

Then my watch vibrated, cutting through the haze like a bad punch line.

We froze, breath still tangled, her lips hovering close enough that the next exhale could have undone us all over again. And it did.

My fingers found her waist, her heat pulling me closer. She laughed once into the kiss, breath catching as she leaned in. I sat back against the machine, and she followed, the space between us gone completely.

She was just starting to shift onto my lap when my watch buzzed again, this time against her hip. We both froze and I glanced down. My agent's name lit up the screen with a meeting reminder. The timing couldn't have been worse.

"Damn," I said quietly. "I have to take this."

She blinked, breathless and amused. "You're kidding."

"I wish I was." I stood, trying to find oxygen and reason at the same time. "My timing's terrible."

She laughed once, shaking her head. "Go do your thing, Mr. Priorities."

I hesitated. "I didn't mean to—"

She cut me off with a look that said, *Don't ruin it.* "We both did. And I'm fine."

I nodded, still caught somewhere between wanting to stay and knowing I shouldn't. "I'll see you later?"

"Count on it," she said, voice steady now, but her eyes betrayed her.

I walked out of the gym, pulse still drumming in my throat, her taste lingering like a secret. The call connected, my agent's voice spilling through the line, but I couldn't focus.

Because all I could think about was the way she looked at me before she kissed me.

And how I already knew I'd let her do it again.

By early afternoon, my pregame routine should've been the only thing on my mind, but my thoughts kept circling the same apartment across the hall. She hadn't texted. Not that she owed me that. We hadn't officially exchanged numbers, and I wasn't sure what you texted someone after a kiss like that anyway. *Nice form* probably wasn't the move.

Still, something in me wanted to see her before I left. I stopped outside her door with my game bag slung over my shoulder, and knocked.

Once. Twice. Nothing. The stillness felt heavier than it should have.

I pulled a folded sheet of paper from my pocket that I'd scribbled a note on this morning between my protein shake and studying film.

> *You never gave me your number, so I'm leaving this old school. I left two tickets under your name for tonight's game at VIP will call in case you and your dad want to see what I actually do when you're not annoying me. — 34B*

I slid it under the door, hesitated, then walked away before I could talk myself out of it.

The sky opened the moment my tires cleared the ramp. Sheets of rain wiped the street into streaks of light and my wipers worked as hard as they could yet still lost ground.

Visibility dropped to near zero as traffic slowed to a crawl. As I sat at a light, I spotted a familiar movement that was small, mighty, and comically stubborn. Three dogs tangled in their leashes were being led by one woman with an umbrella that had already retired from duty.

Bellamy.

She was soaked, ankle deep in runoff, and the corgis appeared to be forming a rebellion. I eased my ride to the curb and rolled the window down, causing warm rain to hit my arm.

"You need a ride?"

She squinted through the gusts of rain. "I'm fine."

"Sure, Bella," I said. "Meanwhile, you're clearly drowning while upright."

MiMi moved to dart toward the street and Bellamy lunged, caught in her leash, and swore. That was answer enough. She wrangled the dogs into the back seat, then climbed in, dripping everywhere.

"Don't say it," she warned.

"I wasn't going to."

"You absolutely were."

"I was thinking it," I admitted.

She tried to glare, failed, and laughed under her breath.

"I was trying to beat the storm," she said, wringing out her sleeve. "Guess I misread the sky."

"Guess so."

She leaned back, watching the wipers lose the fight against the rain. "My dad ran out for groceries. Said he'd be quick. Which, in his language, means he'll wander Costco for three hours and come home with nothing but a rotisserie chicken."

I smiled. "Been there, done that. As long as he's not out putting a hit on me, you'll hear no complaints."

"Quite the contrary," she said softly, then turned toward the window again.

We rolled into the garage, and I parked so she could get out without getting drenched again. Bellamy didn't move right away. Her hands tightened around one of the dogs offering an unreadable expression.

"Oh, before I forget," I said. "I left a note for you under your door."

Her head turned, one brow arched. "Another truce?"

"Tickets," I said. "For you and your pops… if you want them."

Her mouth curved, equal parts teasing and curious. "A new truce. Over a kiss?"

I laughed. "I would hope you don't think that was a truce

move. And for the record… you kissed me first."

She rolled her eyes. "Semantics."

"Convenient memory."

"Well, either way," she said, wiping away a trail of wetness running from her hairline, "thanks. I'll let him know."

"I don't want to rush you," I said, glancing at the clock on the dash, "but I do have to get to the game."

She nodded, the smallest pause before her hand found the door handle. "Good luck, Coach. Don't miss any layups thinking about me."

I grinned. "You assume I ever stop."

That got me a look I couldn't quite read, somewhere between amused and undone, before she pushed the door open and stepped out. The corgis tumbled out after her, tails wagging like nothing about this moment was complicated.

I watched her cross the garage until the door shut behind her. Then I exhaled, shifted into gear, and pulled away, telling myself to focus on the game.

And failing completely.

We won, apparently. The guys were already celebrating, but I was half dressed, staring at my phone, wondering why I cared more about an unanswered invitation than a scoreboard.

"Yo, Cole," Javon called from across the room, towel slung around his neck. "We're hitting the taco joint tonight, you in?"

"Of course he is. The man needs protein," Nico added, grinning. "That counts, right?"

"He already told you knuckleheads he ain't going," Ronan cut in before I could answer. "Let the man go home before he remembers how much of a pain in the ass you both are. Running around acting like y'all were born out the same damn womb. Tell me, who's Tia and who's Tamera?"

The rookies faked a laugh and shuffled away, already arguing over whether to hit the spot anyway. Ronan gave me that captain look, equal parts authority and friendship. "You good?"

"Always."

He didn't believe me, but he didn't press it either. Just gave a nod, one that said he'd seen enough players try to out-stare their thoughts and lose.

When the room finally cleared, I checked my phone again. No messages. Not from Beauty, not from Bellamy. I told myself that was fine, then told myself again until it almost sounded true.

I grabbed my duffel, did my contractual ten-minute postgame dance—which was basically offering up the press room quick quotes and smiles—and made it out without saying anything that'd haunt me later. When I finally I pulled into the garage, my world was silent. A silent that made you realize how much you'd been filling the day just to avoid it.

At my door, I paused. The hallway was still, but something about it didn't feel like silence. Maybe it was instinct, or maybe I just wanted a reason to linger. Her light was on under the door, a soft gold strip against the floor.

I knocked once then waited.

It took a moment before the lock clicked. Bellamy leaned against the doorframe, blanket wrapped around her shoulders, hair tied up in a loose scarf. Her face was flushed, eyes slightly glassy. "You again?" She tried to laugh a little, but I could tell it took some effort.

"Hey," I said. "You okay?"

She cleared her throat, winced. "Define okay."

"You sound like someone swallowed sandpaper."

"Wow. You're just full of compliments tonight."

I smiled, small. "Didn't see you at the game. Figured I'd check in."

She sighed. "Yeah. My dad ended up driving to Austin last minute. One of his friends was playing with some band, and apparently that couldn't wait. I stayed behind. Was getting ready earlier and started feeling off. You know, a sore throat, tired, all that fun stuff."

I nodded, leaning against the door. "So you've eaten?"

She blinked, slow. "Define eaten."

"That's a no."

"Well, I was right about the rotisserie chicken, but it's still in the fridge. I've been asleep." Her lips curved faintly. "You don't have to do the neighborly check-in thing, you know."

"I know," I said. "That's why it counts."

She laughed, the sound cracking halfway through. "You're unbelievable."

I winked, stepping inside before she could object. "Sit down. I'll make you something."

Her brows rose, but she didn't stop me. "You can cook?"

"Let's find out."

TJ's kitchen was a photographer's dream, which sometimes meant it was going to have little substance to offer. I scanned the cabinets and was thrilled to find out I was wrong. There was enough to work with. I got to work pulling out the chicken, rice, chicken broth, frozen kale, soy sauce, scallions, ginger.

Bellamy sank onto the couch, blanket pulled tighter. "You realize this is weird, right?"

"Only if you're awake for it," I said, chopping ginger. "If you fall asleep, it's charity."

"Charity with seasoning. Real fancy."

Steam rose from the pot, carrying the sharp, clean scent of ginger and garlic. She gravitated to the kitchen island, sat down on a stool, and closed her eyes, breathing it in.

"That smells amazing," she murmured.

"See? No need for those delivery apps."

"I don't know, they bring napkins."

"Guess I'll have to improvise." She cracked a tired smile, which turned into a cough she tried to hide behind her sleeve. I stirred the pot, glanced back at her. "You should rest. I'll walk the dogs while this finishes."

"You really don't have to—"

"Bella, you can barely make it to the door. Let me."

Her silence was its own surrender. She nodded. "They'll love you forever if you do."

"Good. I could use fans who don't upload videos of me of my worst moments."

That brought out the faintest laugh.

When I returned twenty minutes later, the dogs were calm, the soup ready, and she was back on the sofa curled under her blanket, in and out of sleep. I plated two bowls anyway and nudged her awake. "Hey. Dinner."

She blinked up at me, dazed. "You're still here."

"Soup's better warm," I said, setting the bowl in her hands. "Eat before I change my mind."

She took a slow sip. The first swallow made her eyes close. "Okay, that's... actually really good."

"I'll take that as a five-star Yelp review."

She smiled around the spoon. "You keep this up, I might start believing you're actually decent."

"Don't ruin my reputation," I said. She set her bowl down, still smiling faintly. I nodded toward her phone on the coffee table. "Hand me that."

"Why?"

"So I don't have to keep knocking like a door-to-door

salesman." She unlocked it and passed it over, amused. I tapped in my number and let it ring once. "There. Now I can text before showing up unannounced. Something tells me next time your pops might be around and won't appreciate it."

"Dramatic much?"

"Guilty," I said, typing her name in before locking the screen. She caught it. "Bella?"

I leaned over and pressed a kiss to her warm forehead instead of answering. "Damn, let me grab you something for that."

I stepped away long enough to search the medicine cabinets for anything that might help with fevers and then made her a cup of tea for added measure.

After she ate, we ended up watching some movie neither of us picked because it auto-played before we could choose another. She laughed once or twice, coughed more than that, and somewhere between scenes, her head slipped sideways against my chest.

When her breathing evened out, I moved her so she could be comfortable then stood, took our empty bowls, and covered her with the blanket. The dogs looked up, unimpressed, as if I'd violated protocol.

"Relax," I whispered. "She's fine."

I finished cleaning up the small mess I'd made and turned off the extra lights. Then I dashed across the hall to my place, found the set of keys Evan had offered in case of emergency, and returned to lock the door behind me.

In the silence of my own apartment, I scrolled to her new contact and smiled.

Chapter 11

BELLAMY

MY PHONE WAS THE FIRST THING TO WAKE ME, BUZZING against the nightstand. I ignored most of the notifications but did open one of the texts.

Dad: Decided to stay over in Austin tonight.
See you in the AM.

I stared at the message, groaned, and sank deeper under the blanket. My head was heavy, my throat rough, and my body made me question if I should've gotten a flu vaccine after all. The dogs, of course, were thriving. Three furry faces hovered at the edge of the bed, tails twitching in sync.

"Fine," I croaked, sitting up. "We'll go."

I stumbled to the front door after slipping my feet into a pair of UGGs, then tossed a hoodie over my gown and pulled on a pair of sweatpants underneath, not caring that I was sure I'd appear to be quite the sight once people saw me. I was already bargaining with God for strength, and now I needed to add minimal public shame to the list. I cracked the door open just as Cole stepped out of his apartment across the hall with a duffel bag slung over his shoulder.

I caught him taking a quick look at me before he did a double take as if what he saw finally fully registered. "You planning to walk them, or are you sleepwalking and have no clue what's going on right now?"

"Walking the dogs," I mumbled, voice scratchy. "Eventually."

He blinked, then crouched to pet the pack and to take the leashes from my hands before I could protest. "You look like you're about to pass out. Go back inside."

"Cole—"

"Bella," he said, tone leaving no room for argument. "I got it."

Before I could form a coherent objection, he and the dogs were gone just like that, leaving me in the doorway with a small, confusing sense of relief. When they returned soon after, all four looked victorious.

"They made friends with a squirrel," he said, heading straight to the kitchen. "Where's their food? I'm sure they need to eat."

I pointed weakly toward the refrigerator, too tired to argue about boundaries. He found the labeled jars and set three bowls down like he'd done it a hundred times. The corgis dove in with their tails wagging.

"Anything else I should know?" he asked, rinsing his hands at the sink. "Favorite snacks? Love languages?"

"Rih's is food. The other two thrive on attention and mild disrespect," I rasped. "Very affectionate disrespect."

He glanced over his shoulder. "So she takes after her sitter."

I would've rolled my eyes if it didn't require energy. "Shouldn't you be at practice?"

"Heading out soon," he said, opening the fridge again. "But you look like you haven't eaten."

He pulled together eggs, spinach, and the smug satisfaction of a man who knew exactly what he was doing. A few minutes later, he slid a plate toward me and set a glass beside it. The last time I saw something green in liquid form just like it, I'd ended up getting fired.

"What is that?" I asked, squinting.

"Immune booster," he said. "Ginger, apple, kale, lemon. Don't throw it this time."

"I didn't throw the last one," I said, feigning offense on behalf of my past self. "I just… tried to share it. That's all."

"Sure." His grin was lazy, too knowing. Then he leaned in, wrapping an arm around me, pressing a slow kiss to the top of my head, the exact move from the dream I swore I didn't have.

"Drink," he said softly. "Then sleep."

I sipped, winced from the rawness in my throat, and set it down. "If I hug you back, San Antonio's going to blame me for ruining the season when you catch whatever this is."

"I'll take my chances," he said, hugging me anyway before picking up his bag. "Text me if you need anything. I'll drop some soup off later."

"More soup?"

He shrugged, halfway out the door. "You didn't die from it last night, and I need to get my sparring partner back on her feet, so whatever helps nurse you back to yourself, that's what I'm gonna do. It's no fun when the competition is down."

He was gone before I could tell him thank you properly.

So I did the next best thing. I texted.

Me: Thanks. You didn't have to do all that.

Cole: I know.

That was it. Two words, somehow louder than a paragraph.

The dogs curled up beside me on the couch, still warm from their adventure. I was between bouts of sleep attempts when the door opened again. This time it was Dad.

He stepped in with a bag in hand, scanning the room like a detective mid-case. "Smells like somebody cooked in here… and cleaned. You been domesticating overnight?"

I pulled the blanket up to my chin. "Nope."

His gaze flicked to the second mug on the counter, the rinsed skillet, the fresh dog bowls lined up neatly in a row. One brow lifted. "Uh huh."

I smirked, pushing off the couch. "Goodnight, Daddy."

"It's ten in the morning."

"Exactly," I said, disappearing into my room. "Perfect time for a nap."

Behind me, I heard him laugh, the sound soft of knowing.

The DMs

You ever try to fall asleep and your brain
decides it's performance review time?

That's one way to start a conversation. But yes.
Mine prefers to hold staff meetings around 2 AM

Same. I thought maybe if I sent the thought out it
would stop pacing.

You're describing insomnia like
it's a roommate you can't evict.

Exactly. The one that doesn't pay rent
on time and leaves dishes in the sink.

Charming. You should probably cook for it.

Already did. Cleaned the kitchen too.
Still wide awake.

You cooked and cleaned? Overachiever.

It happens from time to time.

@BeautyIzHerName
I usually let Netflix try to fight it for me.
Background noise, fake plots, someone else's
drama so I don't drown in mine.

@ChefSwishWhisk
What's on tonight?

@BeautyIzHerName
Some romantic comedy with too much snow
and people falling in love after a week.
I roll my eyes at it but haven't turned it off yet.

@ChefSwishWhisk
That's how they get you.
One sarcastic comment at a time.

@BeautyIzHerName
Guilty. But it's easier than thinking
about the real stuff.

@ChefSwishWhisk
Which is?

@BeautyIzHerName
You first.

@ChefSwishWhisk
Fine. I keep thinking about how much control
I try to have. In every corner of my life.
The more I hold on, the less I sleep.

@BeautyIzHerName
That sounds familiar. I'm the opposite, though.
I let go so fast I make people dizzy. Push them
away, then call it independence. My mom says I
confuse being strong with being untouchable.

@ChefSwishWhisk
Your mom might be onto something.

@BeautyIzHerName

Don't side with her. I hung up on her last week. Or
at least I pretended I did, but I know if I really did
she'd fly in just to slap the Black off me.

@ChefSwishWhisk

She struck a nerve, then.

@BeautyIzHerName

Maybe. She said I sabotage anything that
looks like it might last. That I'd rather leave first
than risk being left. I wanted to argue,
but I didn't have the words.

@ChefSwishWhisk

You had the words.
You didn't want to admit they fit.

@BeautyIzHerName

You're too good at this.

@ChefSwishWhisk

No. Just practiced. My version looks different
but feels the same. I hold too tight instead
of letting go. Either way, the ending's lonely.

@BeautyIzHerName

It's strange, isn't it, how you can know
your own patterns and still repeat them.

@ChefSwishWhisk

Comfort in failure. At least it's familiar.

@BeautyIzHerName

That sentence just punched me in the throat.

@ChefSwishWhisk

Sorry.

@BeautyIzHerName
Don't apologize. It's true. And maybe that's
why I'm still awake, watching strangers kiss
under fake snow. Because part of me wonders
 if it's possible to want something different.

@ChefSwishWhisk
That sounds like a turning point.

@BeautyIzHerName
Maybe. But I'm afraid I wouldn't
 recognize real if it showed up.

@ChefSwishWhisk
You would. It wouldn't need the fake snow or the
countdown clock. It would just sit there stubborn. Keep
knocking even when you don't answer the first time.

@BeautyIzHerName
You sound like you're speaking from experience.

@ChefSwishWhisk
Maybe I'm speaking from hope.

@BeautyIzHerName
Hope is fragile.

@ChefSwishWhisk
So is sleep deprivation.

@BeautyIzHerName
Don't make me laugh when I'm trying
to have a moment.

@ChefSwishWhisk
Laughter is a moment. And maybe hope too.

@BeautyIzHerName
You keep nudging me toward optimism
and I keep resisting.

@ChefSwishWhisk

Resistance is natural. But you opened your phone
instead of shutting down. That's not nothing.

@BeautyIzHerName

I didn't want to feel alone with it.

@ChefSwishWhisk

You're not. Ceiling stares, snow movies,
both of us wide awake.

@BeautyIzHerName

I don't know if I should be comforted
or sad about that.

@ChefSwishWhisk

Both. Mixed feelings are allowed.

@BeautyIzHerName

Okay, let me ask you this. If you're someone
who's always controlled things too tightly,
how do you loosen your grip?

@ChefSwishWhisk

By admitting you can't hold everything.
Which feels like failure until you realize
it's the start of trust.

@BeautyIzHerName

I think you just described the
one thing I'm worst at.

@ChefSwishWhisk

Same.

@BeautyIzHerName

Really.

@ChefSwishWhisk

Really. You're not the only one awake at 2 thinking
about the way you've barricaded your own heart.

@BeautyIzHerName
Well. There it is. Two insomniacs in different
rooms, confessing to walls and screens.

@ChefSwishWhisk
There are worse ways to spend a night.

@BeautyIzHerName
True. At least you don't judge my snack choices.

@ChefSwishWhisk
Not yet. What's on the menu tonight?

@BeautyIzHerName
Dark chocolate and potato chips with a drizzle
of honey. Remember the rule… don't judge.

@ChefSwishWhisk
No judgment. That's championship-level snacking.

@BeautyIzHerName
Championship? Please. It's desperation
disguised as innovation.

@ChefSwishWhisk
Every innovation starts with desperation.

@BeautyIzHerName
There you go again. Making insomnia
sound noble.

@ChefSwishWhisk
No, just survivable.

@BeautyIzHerName
Surviving isn't the same as living.

@ChefSwishWhisk
Maybe not. But moments like this,
sharing the weight when the ceiling feels
too heavy… those are closer to living.

@BeautyIzHerName
You're giving me more credit than I deserve.

@ChefSwishWhisk
No. Just seeing what's already there.

@BeautyIzHerName
Bold thing to say.

@ChefSwishWhisk
True things usually are.

@BeautyIzHerName
Then here's one. I think I'm at a turning point. Like
maybe my heart wants to risk something again.

@ChefSwishWhisk
Same.

@BeautyIzHerName
Just like that.

@ChefSwishWhisk
Just like that.

@BeautyIzHerName
Shouldn't it be harder?

@ChefSwishWhisk
Probably. But maybe it doesn't need to be.
Not here.

@BeautyIzHerName
You're going to make me believe
in snow movies, aren't you?

@ChefSwishWhisk
Only the parts where the right people find each
other. The rest we can skip.

@BeautyIzHerName
Deal.

@ChefSwishWhisk
Then maybe tonight isn't wasted.

@BeautyIzHerName
Not wasted at all.

Chapter 12

COLE

I HAD JUST LOCKED MY DOOR WHEN ANOTHER OPENED across the hall.

Out came Terrence, AirPods in with leashes in hand. It had been a week since our last run-in. All three dogs trotted at his feet, causing a small ruckus before they could even cross the threshold to go outside. The hallway suddenly felt tighter, like I'd been caught doing something I wasn't supposed to, even if all I was doing was heading out to the grocery store. Or maybe because not ten hours ago, I'd been fantasizing about his daughter in a way that would've made a lesser man flinch under the guilt.

I nodded in greeting, hand still on the doorknob, trying not to look like I needed to be saved by a fire drill.

I'd only been back in town a few hours. Four days on the road hitting up Houston, New Orleans, and Dallas, giving us two wins and one loss, and somehow, between each game, my mind kept drifting back here. Back to her. I wondered if Terrence had any idea his daughter and I had been trading messages all week. She'd told me he was staying longer to help with the dogs while her cold ran its course.

"You headed out?" he asked, as if we weren't both clearly in motion.

"Yeah. Gonna run to the store real quick."

He grinned like he'd been waiting for that answer. "Cool. Let's walk."

Before I could protest or decide if I had the moral clarity to walk next to the father of the woman I'd imagined stripping down to her panties, he turned toward the elevator and hit the button.

"I'm just heading to the one around the corner," I offered mildly.

"Perfect," he said without turning. "We like that route. MiMi gets moody without some time on the pavement. And RihRih loves being outside and seen."

I blinked. "Right."

We rode the elevator down together in companionable silence, broken only by the occasional sniff or sneeze from the corgi crew. I held a grocery tote in one hand and pretended my phone deserved the other. Terrence carried a stillness that didn't just come from years in the spotlight. It came from a lifetime of sizing men up. In that small space I could feel him clocking everything. My posture, my quiet, the way I used my hands. Like a father measuring whether I was the kind who invited smoke or someone who made it.

Outside, we walked slow. My longer strides adjusted to the deliberate pace of the pups. We reached the corner before he finally said something.

He said, adjusting his sunglasses, "I've seen a lot of men circle my daughter. Some come bold. Some come quiet. Some show their cards, and some fold before the first hand even plays out."

I stayed silent and let him speak.

"But the ones who worry me most," he continued, "are the ones who don't know they're already in it."

I looked over at him, the weight of that settling heavier than

I expected.

"She's not just smart, or fine, or capable. She's got a depth most people never get to. And when they do? They flinch. Or fumble."

The corgis stopped to sniff a lamppost. He paused with them, then gave a gentle tug on the leashes.

"And let me be real clear about something. If she ever cries and it ain't from laughing too hard, that's a problem. Even the happy tears make me twitch a little. Anything else, and I'm not above getting disrespectful. Verbally or otherwise." He paused, lowering his sunglasses just enough for me to catch his eyes. "My brothers feel the same way. They love their niece something fierce. Troy Alexander's been quiet lately for a reason. Let's just say two of them have records, and I'm not talking about Al Green."

He glanced at me now, not with threat, but certainty. Like he already knew how the scene would go if I messed this up and had made peace with it.

"I don't know what you're hoping this is or isn't yet. But just know the clock's running. The ball's in play. And if you're smart, you'll stop acting like you're just here for the walk."

Then he was gone, heading back up the block with three dogs and the casual confidence of a man who'd dropped a truth bomb and didn't need to stick around for the fallout.

I stood there a beat longer than necessary, still needing to get to the store. But yeah… I had a feeling I'd just been handed something heavier to carry than whatever groceries I had to bring back.

Once I made it back upstairs with one hand full of a grocery bag missing half the things I'd actually gone for, my phone lit up with a missed call from Nina and a voicemail waiting.

"Just a heads-up. Bellamy hit me asking where to find oxtails. Her dad's trying to make them before he heads back out of town, and apparently she has no idea where to go. I told her I'd ask around. So, I'm

asking around. And by around, I mean you. Don't say I never looked out."

She even laughed out loud at the end, like this was some covert matchmaking operation.

I stood at the kitchen counter, thumb hovering over the screen. The grocery tote slumped beside me, holding little more than a bruised ego and a few uninspired choices I hadn't been excited to grab. I'd skipped most of the produce, telling myself the farmers' market would be a better call, still debating whether I felt like making the trip to The Pearl. Maybe it was just an excuse to invite Bellamy into a quiet corner of my world. Or maybe it was Nina's message, pushing me toward what I already wanted to do.

My first instinct was to send a text. Keep it simple. Just food talk. But then I remembered the way Terrence had looked at me earlier. Not only as a father guarding the gate, but as a man who needed you to prove you belonged anywhere near it. That look didn't leave room for shortcuts or charm.

Stop acting like you're just here for the walk.

So I called. It rang a couple of times before she answered.

"Hello?" Her voice was soft, brighter than it had been when I last heard it.

"Hey, it's me. Heard you're on an oxtail mission."

A small, surprised laugh slipped out. "Nina really can't hold water."

"Good thing I can. If you're serious about making them, there's a butcher I trust near The Pearl. He sets up at the farmers' market every weekend, and it closes in a couple of hours. I can take you if you're free."

A pause.

"You offering chauffeur services now?"

I smiled into the phone. "Just making sure you don't end up with grocery-store oxtails when the good stuff's waiting."

"Give me fifteen," she said, already sounding in motion.

Exactly sixteen minutes later, we met in the hallway. She wore a button-up sweater and leggings, a crossbody bag slung across her chest, keys and phone in one hand, a faint floral scent trailing behind her. I nodded, trying not to look like I'd been rehearsing casual all morning.

"You good?" I asked, stepping aside so she could lock up.

"Yeah. Just hope we're not too late."

In the car, she told me her dad had woken up in a mood, craving something he didn't ask for so much as declare *she* was getting. She rolled her eyes, but affection threaded through the sound.

"You making them?" I asked.

"I'm assisting. There's a difference. He doesn't let just anybody in the kitchen when it comes to oxtails. My role is moral support and selective praise. Think sous-chef, but with lower expectations. But he knows how much I love it when he makes them, so you'll hear no complaints from me."

I glanced over. Her eyes were fixed on the window, but I could feel the weight of what she wasn't saying. "Sounds like he raised the bar high."

"The bar was his ego. I just tried not to trip over it growing up. Spoiler alert, I failed twice before I could even drive."

There was humor in her voice, but beneath it I heard splinters. I didn't push. Just drove.

The Pearl farmers' market was still buzzing with its Saturday sprawl. Sun overhead, saxophone in the distance, babies in slings, vendors calling out deals with joy. Bellamy moved with curiosity but never uncertainty. She paused to touch basil, asked if I liked yellow squash, and laughed at a dog riding in a backpack.

We reached the butcher I trusted. He didn't waste time, just nodded, prepped, and handed me the wrap I'd asked him to set aside.

"So you're personally vouching for this?" she asked, brow

arched.

"Wouldn't bring you here otherwise."

She took the bundle, holding it as though it carried more than meat, as though it held something she hadn't let herself feel in a long time. Her shoulders eased, and she looked down for a long moment.

She said quietly, "I don't usually let people ride shotgun on Barnes family recipes."

"Then I'll try not to mess it up."

She didn't smile, not really, but something flickered in her eyes. A quiet reminder that we weren't strangers anymore.

"Well," she said, nudging my arm, "if you're not doing anything later, come by. Taste the finished product. Long as you promise to lie and say it's the best you've ever had."

"I don't lie about food."

"Then you better hope it turns out."

Her gaze met mine, steady and open. Something passed between us that words couldn't hold but both of us felt.

We wandered through the last few stalls, the space between us closing with every step. Her hand brushed mine once. I didn't move. Neither did she. This wasn't just an errand. It was a shift, and we both knew it.

We circled back toward the lot, bags in hand, walking slower than we needed to. She paused near a booth selling fresh-cut flowers and picked one up, turning it gently between her fingers.

She said softly, "this was my mom's favorite flower. My dad used to bring her a bunch every time they made up after an argument. I didn't realize until I was older that we had a vase for them permanently on standby."

I didn't rush her. Just watched her turn that flower in her hand, studying it as if it held a piece of her she hadn't touched in a while.

"And did it work?" I asked.

"Sometimes. Depended on the bouquet or the lie."

Her voice didn't crack, but there was tension in it, fine and taut, something you don't touch unless you were ready for the unraveling.

She set the flower down, then moved to a vendor selling beignets. The way she shifted her stance and took a breath made me wonder if she regretted letting me see that side of her.

Back at the car, she moved slower getting in. I opened her door without comment. She didn't say a word, just hesitated, watchful, before sliding in.

I pulled onto the main road. "You still want company for the taste test?"

She looked over, eyes narrowed in mock suspicion. "That wasn't a pity invite. You sure you can handle my dad's ego?"

"Barely. I think he made me take an emotional timeout halfway through the conversation."

Her brow lifted. "Wait. When did y'all talk again since last week?"

"Earlier this morning," I said, though it had felt more like a psychological obstacle course disguised as a dog walk. "We crossed paths."

She tilted her head, studying me in profile. "And you didn't mention that why?"

"Didn't seem like it needed an announcement."

She let that hang for a moment. Then came an "Mm." Not suspicion. Not exactly trust either. Just an open tab she hadn't decided whether to close or keep running.

"I wasn't lying about you tasting it," she said.

"I know."

"You think I'm still talking about dinner?" she asked, tugging her glossy bottom lip between her teeth for a beat.

The next red light caught us. The car idled as she turned toward me, her expression calm but charged.

"Bellamy," I said quietly, but she leaned in before I could finish.

The kiss found its timing there, under the stoplight's watch. It was unhurried, certain, an exchange that said more than words could. Her mouth was soft, her intent deliberate. She wasn't asking permission, only answering a question I hadn't realized I'd asked.

When the light changed, she eased back into her seat, breath still unsteady, eyes holding mine before she looked forward again.

"Drive," she said.

And I did, though my hands didn't feel steady on the wheel.

She looked out the window, smiling faintly. "You're dangerous."

"Good thing you don't scare easy," I said, still watching the road.

She laughed once, quiet and warm, and the sound stayed with me all the way home.

Chapter 13

BELLAMY

THE KISS STILL LINGERED. HALF AN HOUR LATER AND I could feel it, a low thrum under my skin that refused to fade. I should be helping to prep for my dad, unpacking the things I picked up at the market, doing anything productive, but instead I was perched at the kitchen island with the bounty in front of me.

The condo was quiet, too quiet, in a way that didn't soothe but needled. I rested my chin in my palm, tapping my nail against the counter, telling myself to stop replaying the moment over and over when it was his mouth on mine. The heat of it. The way I forgot, just for a second, how much I was supposed to dislike him when I first arrived.

I reached for my phone, seeking a safer distraction, because of course I did. One tap, and there it was… ChefSwishWhisk.

His new post alert glowed like it knew I was waiting. Before I could second-guess myself, a reel started playing.

D'Angelo's "When We Get By" spilled out of the speaker, soft bass and brushed drums filling the silence like it was made for this moment. The ingredients slid into frame, every color catching the light. Then his gloved hands appeared next taking the screen as if they were made for it.

Large, sure, steady fingers, sliding across potatoes, cutting clean strips that fell into a neat pile. Oil bubbled up when the first fry hit, and he salted them with a flick of his wrist that felt unfairly confident. Then the wings. He seasoned them with smoked paprika, garlic, black pepper, and a pinch of cayenne, working everything into the skin with slow, practiced pressure. The camera followed as he lowered them into hot oil. No rush, no clutter. Just that deep sizzle rising up.

When the wings came out crisp and golden, he set them on a rack and moved to the stove. Butter melted in a small pot, and a handful of finely diced peaches softened into it. Peach preserves loosened and grew glossy. A splash of bourbon hit the heat and lifted a curl of steam. He whisked until the glaze thickened into a syrup that looked decadent enough to count as a sin.

The wings went into the bowl one by one. He rolled them through the glaze until they shone, amber and warm. Then he stacked a few basil leaves, rolled them tight, and sliced them into thin ribbons. The chiffonade slipped through his fingers and fell over the wings in soft green curls, catching the light as if the reel had been waiting on that moment.

A caption under the plated meal read, *Some things come together when you least expect it.*

The loop started again before I could stop it. My stomach growled so loud RihRih lifted her head in judgment. By the third replay I was half convinced the man had hypnotized me through chicken.

The lock clicked and Dad stepped in, keys clinking in the dish, his eyes taking in the oxtails on the counter.

"Where'd you get those?"

"A butcher at the farmers' market."

He arched one brow. "With who?"

I swallowed. "Cole."

He emitted that low dad sound that was half grunt, half hmm, and said everything without saying a thing. He didn't add words, just went to the sink, washed his hands, and pulled out a cutting board.

"I've been thinking about what we talked about… What I said the other night—"

"Don't." He shook his head, eyes on the sink. "That was on me. Leave it there."

I nodded, though the tight line of his lips told me he hadn't left it anywhere.

"Well, there's something else." Trying to change the subject, I smiled, putting on the charm, and leaned toward him. "Kind of have a taste for wings for lunch."

He gave me the slow turn, father's side-eye locked and loaded, before pulling open the fridge. "Of course you do." He rummaged and came out with a bag of party wings, shaking his head like the universe had personally betrayed him.

"And fries," I added, leaning into my sweetest tone.

"Heavenly Father, please help me right now." He went into the pantry then returned, dropping a sack of potatoes onto the counter with exaggerated force. "Anything else, Your Highness? You want banana pudding, too? A fresh batch of sweet sun tea while we're at it?"

I laughed, because I couldn't help it. Then I smiled, batting my lashes at him like I used to as a little girl, because all of that sounded good. "Now that you mention it, I think that would be perfect."

He moved with an ease only years in the kitchen could teach, getting lunch started before rinsing the oxtails after he cleaned them under a steady stream of cold water and patting them dry with the precision of a man who believed food deserved respect. The bones glistened and he lined them up neatly on the board. Then, as if pulling them from thin air, he set out Scotch bonnets, garlic bulbs, and a fistful of fresh thyme like a magician laying out his cards.

"You'll like this," he said without looking up. His tone was casual, but there was something proud threaded through it. "Ran into Nina at Jawn this morning. Told her to swing by tonight."

The corner of my mouth lifted before I could stop it. "I also invited Cole and said he should come over. Maybe he can bring Ronan."

That earned me a grunt. Nothing more, nothing less.

I busied myself with the potatoes at the island, peeling skins into long ribbons that curled into a small pile. The rhythm settled me until the peeler slipped and bit into my thumb. I hissed softly, but before I could even process it, he was already there. My dad took my hand, turned it under the faucet, and rinsed the small nick clean. He took a paper towel and pressed it to my wound before offering a pat to dry it. Then he let go, leaving long enough to find what he thought I needed to dress the cut, offering no scolding and no lecture about being careful. Just quiet care and a return to his board, like it was a natural extension of the work.

Figuring I was doing nothing but getting in the way, I ran my finger over the bandage he'd put in place and moved to leave the kitchen.

"Stay in here with me," he said as he reached for the knife again. "Sous-chef."

It wasn't really a request, and I didn't treat it like one, so I stayed.

Soon my dad showed me how to slap thyme against your palm to wake the oils, the sound sharp in the air. I rolled my eyes because I'd watched him do it my whole life, but I nodded like it was the first time.

"Pay attention," he said, glancing at me with a sideways smile. "You might need this one day."

"Pretty sure I'll survive without ever knowing how to spank an herb," I shot back. "I'll be good without it."

"Survive?" He lifted a brow. "Those delivery apps aren't going to make you a good, solid meal with love worked into the stock."

I snorted. "I'm not convinced love is what you put in there. More like brown liquor."

"Same difference."

The seasoned wings hit hot oil, the sizzle bold enough to make me jump. He grinned, grabbed a pair of tongs, and tossed them with a practiced flick of the wrist, then tilted his head at me. "You see that? Took me years to get it right."

"Or maybe you just still have wrists that work," I muttered.

He cut me a look full of mischief. "Keep talking slick. I'll let MiMi lick your plate first."

I clutched my chest. "You wouldn't."

"Try me."

We laughed, and the kitchen filled with the comfort of it. Garlic curled into the corners of the condo. Scotch bonnet seeds scattered. For a while, I forgot the kiss still stamped across my mouth from earlier, the one I'd been replaying half an hour straight.

"Make me my favorite cake tonight," he said casually, like he was asking me to pass the salt. "You've got the recipe down."

"I will."

And then he started singing the song he wrote when Mom was pregnant with me, back when music felt like the air we breathed. He recorded it in the basement studio of the first home they bought together while singing to her belly like I could already hear him. He only played it once, for our dance at their first wedding.

I could still see it. Him in that cream suit with the shiny shoes. Me in a frilly, puffy white dress, my hair pressed and curls spiraling down my back, standing on his feet while he led us slow across the spotlit floor. The lights were soft, the room glowing, and everyone's eyes trained on our daddy-daughter dance.

Now his voice had deepened with age and was smoother than it used to be, but it still filled a room the same way, steady and sure.

"Dad," I murmured, "you're going to make me cry in the collards."

He grinned without looking up, and the moment was so easy, so full, I wanted to bottle it. "Then at least cry off the stove. I just got that pot right."

We moved around the kitchen like it had always been this way, with him chopping, me peeling, laughter floating through the air like another spice in the pot.

Then a sharp, jarring buzz came from the intercom.

Dad looked up. "You expecting somebody else?"

I shook my head and wiped my hands on a towel. "Maybe Nina's early?"

But my gut knew better.

I crossed the kitchen, hit the panel. Daryl's voice was polite but buzzing, like he knew something.

"Miss Barnes? You have a guest."

"Who?"

A pause. "Your mother."

The towel slipped from my fingers.

Behind me, Dad stilled. He didn't say a word. His shoulders just shifted the slightest bit before he picked up the knife again and went back to his cutting board, deliberate as a man cutting through stone.

I didn't wait for more. My feet carried me down the hall, into the elevator, pulse running like I was sixteen again, sneaking home late.

Five minutes later, I was in the lobby, and sure enough, there she was: my mother, standing in a travel trench with a roller bag at her side, already looking like she was scouting the property for flaws in the marble tile.

"Surprise," she said, sweeping me into a hug that smelled like Tom Ford perfume layered over airplane air. Her lips brushed my cheek, then she leaned back, giving me a once-over only a mother could manage. It wasn't mean, just forensic, like she was reading my pulse through my skin. "You look tired."

"Hello to you too," I mumbled, wheeling her bag toward the elevator.

"Don't roll your eyes. Fatigue shows first in the under-eye, then in the posture. I knew I was right to come out to check on you, baby. You've been worrying me."

"Mommy, I told you the other day that I'm fine."

"If you're so good, then why have you only answered half of my calls?"

"Oh my goodness, between you and Daddy," I muttered. I swiped the fob while nodding toward Daryl. "I am fine, living my life and trying to keep TJ's dogs alive until she gets back. There really was no need to fly out."

"Well, since I'm here, we can hang out and catch up. Have a little girl time."

We rode up together, her filling the space with travel updates about the woman seated next to her on the flight who'd "believed peanuts were still a lunch option." I nodded, trying not to think about the fact that in approximately sixty seconds, I'd be responsible for housing both of my parents in the same condo at the same time.

I reached for the door and started as I turned the handle, "Mom, about that girl time—"

Mom halted in the entryway and I followed her line of vision. Her eyes cut to him with arched brows as her shoulders lifted with tension.

"You're here," she said, in a tone that was equal parts statement, question, and judgment.

My father was at the stove. Wings crackling in oil. Heat shimmering above the skillet. He didn't look up. He didn't need to. His presence filled the kitchen the way bass filled a song. Without missing a beat, Dad flicked a wing with his tongs. "Clearly."

Dinner smelled like home, hinting at the ability to start arguments and end them just as quick once plates hit the table. Oxtails in gravy. Collards simmering with smoked turkey. Mac and cheese with a crust so golden it ought to have a halo. Fried plantains crisp at the edges, jasmine rice soaking up whatever it could catch, and cornbread cooling beside a honey-butter dish that wouldn't survive the hour.

Dad moved like he owned the place, stirring pots, and Mom floated behind him, straightening, seasoning, adjusting as if the Food Network crew was about to show up. Every corner of this kitchen was claimed. I poured a glass of merlot just to keep my hands busy, pretending that counted as helping.

Not long after she'd arrived, they slipped out to the balcony for what was supposed to be a quick talk, five minutes that stretched into a whole act. When the door finally slid open again, Dad was carrying her suitcase down the hall to TJ's room, and Mom followed, unreadable. A few minutes later they were both back, moving around each other like nothing had happened, her hands busy at the counter grating cheese for the macaroni while he checked the heat under the oxtails. The silence between them wasn't cold. It was practiced.

A knock came right as tension tightened the air. Cole stood in the doorway, sleeves pushed up, a towel draped over a large rectangular dish he held in both hands. Ronan was behind him, grinning like he was already part of the family.

"I brought dessert," Cole said, voice low, eyes steady.

Dad turned from the stove, spatula in hand. "You bake?"

"When it matters." Cole set a glass dish on the counter. "Peach cobbler. From scratch."

That got my attention—the scent of brown sugar, cinnamon, butter, and a sweetness that snuck up and stayed hit first.

Mom leaned forward, half teasing, half impressed. "Now that's a man raised right."

Dad nodded once. "We'll be the judge of that."

Cole only smiled. He pulled the towel away, revealing a crust that was browned just enough to earn respect. Syrup slipped down the edges, bubbling in quiet defiance. He checked it with a wooden spoon, then looked satisfied.

I tilted my head. "That looks unfair."

He grinned. "Depends on who you're serving."

I laughed softly. "I've tried making peach cobbler. One attempt that led to one regrettable failure."

"That's because you probably were overthinking it." His voice was soft enough to pull me closer without moving an inch. "You just need the right person showing you what to look for."

The comment settled somewhere between challenge and invitation. I wasn't brave enough to answer before Nina's voice broke the moment.

"Who do I have to thank for this smell traveling down the hall?" She breezed in, curls twisted up, hoop earrings catching the light, and a tote bag slung over her shoulder. "If I faint, someone catch me gently."

"Perfect timing," I told her.

"I hope I didn't miss the blessing," she said, already hugging me.

"You made it," I said, grateful for the interruption.

Dad was already smiling. "There she is. The heartbeat of Jawn."

"Look at you, trying to sweet-talk your way to another meal on the house," she said, moving on to hug him next. Nina lit up the moment she stood face to face with my mom. "Okay, I really have to faint now. I know I'm not standing in front of my shero, *the* Jacqueline Barnes. I still have the VHS tapes from every appearance your group made on *Video Soul.* My cousin and I tried to copy your hair for a whole summer."

Mom laughed, caught off guard by the warmth. "That feels like a lifetime ago."

"And a pen game so strong, you wrote half the songs that raised us," Nina added. "You don't get to downplay that."

Dad glanced at her, pride cutting through the years. "She's the reason half the folks in this business ever sounded good."

Mom looked away, trying to pretend his words didn't affect her. Once we settled into our seats, the table was filled with conversation and plates being devoured.

Ronan leaned back in his chair, napkin still in hand, wearing that look that always meant mischief. "Quick question, Bellamy," he said casually. "You signed the Storm Joint Likeness and Media Compliance Addendum, right?"

I blinked. "The what?"

He looked genuinely confused by my confusion. "The Storm Joint Likeness and Media Compliance Addendum. Any time two or more active players are in a non-team environment, everyone on site has to sign off on limited image rights. Protects the franchise from unauthorized association, media leaks, or accidental endorsements."

I stared. "You just made that up."

"Did I, though?" His voice was steady, too professional for a dinner table. "It's in the CBA somewhere. Appendix D or E. The one with all the commas. Storm's a strict franchise, Bellamy. They had a whole thing last season when two players showed up in a TikTok challenge holding a protein shake from the wrong sponsor. League fined them ten grand each for 'brand confusion.' You think

I'm risking that over some bomb-ass soul food?"

"That's not real," I said. "No one's paying a fine for being in a video."

Nina nodded solemnly, straight-faced as a witness on the stand. "It's real enough. We had to do it for Jawn, remember? I sign a new one every quarter just to be safe."

"Safe from what? Collateral branding?" I asked, watching both of them for tells I couldn't find.

Cole was busy with his plate, head down, but his shoulders shifted slightly like he was fighting something.

Ronan leaned in, perfectly calm. "It's really just a liability thing. Ever since the NIL rule changes, legal wants everything documented. You'd be surprised how fast a dinner turns into a dating rumor or an unauthorized campaign. Protect your likeness, protect your bag."

It sounded so official that I came close to believing him.

I narrowed my eyes. "You're serious?"

He gave the smallest shrug. "Believe what you want, but if someone posts this and Gatorade calls legal, I'm forwarding them your number."

I thought he meant it. Then Nina snorted into her drink, Cole lost the fight to hide his laugh, and it all clicked.

"You're kidding me," I said, groaning.

Ronan grinned, way too pleased with himself. "Welcome to the team, sis. Consider this your rookie orientation."

"You're all ridiculous," I said, laughing now because I couldn't help it.

Cole wiped his mouth, still smiling. "They only mess with people they like."

"Good to know," I said, tossing my napkin toward Ronan. "Because next time, I'm suing for emotional damages, and you don't want to get my daddy started when it comes to threats of lawsuits."

Dad didn't miss a beat. "You're damn right. I already tried to sue the internet once. Don't think I won't come for the Storm next."

Mom gave him the side-eye over her glass. "Terrence, please. The last time you threatened legal action, you were yelling at a meme."

He waved her off, dead serious. "A *defamatory* meme."

The table burst into laughter again, and I hid my smile behind my glass, realizing I'd never live this one down.

Ronan pointed his fork toward the spread. "Whoever cooked this deserves their props."

Dad raised his hand slightly. "That'd be me."

"Then I'm ruined," Ronan said. "No restaurant stands a chance after this."

Nina shook her head. "He's not lying. This jawn just put my whole brunch menu to shame."

Dad grinned, looking toward Cole. "Credit where it's due. Cole's the one who put Bellamy onto his butcher. Fresh cuts make all the difference. A good man doesn't gatekeep flavor."

Ronan leaned back, still eating. "Look at you, number twenty-four, playing teacher's pet. Bring dessert, talk meat, win over the girl's dad… That's elite strategy." He took another bite. "Speaking of food, Nina, you still running open-mic nights at Jawn? My rookies could use a little public humiliation."

Nina hesitated. "Not lately."

Cole glanced her way. "Why not?"

She shrugged, pride steady even as her tone dipped. "It's just not what it used to be. Weeknights are light. Brunch keeps the lights on, but those community nights cost more than they bring in. I've been thinking it might be time to let them go."

Dad nodded slowly. "Still sounds like something worth keeping."

She sighed. "Maybe. But it feels like the end of a chapter. I was going to cancel this Wednesday. No need to prolong the inevitable."

Ronan looked up. "Wednesday?"

"Yeah. Games and Grub night."

He shook his head, already reaching for his phone. "Don't cancel. Maybe switch the theme, but keep the doors open."

"Ronan—"

"You'll have a crowd," he said, thumbs moving fast. "Trust me."

Nina groaned. "Chill wit' all that. You are not turning my café into a spectacle."

"Too late," he said, smirking. "And it's not what you're thinking."

Cole's phone buzzed. He checked it, laughed, gave Ronan a nod. "You're out of control."

Ronan shrugged. "But I get results."

My phone buzzed next. Cole's text appeared first, telling me to add my dad to the group chat he'd just looped me into with Ronan.

Nina crossed her arms. "Why is everyone's phone lighting up but mine?"

"Because it's a surprise," I said, smiling. "A good one."

Dad leaned back in his chair. "If you're turning this into something, you'll need sound. Let me handle that."

"Terrence," Mom started, but he waved her off.

"I mean it. Text me the contact info for whoever handles booking the talent for you. I'll take care of the rest."

Nina studied him, unsure whether to argue or thank him. "Y'all are doing too much."

"Maybe not enough," I said. "I'll handle promo. You just focus on showing up and turning the lights on."

She reached across the table and squeezed my hand. "You don't even know how much that means."

"I think I do."

Ronan lifted his glass. "To Wednesday, to Jawn, and to family… by blood and by choice."

Glasses clinked and the air lightened.

When dessert came out, Cole stood to serve it himself. I observed, ready to assist, as the crust cracked under the spoon with syrup pooling at the corners as he plated it all, adding a scoop of vanilla ice cream to everyone's bowl. He then sat, calm and waiting.

"Moment of truth," he said.

Dad was the first to taste. He chewed, swallowed, nodded. "Son, you did that."

Mom mumbled her agreement around a mouthful of cobbler. "He really did."

Cole smiled modestly.

I leaned forward. "You'll have to prove that sometime."

His eyes met mine. "Just say when."

The heartbeat of the table carried on with laughter and stories, but my attention stayed on Cole. That cobbler might've been dessert, but something else got served at that table.

And I was still tasting it.

The condo exhaled after the last goodbye. Dried plates were stacked and put away, counters gleamed, and the cobbler dish sat scraped clean, the only proof a good night happened here. Out on the balcony, my parents leaned into the railing with the city stretched wide beneath them. Their voices were low, measured. Mom talked with her hands, her rings catching the faint reflection from the glass door. Dad listened with his chin tipped down, a slow curl of smoke rising from the cigar balanced between his fingers. The Dalmore in his glass caught the light from the room behind him. The sight was so rare I didn't move. I just stood there, memorizing peace while it lasted.

Cole rinsed the final wineglass, turned it upside down on the rack, then folded the dish towel between his hands. The kitchen light softened across his face, making him look steady in a way that felt unfair. When his gaze found mine, it lingered a second too long.

He tipped his chin toward the hallway. "Walk me home, Bella."

I blinked. "First of all, it's Bellamy. Second, your door is three steps away."

He shrugged. "Humor me."

"You want an escort in case you get lost crossing the hall? Are you worried about Ms. Patel jumping you or something?"

"Could happen," he said, that half-smile tugging at his mouth. "Never know what kind of trouble's waiting in a hallway at midnight."

"You really have no idea what might happen if I leave those two alone unsupervised." He just laughed, so I rolled my eyes and reached for the leashes, needing something to do with my hands. "Fine. But only because MiMi needs the walk."

He grinned. "Sure. Let's call it that."

The elevator ride down was quiet, heavy with everything we didn't say. He stood close enough that I felt the warmth radiating from him, and I told myself it was only because the dogs took up space. My pulse disagreed.

Outside, the air was cool and soft against my skin. The corgis took off with purpose, little legs pumping as if they had somewhere to be. Cole walked beside me, his hands loose at his sides, movements unhurried. For a moment, the city felt smaller.

"So," he said finally, "is this where you pretend certain things didn't happen?"

I glanced over. "Which part?"

"Kissing you."

Heat crawled up my neck. "You mean the accidental, spur-of-the-moment lapse in judgment?"

"Which time?" he said evenly. "Neither felt accidental."

I gave him a look. "I was being polite."

"That's polite?" His brow arched. "Good to know."

I groaned. "Do you ever stop?"

"Not when I'm right."

I picked up the pace, forcing the dogs into a fast trot. He matched me step for step, calm in a way that made me more aware of myself than I wanted to be.

"Look," I said finally, trying for lightness, "I'm not the type to complicate things. Been there, done that, got the therapy bills to prove it. So if you're looking to start some bull—"

"For real?" He laughed. "Pretty bold coming from someone who doesn't find drama. You create it."

I stopped long enough to glare at him. "Wow. Rude."

"True," he countered easily.

I sighed, the fight leaking out of me. "I just mean I'm not trying to repeat history, okay? I have a bad habit of choosing men who… keep half their life behind a locked door. Men who make me guess. Men who never actually show up."

The words slipped out softer than I intended. He didn't rush to fill the silence.

"So that's why you're here," he said after a moment. "Starting over. Doing it different."

"Exactly," I said too quickly, defensive out of habit.

He studied me, his mouth curving slightly. "And yet here you are. Walking me home."

I frowned. "You asked me to."

"You could've said no."

"You're insufferable."

"And you're still here."

The dogs paused to sniff a bike rack, tangling the leashes. He crouched to help, fingers brushing mine just long enough to knock the air out of me. When he straightened, he didn't step back.

"You want different?" he said quietly. "Then stop acting like a kiss is something you need to apologize for."

My pulse stumbled. "And stop calling me Bella."

He smiled. "Not a chance."

The corgis tugged the leashes again, breaking the spell. He laughed and stepped back into stride beside me, and the two of us walked home like nothing had happened. But the night knew better.

By the second night of Barnes vs. Barnes, I'd learned TJ's condo was built for echoes, not secrets. The walls caught everything. Sighs. Side comments. The quiet before someone remembered they still had a point to make. I was spoon deep in butter pecan ice cream when the first note hit.

Dad started with "Let's Chill" by Guy, his signature move. The volume was low, persuasive, a song that pretended to be patient while begging in plain sight. I pictured him in his room, head tilted back, mouthing the words like he wrote them.

Mom answered without hesitation. "Before You Walk Out of My Life" by Monica slid in with perfect timing, her voice smooth and steady. She wasn't shouting, not even arguing. She was just reminding him that some doors closed for good.

He tried to charm his way back with "Soon As I Get Home" by Babyface, layering guilt and sincerity in equal measure. That song has gotten too many men forgiven. He should've known better.

She reminded him why that tactic didn't work anymore. "Not Gon' Cry" by Mary J. Blige rose from the speakers, deliberate and devastating. The dogs lifted their heads at the first chorus, glanced my way, and dropped back to sleep. Seasoned professionals.

Dad pivoted. He cued "Spend My Life with You" by Eric Benét and Tamia, probably smiling like he just played his ace. That was his duet strategy. Pretend it was about unity while she did all the heavy lifting.

Mom laughed, the sound soft but knowing. Then, without warning, Kelis's "Caught Out There" exploded into the room next door. Her scream hit the wall like a fire alarm. I nearly dropped my spoon. "Oh, this man's in danger," I muttered.

He regrouped with "Nobody" by Keith Sweat, crooning through the speakers, falsetto straining for sympathy. It was the musical equivalent of flowers after betrayal.

Mom didn't even blink. "Take a Bow" by Rihanna answered, silk over steel, every lyric dipped in quiet grace. She wasn't mad anymore. She was done.

He must've sensed it, because suddenly Luther Vandross took over with "Forever, for Always, for Love." It was rich and familiar, a plea disguised as devotion. I could hear the shift in her breathing through the wall. She was listening, but she wasn't giving in just yet.

Then Keyshia Cole showed up with "I Should've Cheated." That was all Mom. Petty, justified, flawless in her timing. The dogs sighed again. I whispered, "Pray for him," to no one in particular.

Dad reached for nostalgia. "When Can I See You" by Babyface returned, low and tired. It was an olive branch wrapped in regret.

And just when I thought she was done with him, I heard "We Belong Together" by Mariah Carey bleeding through, and everything changed. That was her tell. The soft spot she still swore didn't exist.

He knew it too. "Love's Holiday" by Earth, Wind & Fire glided in next, his voice carrying just under the chorus. She laughed… a real one this time… and I knew he was winning.

"Oh no," I whispered, setting my bowl aside. "He brought out the falsetto."

By the time "If I Ain't Got You" by Alicia Keys joined the rotation, it was over. He had her. They were probably swaying in the hallway between the two rooms like they were twenty years younger.

That was my cue. I grabbed my tote, slipped into sneakers, and headed for the door before the reunion ballads started. Mom's laughter followed me out the door, softer now, threaded with something carefully tender. It was too much to witness sober.

The hallway smelled faintly of jasmine from someone's diffuser. I scrolled through my phone, thumb hovering over *his* name, deciding if this counted as an emergency or just self-preservation. I texted anyway.

Me: You awake? Kind of having an urgent nonemergency.

Cole: Which kind of nonemergency?

Me: Parental Verzuz. I'm stuck in the hall and requesting asylum.

A pause—then the sound of a door unlocking. Cole stood there shirtless, wearing only joggers, water trailing down his shoulder. His skin smelled faintly of soap. He looked at me once, slow and assessing, then stepped back. "You good?"

"Define good," I said. "My parents are currently holding an R&B battle through TJ's sound system. I left before they ended up before I overheard sounds of reconciliation."

He nodded, mouth curving into that small, knowing smile as he stepped aside. "Then you made it out just in time."

"I'll take the couch," I said.

"You will," he said, "and you'll get the good blanket, because I'm civilized."

"That remains to be seen."

He filled the kettle at the sink. "Tea, water, or stronger?"

"Tea works. I have to get up early to work on press for Jawn."

He didn't ask for details. The silence between us held. A bowl of popcorn sat on the coffee table, still warm, salted just right, with a hint of cayenne that hit the back of my throat when I took a handful.

"You made this?"

He nodded. "You don't season your popcorn?"

I shook my head, smiling. "Not like this. Damn this is good."

While he moved around the kitchen, I dug through my tote like I was mining for treasure. Out came a bag of kettle chips, a pack of M&M's, and a full jar of peanut butter that clanked against the table when I set it down. I lined them up like a miniature buffet.

He glanced over his shoulder. "You planning a siege?"

"Just being prepared," I said. "I get snacky when emotionally displaced."

He nodded toward the spread. "You need anything else?"

I looked at the bowl of popcorn on the table and lifted a brow. "You wouldn't happen to have chocolate syrup, would you?"

He paused. "For what, chocolate milk?"

"For the popcorn," I said, as if it should be obvious.

He studied me. "You dip popcorn in chocolate syrup?"

"Not always. Sometimes caramel if I'm feeling fancy."

He shook his head. "You might be the only person on earth with popcorn trust issues."

"Don't knock it till you try it," I said, already popping a few kernels into my mouth. "Sweet, salty, slightly unhinged. It's a metaphor."

He laughed quietly as he poured the tea. "I'll take your word for it. You want background noise?" he asked.

"Something without emotional risk."

"*Bake Off* it is."

We settled into the couch, a safe distance apart. The TV filled the space with polite accents and failed meringues. The dogs would have approved of the civility.

When one contestant opened the oven too early, Cole shook his head. "She knew better."

"You sound personally betrayed."

He smiled without looking away. "Patience is half the work."

I studied him in the screen's reflection. He looked impossibly steady, not still in the way men performed, but grounded. Every gesture had its place. Every silence had intention.

"Thanks," I said. "For not asking."

"You'd tell me if you wanted to."

I sipped my tea, the citrus bright and grounding. "You said you respected my need for different," I said, fingers tracing the edge of my mug.

"I do."

"So what do you need?"

He didn't answer right away. The screen flickered across his face, light and shadow shifting like thought. "Something calm that doesn't cost me myself."

It sat between us for a moment, heavier than the steam from my tea. "That's a good answer."

"It's the truth."

His voice lower now, quiet enough that I felt it before I thought about what to say next. I looked away first, pretending to focus on the show, but the room felt too small to keep pretending.

"You ever feel like people decided who you are before you even had a say?" I asked.

"All the time."

"What do you do about it?"

He leaned back against the couch, his hand resting loosely on his knee. "I stop performing. Let the silence tell the truth first."

I tilted my head toward him. "And does it?"

"Sometimes," he said. "Depends who's listening."

The air between us softened. He turned his head then, and we were just looking—no rush, no hiding—in a way that felt more like conversation than sound.

I shifted slightly, pulling the blanket higher, but my knee brushed his leg and lingered. He didn't move away. He just watched me with that steady calm that felt like an answer to questions I hadn't dared to ask yet as his hand settled for a resting place on my thigh.

"You make calm look easy," I whispered.

"It's not," he said, his voice rougher now. "But right now, it is."

The show continued on in the background, offering us the go-ahead to stay exactly where we were. I sipped the last of my tea just to have something to do with my hands, but his attention never drifted.

When I set the mug down, he pulled me to him and reached out, just a light touch along my wrist, enough to steady me. It wasn't forward, not demanding. It was a quiet statement, as if he was saying, *I'm here and I see you.*

My pulse stumbled. "Cole."

"Yeah?"

"I should probably move."

He studied me for a moment, then shook his head slightly. "You could. But you don't have to."

His hand slid up, cupping my face. My pulse tripped, but I didn't stop him. He leaned in slowly, giving me every chance to turn away. I didn't take it.

The kiss was soft and patient, tasting of tea. It deepened, just enough to ruin the idea that it was accidental. When we parted, the air felt different, thinner yet charged.

He rested his forehead against mine. "You good?"

I nodded, my voice gone.

"Then sleep," he said, brushing his thumb across my cheek before he leaned back.

The sleep he spoke of soon found me before I realized it.

When I woke, morning light spilled across the room. My head was on his shoulder, his arm stretched behind me, not holding but close. He was already awake, eyes on the skyline. He turned slightly, careful not to wake me all the way. "Coffee?" he asked.

"Please," I whispered, still half dreaming.

He stood, the space he left behind still warm. When he came back with two mugs, the smell of dark roast filled the room.

"My parents are probably doing something someone will regret," I said into my coffee.

He smiled, faint but real. "You can stay until it's safe."

"I probably should." I took another sip, grounding myself in the heat of the mug and the stillness he made possible. "Thank you. For the couch. For last night. For not making it something it didn't need to be."

He looked up, eyes steady. "Who says it wasn't something?"

The question landed before the world outside swallowed the rest of it up and the morning felt suddenly new again.

Chapter 14

COLE

I STEPPED OUT TO TAKE THE TRASH TO THE CHUTE AND there she was, and suddenly I felt my body respond to the nearness of her in ways I hadn't wanted to notice before. Bellamy glanced up, froze for a beat, and gave me *that* look. The one that said I was an irritation and a welcomed sight at the same time.

"Your fan club is loud," I said, leaning one shoulder to the wall.

"They're residents," she replied, chin lifting. "And they have every right to enjoy their domain as much as the rest of us."

"I heard they nearly took out Mrs. Riley at the elevator this morning."

Her mouth curved, something between a smile and a warning. "Mrs. Riley survived Studio 54 and two divorces. She can sidestep a corgi."

"Barely."

"Maybe she tripped over your attitude."

"Wouldn't be the first casualty."

That nose flare again. The quick bite of her lip, like she was trying to keep from saying more. I should've walked away. I didn't.

"Say what you want to say," I told her, pushing off the wall, closing half the space between us.

She looped the leashes on the hook by TJ's door and stepped closer. The dogs sat in a perfect triangle, silent witnesses.

"What I want," she said, "is for you to stop pretending you don't know what you're doing."

I tilted my head. "And what am I doing?"

"Looking at me like that."

"Like what?"

"Like you're deciding whether I'm trouble or worth it."

A smile pulled at my mouth before I could stop it. "Maybe both."

Her breath hitched. "You really don't make things easy."

"Probably not. But you're still standing here."

"Don't flatter yourself."

"Too late."

We went still, the space between us alive with something neither of us bothered naming. One of the dogs exhaled, unimpressed. Somewhere down the hall, an elevator dinged. I should've been tired from travel, from the game, from everything that had been sitting on my back this week. Instead, I was awake in a way that felt reckless.

"You do this thing with your nose when you're mad," I said quietly. "Right before you decide to cut somebody."

She blinked. "I do what?"

"It flares. Barely. Like you smell the lie before you expose it."

That earned a slow breath, her eyes flickering. "You notice too much."

"Only when it's you."

"Don't try lines on me."

"They're not lines. They're facts."

She stepped forward, close enough for her perfume to thread the air between us, warm and clean.

"Here's one," she said. "You annoy me."

"Likewise."

Her mouth tilted. "And you fascinate me."

I heard it—the honesty buried beneath the challenge. I moved in without touching. Her breath caught and her eyes went darker, a shift I had been pretending not to obsess over since the first day she said my name like it was a problem.

"Tell me you don't want me to kiss you," I said.

Her mouth opened and closed. No sound. Then the smallest laugh that tasted like surrender. "I will not lie on a Monday."

"Good."

The first kiss was a test and a truth. Soft at the edges, firm where it counted, my mouth catching hers and holding, not taking more than I was offered. She answered with a sound that started deep and slid forward into my mouth. I tilted her chin and went in again, deeper, slower, tongue easing against hers in a way that made her fingertips curl in the front of my shirt.

"Inside," she breathed, closing the door behind her.

I pushed my door open with the heel of my shoe, backed us into my place, and kicked the door shut without breaking contact. The dogs did not follow. Bless them.

In the kitchen, the city threw pale light across her cheekbones. I set my hands at her waist and waited. She nodded once, giving me the consent I sought. I lifted her onto the counter and stepped between her knees, catching her mouth again with more intent. She kissed like someone who had been starving and finally decided to eat.

"You are trouble," she said against my lips.

"Not tonight. Tonight I am intentional."

Her fingers slid to my chin and held me still, her eyes reading me like I was the story. "Then be."

I peeled her top away. No rush. I wanted the reveal, the way her skin warmed beneath my fingers, the way color moved high on her chest when I paused to look. Lace cups framed breasts the exact size my hands were made to hold. "You are beautiful."

She rolled her eyes, but the breath she let out told me it got through. I kissed the top swell, slow, then lower, then lower still until I tugged a cup down and caught her nipple with my mouth. She arched and inhaled, one hand braced behind her, the other in my hair as I circled my tongue and then pulled with just enough pressure to make her curse. I gave the other the same devotion until her hips started to shift and her throat gave me these broken sounds that told me exactly where she was headed.

"Put me down," she whispered, and I dropped her to standing, crowding her deeper into the counter while she dragged her leggings down. I knelt and looked up at her, hands sliding to the back of her thighs. She nodded. I kissed the inside of one knee, then higher. She widened, and I pulled the last barrier aside, revealing the wet shine that made my mouth ache. I dragged the flat of my tongue through her, slow from bottom to top, then closed my lips around her clit and sucked.

Her answer was a gasp that turned into my name. I held her there with my hands cupping her ass and my tongue drawing circles that tightened as she started to climb. She rolled her hips, and I met her with pressure that fit her exactly. I slid a finger inside, then a second when she breathed me in. Slow, then deeper, then curled just right. Her legs trembled against my shoulders and she bit her lip until it shook.

"Do not be nice," she said, voice rough.

I did not. I worked her with my mouth and hand like I planned to live there, unbothered by the way my knees were protesting on the tile. This was worship. This was correction. This was a man who'd decided he was done pretending he did not want the woman who drove him insane. She broke against my tongue, hard and messy, thighs clamping, head tipping back, one hand slapping the counter like she was trying to steady herself.

I stood, and she dragged me up by my shirt, kissing me like she wanted every taste back. Her hand slid into my sweats, finding me hot and heavy, and stroked in a slow pull that made my vision tilt.

"Condom," I managed.

"Where?"

"Bedroom."

We walked there without separating, mouths finding each other between short steps, hands everywhere. I fumbled in the drawer and tossed a packet to the bed. She peeled my shirt away with a look that sat somewhere between appreciation and impatience. I returned the favor with her bra, then took one second to just look at her. If I said something, it would be praise that embarrassed us both. I left it in my eyes.

She pushed my sweats down, and my dick sprang free. She wrapped her fingers around the base and gave one firm stroke that made me curse. Then she sank to her knees on the rug and glanced up like she wanted a record of my face before she took me into her mouth. Warm. Wet. Slow. She was not trying to prove anything. She was tasting. Learning. Hollowing her cheeks and then backing off to stroke me while her tongue teased that sensitive strip underneath. I braced a hand on the dresser and the other in her hair, not to force but to feel.

"Bella," I warned.

She rose, smug and flushed, and kissed me while I rolled the condom on with hands that did not want to be patient anymore.

"Tell me where you want me," I said.

"Right here." She climbed onto the bed and turned on her knees, palms down, spine bowing as she looked back over her shoulder. The challenge in her eyes found something feral in me.

I lined up and pushed in inch by inch, letting the stretch take me. She was tight and slick and perfect, and I had to shut my eyes for a breath to keep from losing it. We both held. Not a pause. A recognition.

"Fuck," I whispered.

"Yes," she replied, eliciting a soft moan.

I started slow, a deliberate drive that dragged along every place that made her shake. I found the angle that pulled a sound from deep in her chest and ground there. She gripped the sheets and pushed back to meet each thrust. The bed complained, wood giving a low note that only made me want to ride it harder. I slid one hand around and circled her clit, tight strokes that matched the pace of my hips. She was loud now, unguarded, each sound a gift in a room that would remember us.

"That," she said, breath catching. "Do not stop."

I did not. I held her there with an arm around her waist and worked her with the other, building her up and keeping her on the edge until she slipped over it and dragged me with my name spilling out in a tone I had been waiting my whole life to hear. She clenched around me, and I swore it felt like the world narrowing to a single point of heat where we met. I kept moving through her release and felt another wave hit, smaller but deeper, the aftershock that ate my breath.

I pulled out slow and rolled her to her back. Her hair fanned out on the pillow and her mouth was swollen, her eyes gone soft and glassy. I hooked one of her knees over my forearm and slid in again, deeper like this. I kissed her while I moved, and the kiss was different. Less fight. More *yes*. She cupped my face like she had been waiting to hold it this way since the lobby.

"Look at me," I said.

She did. I set a pace that was all control until it snapped. I told her what she did to me. How good she felt. How I had thought about this every night since she answered her door with a hard voice and soft eyes, taking my offering at the time. She met every thrust and took it, nails marking my back, legs locking around my waist. When my edge rushed up I breathed through it, changed the angle, and watched her unravel again, her body milking me until I groaned into her neck and let go.

We lay there, breathing hard, sweat cooling, the room quiet except for us and the city outside. I brushed her hair back and kissed the corner of her mouth. The tender place where laughter lived.

"You good?" I asked.

She smiled up at the ceiling like she did not trust happiness in direct eye contact. "I am excellent."

"Anything hurt?"

"Only my resolve." She turned her head and met my eyes, open now, real. "We technically do not like each other."

"Not always."

"We should not do this."

"Probably not."

"We are going to anyway."

"That sounds correct."

"We're terrible at boundaries."

"Excellent at chemistry, though."

We started laughing, laughter that shook your chest and reset something in your spirit. I got up, took care of the condom, grabbed water, came back. She was watching me like she might memorize how I moved. I slid in beside her, and she tucked into me like her body had finally found a room temperature that fit.

"We will talk," I said. "Soon. About lines and what happens if we cross them again."

Her fingertip followed the ink on my chest, slow and deliberate, like she was memorizing the shape of me through it. "You mean when."

I didn't argue. I ran my palm down the back of her neck and felt the last of her tension let go. For a while we did not speak. The city lights moved across the ceiling. Somewhere down the hall, a dog gave a sleepy protest and settled again.

"I should go," she said, though she did not move. "If I stay, we will test your cardio again."

"Let me stretch first. You say that like it's a threat."

"It might be."

I kissed her once, slow enough to feel my heart change. Then I let her go, because discipline was not the opposite of desire. It was the container that made it repeatable.

She dressed, checked her hair in the black glass of the window, then leaned over me and stole one more kiss that felt like a promise and a warning. At the door she looked back and softened just a little, like she was letting me see something no one else did.

"Goodnight, Cole."

"Night, Bella."

She slipped out. I lay there staring at the ceiling, waiting for my mind to start its usual pacing. It didn't. The room felt settled, and so did I. I wasn't built for games or coincidence. I was built for intention. I reached for my phone out of habit, then left it on the nightstand. Whatever was waiting could keep waiting. For the first time in a long time, I thought I might actually sleep.

The DMs

@BeautyIzHerName

Explain to me why this heroine just agreed to
a marriage pact with a man who alphabetizes
his spice rack by color. He said they should
marry at thirty if they're both still single. Thirty.

@ChefSwishWhisk

Color coding is the only red flag I'll defend.
That pact clearly happened over mulled wine.
Bad decisions thrive when cinnamon's in the air.

@BeautyIzHerName

So you admit it's bad.

@ChefSwishWhisk

It's storybook. On screen, "if we're both single at
thirty" sounds romantic. In real life, it's how you
end up at a courthouse with a man who files his tax
receipts in a blue cookie tin.

@BeautyIzHerName

Not the blue tin.

@ChefSwishWhisk

You know the one. Every auntie's got it.

@BeautyIzHerName

He just said he still keeps her old mitten because
it "smells like peppermint." Sir. Seek help.

@ChefSwishWhisk

Or maybe the mitten reminds him of a memory.
Peppermint can do that, you know. It cheats time.

@BeautyIzHerName
Look at you getting poetic.
Since when are you Team Mitten?

@ChefSwishWhisk
I'm Team People Want to Be Chosen.
The mitten's just the proof.

@BeautyIzHerName
If these two end up slow-dancing in
a barn under twinkle lights while a dog
in a sweater watches, I'm turning this off.

@ChefSwishWhisk
You won't. You'll talk through it while your
snack bowl disappears. What are we eating?

@BeautyIzHerName
Hot sauce on kettle corn with
chocolate-covered wasabi peas.

@ChefSwishWhisk
That's bold. Confusing but bold.

@BeautyIzHerName
It's fire. Literally.

@ChefSwishWhisk
I respect it. I'm making kimchi fried rice, but I got
carried away with the chili paste. Might be joining
you in the flames.

@BeautyIzHerName
This is what I get for flirting with a man whose
comfort food has a passport.

@ChefSwishWhisk
You called it flirting. Noted.

@BeautyIzHerName
Don't get cute. I flirt with outcomes not people.

@ChefSwishWhisk

That might be the most honest
thing you've said all week.

@BeautyIzHerName

It's also true. My track record is... not stellar.
Men who need fixing. Men who look finished but
aren't. Men who love me in private and forget me
in public. Pattern recognition is a skill and a curse.

@ChefSwishWhisk

Pattern recognition's the first step
to breaking it. That one's free.

@BeautyIzHerName

Hypothetically, say someone's starting to care
about a person. Not a pact person, not a mitten
hoarder. A person with gravity. And she doesn't
trust herself not to blow it up because the burn
rate's high. What does a sane person do?

@ChefSwishWhisk

She says that sentence out loud.
Which you just did.

@BeautyIzHerName

To you. Not to the person with gravity.

@ChefSwishWhisk

Sometimes saying it here is the warmup.

@BeautyIzHerName

Don't feed me coach talk like it's medicine.

@ChefSwishWhisk

It's not. Some things can't be rushed. You need time,
heat, and patience. Open the oven too soon,
you lose it. Never open it, same thing.
You learn when to check and when to trust.
That's not coach talk. That's life.

@BeautyIzHerName
You really said love is mise en place.

@ChefSwishWhisk
I did. Get your station together, then cook.

@BeautyIzHerName
I hate how much I like that.

@ChefSwishWhisk
Hate it gently.

@BeautyIzHerName
He just pulled the mitten out at the tree lighting.
If anyone claps...

@ChefSwishWhisk
They're already clapping. The mayor's crying.

@BeautyIzHerName
You aren't watching this. Wait... Are you?

@ChefSwishWhisk
All these holiday towns share a script. I
don't need to.

@BeautyIzHerName
We're a mess together.

@ChefSwishWhisk
We are. But your hypothetical made me think.
Wrong woman, right timing. Right woman,
wrong me. I've been good at looking steady.
Terrible at staying open. Lately someone's
been changing that.

@BeautyIzHerName
Complicated good or complicated ruin your life?

@ChefSwishWhisk
Complicated human. That's enough.

@BeautyIzHerName
Jealous and relieved. Jealous because
complicated human sounds like a miracle.
Relieved because it means you won't be
waiting at thirty with a spare mitten.

@ChefSwishWhisk
I don't do peppermint knitwear. But miracle's
the word I don't say in daylight.

@BeautyIzHerName
You could say it at night.

@ChefSwishWhisk
I just did.

@BeautyIzHerName
Do you ever think we're cowards?
Not to each other but to the idea of it.
With the people we could actually lose.

@ChefSwishWhisk
Honest answer—I'm brave with the things
I can control. Feelings that might come back?
That's a different kind of risk. Respectable
way to starve, though.

@BeautyIzHerName
Say it louder for the row in the back.

@ChefSwishWhisk
I'd rather say it quieter for the two of us.

@BeautyIzHerName
Don't do that.

@ChefSwishWhisk
Do what?

@BeautyIzHerName
Be tender and make it sound like a dare.

@ChefSwishWhisk

It's not a dare. It's where I am.

@BeautyIzHerName

Where's that?

@ChefSwishWhisk

Somewhere between knowing too little
and saying too much. That's where
naming usually goes wrong.

@BeautyIzHerName

Look at you getting all poet chef again.

@BeautyIzHerName

Speaking of naming, he just asked her to be his
backup plan again. Why is that so sad?

@ChefSwishWhisk

Because it hides a fear. It says I'll be your safety
net when the truth is I'm scared I'm not your first
choice. Sweet on the surface, which somehow
makes it worse.

@BeautyIzHerName

So you wouldn't be someone's backup plan?

@ChefSwishWhisk

For you? Maybe. But I'd want to be the plan that
doesn't need a backup. Still, I'd bring a ring pop
just in case.

@BeautyIzHerName

You just made me laugh and feel something
at the same time. That should be illegal.

@ChefSwishWhisk

Crimes of charm. I plead guilty.

@BeautyIzHerName

I hate that I'm smiling at my screen
like a teenager in pajamas and a bonnet
on that's trying to escape. Not cute.

@ChefSwishWhisk
It is. Somebody could look at you like
that and think this is the scene.

@BeautyIzHerName
You talk like a man who knows how to make
women feel seen.

@ChefSwishWhisk
I talk like a man still learning how to.

@BeautyIzHerName
Don't make me like you more.
My ecosystem's fragile.

@ChefSwishWhisk
Then I'll be careful with it.

@BeautyIzHerName
You're a trip.

@ChefSwishWhisk
I've been told. Tell me one thing about your
hypothetical person. The part that scares you.

@BeautyIzHerName
They don't rush me, but they don't let me hide.
They see the mess and stay. They listen without
trying to fix me. It makes me want to be braver.

@ChefSwishWhisk
Sounds like someone worth catching up to.

@BeautyIzHerName
It is. Which is why my stomach hurts.

@ChefSwishWhisk
My grandmother used to say that kind
of ache isn't fear. It's the hinge turning.
Doors hurt before they open.

@BeautyIzHerName
Now you're wise and grandmotherly.

@ChefSwishWhisk

She believed butter solved most conflicts.
She wasn't wrong.

@BeautyIzHerName

Tell me one thing about your complicated human.

@ChefSwishWhisk

She's funnier than she means to be. Refuses to be
handled. Argues like she's letting air into a room
that needs it. And when she's tired, she lets it
show. It shouldn't feel intimate but it does.

@BeautyIzHerName

You're gone.

@ChefSwishWhisk

A little.

@BeautyIzHerName

Okay. Reckless game. Would you ever
want to hear my voice? Just a call.
We could hang up if it felt wrong.

@ChefSwishWhisk

Yes. Too fast an answer but yes. Still, if we shift the
frame we risk what makes this work. This version is
not pretend. It is just the one we can manage right
now. And before you ask, no other lives, no secret
families, no hidden complications. Just nerves.

@BeautyIzHerName

Same. And thank you for saying it out loud.

@ChefSwishWhisk

Then we keep the frame. We do not have
to define forever tonight.

@BeautyIzHerName

Look at the mitten couple.
The lights are twinkling, giving off all
the hopeful vibes. He's going to ask again.

@ChefSwishWhisk

He is. And she'll say no to the pact
and yes to him. That's the point.

@BeautyIzHerName
What's the point?

@ChefSwishWhisk

Choose the person, not the deadline.

@BeautyIzHerName
I hate that you're right.

@ChefSwishWhisk

Hate me softly then answer something for me.
Do you ever wonder if we're missing something
by keeping this in the box?

@BeautyIzHerName
I thought about it then shut it down.
You know how it is when you
hyperfocus on a cloud out of fear
that it might rain during a picnic.

@ChefSwishWhisk

If it rains, we move under a tree.

@BeautyIzHerName
Says the man with good umbrellas
and no fear of lightning.

@ChefSwishWhisk

What if just for tonight we do go ahead
and name it without wrecking it?
Not call it soul mates. That word is too shiny
and too easy to sell on a t-shirt.
Something smaller and truer.

@BeautyIzHerName
Like what?

@ChefSwishWhisk

Clickmates. The click is what we have. The flow
of it. The pace. The way the screen lights up and
it feels like a room we built. It doesn't promise a
wedding or a pact. It promises that when we talk,
the world arranges itself for an hour.

@BeautyIzHerName

You really said clickmates like you invented fire.

@ChefSwishWhisk

It is my one good coinage for the month.
Spend it wisely.

@BeautyIzHerName

I'm actually obsessed with it. It takes the pressure
off. Like you said, it's not forever. It's right now. It's
a confession that doesn't demand a ceremony.

@ChefSwishWhisk

Exactly. So, for now until or unless we decide
we want to hear each other to breathe on the
other end of a line, we can be that. Clickmates.
I still reserve the right to bring a ring pop to your
hypothetical pact, though. I do have a rep to
maintain.

@BeautyIzHerName

You're too much. Also, thank you. You say things in
a way that makes the room feel bigger.

@ChefSwishWhisk

You fill whatever room you are in.
I am only rearranging chairs.

@BeautyIzHerName

They just kissed in the hardware store. The dog in
the sweater approved. I'm embarrassed.

@ChefSwishWhisk

I told you the mayor would cry.

@BeautyIzHerName

He is sobbing into a box of nails. Fine, I'm keeping
the movie on. But only because I need to see if
they finally throw that mitten in the wash.

@ChefSwishWhisk

Never. It's a relic now.

@BeautyIzHerName

Goodnight, Chef.

@ChefSwishWhisk

Night, Beauty. Sleep without pacts and dream
without deadlines.

@BeautyIzHerName

And if I panic?

@ChefSwishWhisk

Hit me up. That's what clickmates are for.

@BeautyIzHerName

Bet.

Chapter 15

BELLAMY

I'D BEEN RUNNING ON CAFFEINE AND NERVES SINCE sunrise. Another night of "parental togetherness" left me wide-eyed until dawn, and when I finally stepped into Jawn, I was one good cry or shy one strong latte away from collapse.

The café looked more like a construction site than the heart of a community event. Folding chairs lined the walls, boxes of supplies cluttered every surface, and the scent of hot oil drifted in from the curb where the food trucks were warming up for tonight's crowd. Someone's playlist leaked through a Bluetooth speaker, low and scratchy, keeping us on our toes about the time. Every choice felt personal, from the way the stage should face to where the mic stand belonged.

"You sure you're good?" Nina asked, catching me staring up at the string lights she'd insisted on hanging. Her apron was dusted with flour from the breakfast menu she'd decided to run this morning so her team could still earn their tips before the big event.

"I'm fine," I lied, tugging a strand of light so it sat straighter. "Just measuring how many hours I have before I start talking to walls."

"Eat before you get dramatic," she said, eyes twinkling. "No one gets extra points for burnout."

By sundown, Jawn had been transformed. The tables that

usually held laptops and latte cups now shimmered under string lights, and laughter filled the air in place of morning chatter. I had gone through a transformation too, after a spontaneous trip to The Shops at La Cantera with my mother. She insisted I needed a wardrobe refresh, and now here I was, wrapped in buttery leather that felt like confidence made tangible.

The glow from inside softened every hard line of the day. Music poured through the café, steady and full, threading between conversations. Outside, the food trucks glowed like lanterns against the night, their windows fogged with steam. Each time the door opened, a wave of scent drifted in, bringing us the aroma of jerk seasoning, roasted corn, and something fried, tempting enough to make promises it would never keep.

Ronan's rookies had shown up just like they promised, wearing all black. They moved between tables carrying trays, collecting trash, pretending they weren't pro athletes disguised as waitstaff. One woman tried to flirt with Javon while her husband wasn't looking, and his blush gave him away before his stammer did. We eventually moved him near the back for his safety.

My father owned the stage. "All right, San Antonio!" he boomed into the mic, voice polished and proud. "Y'all came out here looking too good to be quiet. Let's make some noise for our girl Nina and her crew tonight!"

The applause felt like it reached the ceiling. Nina gave a mock bow behind the counter and mouthed, *You're welcome.*

I was in my corner by the bar, balancing my phone on a stack of napkins and filming for Jawn's social feed. The light caught everything, from the gleam on the domino tiles and the way couples leaned close to the sway of laughter that moved through the room like music.

And then Cole walked in. He scanned the crowd once and

found me. Immediately I felt my stomach drop before it eventually steadied. He reached me with that quiet swagger that had no business being this attractive. "You survived," he said, leaning one elbow on the bar.

"Barely. I'm one spades table showdown away from hiding in the kitchen for the rest of the night."

"Tempting if I can join you," he teased, making my cheeks suddenly go warm. "Nina told me your posts are blowing up. People already want to know when the next event is."

Before I could come up with a comeback, he set a plate in front of me. Jerk shrimp skewers rested on a bed of rice with a side of fried plantains and cornbread muffins that smelled so sweet and buttery I almost moaned.

"Eat," he said.

"Are you serious right now?"

"Yes. You've been moving for twelve hours. Eat before you face-plant and give Nina a reason to yell, and no one wants to be called a dickhead over something avoidable."

I wanted to argue. Instead, I picked up a fork. The first bite melted, bright and spicy, and I forgot what I was supposed to prove.

"Fine," I said. "You win."

"I usually do."

I glared, but my mouth betrayed me with another bite.

The band slipped into "Spanish Joint," and the whole room shifted. The bass came first, round and playful, then the horns followed, gliding in easy enough to make the air itself lean forward. My father caught the cue instantly. Host or not, the stage had always been home.

"You all feel that?" he asked, grin wide as the drummer locked in to the pocket. He gave a nod, and his voice joined them, instinctive and sure. Around us, heads tilted with the beat, bodies swaying before anyone realized they were moving.

He let it simmer just long enough to warm the room, then lifted a hand toward the band. "All right now, let's take it home."

The horns brightened in response, teasing the first few notes of something funkier. The bass answered with a familiar roll that made couples rise without discussion, hips finding the time that turned movement into joy. Laughter rippled through the room, easy and unforced.

My father chuckled, returning the mic to the stand with a shake of his head. "That's what I'm talking about, but what y'all *not* gonna do is trick me into a performance."

My mother, seated a few feet from the stage, didn't miss a beat. "Then don't start something you can't finish, Terrence."

He flashed a grin and a wink. "I've been finishing since '88, baby."

The place exploded with laughter. I covered my face. "Every single time."

Cole laughed. "That's where you get it."

"Get what?"

"That tone. Soft, but it carries teeth."

I met his eyes. "I'll take that as a compliment."

"It was one," he said. And for a second, the crowd around us blurred.

Then Nina appeared, towel over her shoulder, eyes cutting straight through the moment. "You two goofballs better not be hiding back here flirting. Come on. Your parents want you up front."

"I'm working," I tried.

"You're clocking out," she said. "Your mother didn't ask. She actually *commanded*. 'And bring the tall one.'"

"The tall one has a name," Cole said, amused.

"Not tonight," Nina countered, eyes cutting between us.

"Tonight you're staff, remember?" Her grin said she knew exactly what she was interrupting. She tossed the towel onto the counter and waved us toward the front. "Go before I tell your mama you're hiding from her."

We wove through the tables, shoulder to shoulder, moving at the slow pace of people who weren't ready to break whatever current had started between them. Along the way, a few guests stopped Cole for selfies, and he obliged them with a quiet smile that managed to look genuine. My hand brushed against his back once… accidentally, maybe… and the heat that shot through my palm made me wish it wasn't.

Ronan waved us over to the table closest to the stage. The sight was pure comedy. My father was now seated and talking trash with the confidence of a man who hadn't realized he was losing, my mother sat next to him like a queen guarding her throne, and one of the rookies looked seconds from tears.

"Sit down, Bellamy," my mother said, fanning herself with her cards. "Save your father before he embarrasses himself twice in one night."

"I'm holding my own," Daddy said, right before Ronan slammed down a wild card with enough drama to win an award.

"Change to blue!" Ronan shouted.

The table erupted. Cole slid into the chair beside me, our legs brushing beneath the table, that small point of contact sending awareness through every inch of me.

"Feels like I walked into a family sitcom," he murmured.

"Welcome to syndication," I said, sliding my cards together so I wouldn't fidget.

He leaned in, his voice low enough to feel against my neck. "You look good tonight. The way that skirt is riding up on those succulent thighs of yours is daring me to disrespect you in front of your folks."

The compliment caught me mid-breath. I focused on the cards, pretending they mattered more than they did. "Flattery won't help your hand."

"I'm not here to play," he said. "Just to watch."

"Moral support doesn't usually stare this hard."

He smiled. "It does when something beautiful is sitting right next to it."

The warmth in his tone wrapped around me like a touch. The noise of the room thinned until I could hear the slide of his sleeve brushing mine. I looked up, ready to say something clever, but the words fell apart under the weight of his gaze.

My father's voice cut through before I could recover. "Bellamy! You gonna play or fall in love at my table?"

I nearly choked. "Daddy!"

The table roared. My mother covered her mouth, laughter shaking her shoulders. Cole didn't move, didn't even blink.

"She's multitasking," he said smoothly, all charm.

My mother dabbed her eyes, still laughing. "He's quick. I like him."

"Do not encourage this," I said, trying to regain composure.

"Oh, I absolutely will," she said, leaning back with satisfaction. "We've been waiting for someone who can keep up."

Cole looked at me then like he'd just been handed clearance. My pulse stuttered. The cards blurred in my hands, the room spinning with laughter and music and the warmth of belonging I hadn't realized I'd missed until he was sitting this close.

The next hour blurred into laughter. We watched my parents dance together between rounds, Ronan narrated every hand like a sportscaster, and the rookies drifted between serving and playing backup DJs. Nina popped by our table to drop a basket of beignets and then dropped low enough to whisper into my ear, "I see you, but I'll let you cook."

Every time I looked up, Cole's eyes were already on me. Not in a possessive way—he was just present, attentive in a way that made all the static in my life feel muted.

Eventually the crowd thinned, and my father took the mic one last time. "Before we go, make some noise for the folks who made all this happen." He rattled off our small tribe one at a time, from Ronan and the rookies to the musicians behind him, but then he paused and, with pride in his eyes, looked at me and called out, "And my babygirl, Bellamy. All this love being poured out in this space only happened because she managed to miraculously squeeze it out of us in less than three days."

The applause rose like light through water. I laughed, started to wave him off, but the sound caught in my chest and stayed there.

When the lights dimmed to alert everyone that Jawn was officially closed and the last plates were stacked, my parents made their rounds to say goodbye. Daddy hugged me tight. "You did good, babygirl. This right here? This is love made visible."

"Thanks, Daddy."

"And I'm not talking about the event," he whispered to me before letting go. Then he turned to Cole, all ease gone from his tone as they dapped each other up. "Take care of her, son."

Cole nodded. "Always."

"And don't forget… a father with access to unlimited resources is a motherfucker to contend with if shit ever goes left on his Babygirl. So treat her like the fine china she is to me."

Laughter rippled nearby. My mother tried to look unimpressed but failed. "You two make a nice picture."

I rolled my eyes. "Goodnight, Mommy."

She waved and left with my father, pretending not to hold his hand as they slipped through the door.

When it shut behind them, the silence landed softly. The room glowed under the remaining lights. Cinnamon and sugar from the baskets of beignets that were served at every table still hung in the air.

Nina appeared. "Y'all can finish sweeping up," she said, her smirk impossible to miss. "I'm going home before this turns into a scene I'm too envious to witness."

She winked and disappeared through the back.

Cole moved to the counter and flicked off the overheads, leaving only the string lights glowing over us. "They're not wrong."

"About what?" I asked, quieter than I intended.

He took in the café, the tables, the warmth that lingered. "You. This. The way it feels in here."

Something in me went still.

"You ever stop long enough to enjoy what you build?" he asked.

I looked around at the crumbs, the chairs, the glow clinging to the walls. "I'm trying."

"Good," he said, stepping close enough for the air to shift. "Because you built something that feels like belonging."

My pulse stumbled. "That lowkey sounded like another compliment."

"It was."

A quiet jolt ran through me. The last time belonging sat this close, I'd gotten blindsided. My mouth tried to play it cool before my nerves gave me away. "Don't start reading into things."

He stayed still, watching me. Something flickered across his face, quick and cautious, like he was deciding whether to pull back. He looked like a man who'd learned that too well. But this time, he didn't.

"I'm not reading into anything," he said quietly. "I'm reading *you*."

My breath tightened. "And what does that mean?"

"That you retreat into yourself when something gets real," he said. "You just did it."

The air between us warmed, the truth settling where it needed to.

"And you?" I asked, trying to sound unbothered. "You think you're different?"

He exhaled once, slow. "I'm trying to be."

What disarmed me wasn't confidence or certainty. It was the quiet honesty of a man choosing not to hide.

"Careful," I murmured. "You sound like you're getting close."

His gaze didn't budge. "Maybe that's the point."

His hand brushed my cheek, warm and deliberate. There was nothing uncertain about the way he leaned in slow enough for me to stop it, yet certain enough to make me forget how. The kiss landed soft, sure, patient. Trading breaths instead of stealing it.

When he pulled back, our foreheads touched.

"Still think this was a bad idea?"

"I never said bad," I murmured. "Just dangerous."

He smiled against my mouth. "I can live with that."

I kissed him again, because I didn't want to overthink what already felt inevitable.

Outside, the city moved on. Inside, the world narrowed to just us.

And I finally stopped moving.

Cole unlocked his door and stepped back, giving me room to enter first. The quiet wrapped around us like something alive. He lingered behind me, close enough that I felt the trace of his presence before I heard it. I set my bag on the counter and glanced over my shoulder.

"Still not used to this silence," I said. "It's constant motion on our side of the hall. I love my parents but can't wait for them to leave tomorrow."

He dropped his keys beside my bag, the faint clink echoing

through the stillness. "You filled this place with plenty of sound once before," he said quietly. "Last night wasn't exactly quiet."

I turned, slow enough for him to notice. "That was your fault."

He lifted a brow. "You're really sticking to that."

"I'm right," I said, deadpan.

"You always think you're right."

"That's because I usually am."

His smile shifted, small and lethal, giving away more than he meant. "And what happens the one time you're not?"

"I don't know," I said, stepping into him, "why don't we test it and see?"

That stopped him, not in retreat or pushback but in that subtle shift a man makes when he's willing to let me lead.

A small smile curved his mouth. "Is that right?"

I closed the distance until we shared the same air. The kitchen light glowed across his face, softening the sharp lines I'd learned too well. He leaned against the island, steady, watchful, his restraint visible in the pulse at his throat.

"You've been staring at me all night," I said.

"Observing," he replied. "Not staring."

"Then observe this."

My hand found his collar, fingers sliding down the front of his shirt. Heat gathered under the fabric, spreading through my palm. The air thickened. He didn't move, didn't speak, only breathed slow and measured, a breath that felt held for me.

"You remember last night?" I asked.

His gaze dropped to my mouth. "Every detail."

"Then you remember what happens when I do this."

I rose on my toes and found that place at his neck, the one that had made him lose composure before. I brushed my lips there once, then again, and his breath caught, rough and unguarded. Water clung to his skin, warm beneath my mouth.

That was when I saw it again, the faint ink near his collarbone, half hidden by his shirt and the shadow of his skin. I followed the line with my tongue slowly until his hand tightened at my waist. My other hand drifted to the back of his neck, tracing the tight coil of his hair before sliding down to rest against his chest, feeling the steady pound beneath my fingertips until it stumbled.

"Bella," he said, voice breaking.

"See?" I whispered, still tasting salt and heat. "Memory still works."

He exhaled against my ear. "You keep that up and I'll forget every promise I made about taking things slow."

"I think we're past the syllabus."

He laughed then, the sound resonant enough to move through me. When I tilted my head back, he found my mouth and kissed me like he was tasting something he'd been craving all night. The kiss was deliberate, his lips dragging slightly before he deepened it, tongue coaxing, testing. My body leaned into him before my mind could catch up. His hand slid down my spine, guiding me closer until thought felt distant and unnecessary.

I shifted against him, teasing, and this time I nipped lightly at his lip, catching the bottom one between my teeth. His breath stumbled. "You trying to start something or finish it?" he asked.

"Maybe both."

The air between us changed. I felt the tremor beneath my hand, the pull of muscle under his skin, the small grind of his jaw. When I moved again, he exhaled through his teeth.

"You came here tonight with a plan," he murmured.

"I recall what worked," I said, brushing my thumb along his lower lip. "You didn't complain then, either."

"I'm not about to start now."

I pressed my palm against his chest, urging him backward until the backs of his legs met the couch. He sank down without resistance, gaze steady, pupils dark. I followed him, settling across his lap until the world tilted slightly in our favor. His breath deepened. His hands hovered near my thighs, waiting for a cue neither of us had to name.

"Still following instructions?" I teased.

"For now."

The quiet around us shifted, becoming its own language. Our breathing synced. The faint rustle of fabric, the soft press of movement, the heat of skin meeting skin. I moved my hands up his chest, tracing the steady rise, the rhythm of him under my palms. He returned the favor, removing my top and unclasping my bra with careful precision, letting the straps slip down my arms until my breasts fell free.

Cole's hands rose to cup me, his thumbs brushing lightly before his mouth replaced them. The first flick of his tongue drew a sigh from somewhere I didn't control. The second made me grip his shoulders. He alternated between gentle and deliberate, his teeth grazing, his breath warm against wet skin.

Each movement became instinct, each sound a reply. When I pulled back, his eyes were even darker.

"You don't fight fair," he said quietly.

"Neither do you."

He smiled against my shoulder, then met my gaze again. I reached for his waist, unbuckling, unzipping, easing him free. His exhale brushed my cheek, hot and shaky. My hand closed around him, and the tremor that ran through his body felt like an admission. His hand slid up my thigh, thumb circling until I forgot what came before.

"You keep doing that," he said, voice uneven, "and we won't

make it to conversation."

"That's not a threat," I whispered. "That's incentive."

His hand moved higher, finding the curve of my back again, guiding but never taking.

"Tell me what you want," he said, voice a murmur that lived more in my skin than in the air, as his fingers teased the lacy edge of my panties.

"I already am," I breathed against his ear.

He let out a sound that was part laugh and the rest surrender, the vibration running through both of us. I moved closer, our foreheads still touching, and his next breath came unsteady as he slipped his fingers deep inside me.

"You sure you're ready for where that leads? I don't have it in me for anything fleeting."

"Me neither." I slid my palms up his chest, feeling the slow rise and fall beneath them. "Now hush. I'm the one leading."

He laughed quietly, but never once broke the rhythm of his strokes. "That so?"

"Mmhmm. Now tell me, Cole. What's my name? And you only have one shot at getting it right," I said as I rocked my hips back and forth against his palm.

"Bellamy."

"Say it again."

"Bellamy."

The way he said my name found its way under my skin. I brushed my lips along his cheek. "Good."

His restraint fractured as I squeezed tighter with the next stroke. "You like being in charge?"

"Tonight, I like seeing what happens when you're not."

"Be careful with that."

"Why?"

"Because I'll let you."

I slid my hands beneath his shirt, feeling warmth and muscle and the steady rhythm of his breathing. He was solid but waiting, patient and ready to be unraveled. I tilted my head up, and his mouth found mine again. This kiss was different. It was deeper, heavier, and left no question about where this was going.

I broke it first, whispering against his lips, "Lie back."

His eyes searched mine, then he obeyed, sinking into the couch cushions. "Now what?" he asked.

"Now," I said softly, "you let me see you."

"You already do."

"Not like this."

I traced his collarbone, felt the pulse jump beneath his skin. He watched me as if I'd taken something sacred in my hands. His palms rose to my hips, but I pressed them back down. "Still."

"You like testing limits."

"Only when I trust the person I'm testing."

That quieted him. Something in his expression softened, then sharpened again. I kissed him deeply, lingering until I sensed his resolve unraveling while moving against him as I let the heat between my thighs meet his growing erection. His body answered in small ways, from the shift of his thigh beneath me to the sound caught in his throat when I moved just slightly closer.

"Bella," he breathed, "if you keep doing that…"

"I know." I brushed my thumb across his lower lip. "That's the point."

When he finally reached for me again, it wasn't to take control. It was to match me, every touch meeting where I'd already set the pace. It felt less like surrender and more like translation, two people speaking the same language without interruption.

There was laughter, the soft kind that happened between

collisions of breath. There was a moment as I slipped my panties to the side and lowered my heat-slicked body onto his, taking him deep inside, and he whispered my name like it was a full sentence. And when the rest of it blurred into passion and motion as we made love well into the night, it felt like something that didn't erase what came before but expanded it.

"You're a problem, Bella," he said once we both were able to come up for air.

I smiled against his shoulder. "You were warned."

He laughed, the low sound curling through me. "Remind me not to argue with you again, because I don't think I'll ever win that fight if you play dirty like this."

"There was never a chance of that. And speaking of warning, you've got one more time to call me that before—"

He traced a quiet line along my hip, nothing urgent, nothing demanding, just enough to pull the words right out of me.

We stayed like that, breathing each other in until his heartbeat steadied beneath my ear. Then his voice dropped, quieter now, a little careful. "You really don't like when I call you Bella, do you?"

I lifted my head just enough to meet his eyes. "You've got a habit of shortening things that don't need fixing."

He studied me for a long moment. "Maybe. But Bella means beautiful. And that's exactly what you are."

Something in me shifted at the way he said it with no hesitation. His words weren't a performance, just truth, and it landed deep and left nowhere to hide.

"You're ridiculous," I whispered, the words coming softer than I intended.

He smiled. "You say that every time I mean it."

For once, I didn't feel like anyone's spectacle. I felt like a woman who'd asked for what she wanted and got exactly that.

Chapter 16

COLE

THE HIGH SCHOOL'S GYM SMELLED LIKE EVERY PLACE THAT ever taught me who I was supposed to be. A hand-painted banner that was clearly done by the kids sagged from the rafters reading, *Welcome to the Storm Youth Skills Clinic.*

A group of boys and girls looked ready to turn it into the Finals.

Ronan was already in the thick of it, whistle around his neck, giving pointers to a kid half his height and twice his attitude.

"Eyes on the target," he said. "Elbow under. Breathe. Don't heave like you're throwing out the trash."

The shot went wide, clanging off the rim so hard it startled half the line. Ronan didn't hesitate. "Progress," he said, nodding like the kid had just hit a buzzer beater in June.

I crossed the court, dribbling a spare ball. "You get here early just to show off?"

He smirked, not looking up. "That's what captains do. Lead by example."

"Pretty sure that's what coaches are for."

He glanced over, that familiar grin breaking through. "And you're pretty sure you still get to talk back to the captain?"

I passed him the ball, spinning it once before it left my hand. "Old habits. Hard to shake."

The next hour ran on adrenaline and sneakers squeaking against polished wood. Kids sprinted, parents cheered, and the scoreboard blinked digits that somehow still mattered. Ronan made the drills look like choreography. I just tried to keep up, correcting footwork, shouting encouragement, handing out water bottles like a sideline uncle.

When the whistle blew for the last time, the noise softened into that satisfied buzz that only comes after effort. Pizza boxes appeared on folding tables, and the smell of melted cheese overpowered the funk of prepubescent adolescents who have yet to discover deodorant. Ronan sat beside me on the bleachers, both of us watching the excited energy that we'd helped create moving about.

He said, twisting the cap off his water, "I like you better when you're sweating for a cause."

"You saying I don't normally give back?"

He smirked. "I'm saying you usually give press ready gratitude. This right here? This is real."

I leaned back, letting the wood cool my shoulders. "Feels good. Haven't been around this kind of energy in a while."

"In other words, you're finally touching grass."

"Hardwood," I corrected him.

"Same concept. You're outside your bubble, and it shows." He paused, studying me. "You been smiling at your phone lately. That Bellamy?"

I should've seen it coming. "You keeping tabs on me now?"

He shrugged. "Just pattern recognition. You went from radio silence when you first landed in San Antonio to now checking notifications like a teenager."

"She's different."

He stretched his legs, nodding toward the court where a group of kids argued over who'd hit more free throws. "Different good or different 'I might need to lawyer up'?"

"Good," I said, smiling despite myself. "She sees me like I'm still a person, not just whatever the world decided I was."

Ronan glanced over, brow raised. "You sound like a man getting in deep."

"I'm taking my time."

He chuckled, shaking his head. "That's not how it works, brother. You can pace your steps all you want, but falling still feels the same when you hit the ground."

I laughed under my breath, but it lingered.

He leaned forward, elbows on his knees. "When's the last time you were around somebody who made it easy to breathe?"

I thought about her laugh, how it filled the space like it belonged there. How quiet felt different with her in it.

"Right now," I said.

"Then don't overthink it. She's not a test, she's a person. Treat her like the good thing she might actually be." He stood and grabbed another ball, spinning it on his finger before sending it arcing toward the hoop. It dropped clean. "Still got it," he said.

"Barely," I muttered.

He pointed at me. "You? Definitely lost it."

I caught the ball. "And you're the authority on love now?"

"I'm the authority on your face, man. You look relaxed. That's new."

A little boy ran up before I could respond, clutching a slice of pizza and a Sharpie. "Can you sign my shoe?"

I bent down, took the marker, and wrote my name across the side of the kid's sneaker. "You sure? This gonna make it worth less."

He grinned. "Nope. My friends gonna think it's magic."

Ronan winked at me as the kid ran off. "See? You still got a little somethin' somethin' left."

"Don't start."

"Too late," he said. "And since you borrowed Grim and Doom this weekend, I already know whatever you're planning isn't small."

I frowned. "How do you even know that?"

"Because you've had that secret mission face all morning. And because you just told on yourself."

"Maybe it's nothing."

"Then why are you nervous?"

I didn't answer.

He clapped me on the shoulder. "Relax, man. She already likes you. Just make sure you don't stop liking yourself in the process."

He walked off to help the volunteers pack up, leaving me with my thoughts.

My phone buzzed. Bellamy's name flashed on the screen, alerting me of her latest text. The name had become a quiet pulse in the back of my mind, steady and grounding. The way she smiled when she thought no one was watching. The softness in her voice when she said my name. The way she didn't start when I was silent for too long.

Bella: You survive the madness today?

Me: Barely. Considering new career as guidance counselor.

Bella: Ha! Bet you were great.

Me: Not as great as my company's about to be.

The typing bubbles flashed, paused, then returned.

Bella: Should I be nervous?

Me: Only if you hate surprises.

Bella: I don't.

I caught myself smiling at the screen. Ronan's laugh echoed in my head. He was right. I wasn't trying to control the outcome anymore. I just wanted to show up.

When the last of the kids filed out and the gym lights dimmed to half, I lingered a little longer, the air still warm with the day's noise. I thought about how easily Bellamy had begun to fill the quiet parts of my life. How she'd made space where I didn't think any existed.

As I left the gym, I sent one more message.

Me: Keep Friday open. I've got plans for us.

Her reply came fast, and after answering I pocketed the phone, smiling to myself as the door shut behind me.

Maybe Ronan was right. Maybe I was falling. And this time, it didn't feel like a loss. It felt like something I could trust.

Chapter 17

BELLAMY

BY THE TIME FRIDAY ARRIVED, THE APARTMENT HAD FALLEN back into the flow I'd longed for when it was just me alone with my thoughts. My parents were gone, their laughter and low-grade arguing trailing behind them like perfume that lingered too long. At last, I could hear myself think. I had a few mornings to myself before TJ and Evan returned, and the peace felt like a luxury I didn't want to question.

The corgis were piled near the balcony door, three small bodies arranged in perfect indifference. Cole had texted earlier in the week with a message that made me smile before I finished reading. *Keep Friday open, and you might want to leave Saturday morning clear too, just in case. Dress comfortable. Trust me.*

No explanation. No details. Just Cole, confident in that way of his that always made me want to say yes before knowing what I was agreeing to. When I asked if I should pack anything, he'd replied, *Just your appetite and comfortable shoes.*

I didn't ask again.

Now it was barely seven, and the stillness in the apartment felt almost deliberate. I moved through it slowly, gathering what I needed, feeling my own anticipation stretch and settle. His next message buzzed through letting me know he was downstairs, I was already ready. Soft joggers, a black tee, sneakers, and the gray hoodie that lived on the line between mine and not mine.

My hair was freshly washed and pulled back. My face was clean, skin dewy from moisturizer, with just enough makeup to suggest I'd woken up like this. Before leaving, I knelt beside the dogs. "Nina's coming by later. Try to act civilized." MiMi blinked. Nippy yawned. RihRih didn't bother to respond.

The elevator was quiet, moving slow enough to give my nerves a little room to stir. Not anxious, just aware that something about the day might matter. Lately, Cole and I had been orbiting each other without declaring what it may or may not be. Every day seemed to begin or end with his voice, either in person or through late-night texts that drifted between teasing and confession.

He made sure I was in the arena for every home game, always in the same section, beside Nina, where cameras seemed to find us without trying. Clips began circulating online soon after. Captions called it an unexpected courtside reunion along the lines of, *Cole Howard's companion identified as former morning show host Bellamy Barnes.* The comment sections were split in half, with some rooting for redemption while others relitigated old rumors. It started to get noisy, speculative, and impossible to ignore, but for once I didn't care.

Daryl greeted me when the elevator doors opened and gestured toward the front entrance instead of my usual route through the garage.

Cole was waiting by the curb, leaning against his Range Rover that reflected the early light. He wore a dark sweatsuit that made casual look composed, and when he saw me, he pushed away from the door as I stepped out, opening the passenger side with an ease that felt old-fashioned, prompting me to think of my dad's annoyance whenever I reached to open a door. Inside, two drinks waited. Mine was a dirty chai latte.

"You remembered," I said, smiling despite myself.

"Of course," he replied. "I like my company caffeinated."

"Am I going to need it?"

He looked slightly boyish then, a hint of mischief softening the lines of his face. "Probably. We've got a flight to catch."

"Flight?"

"That's the surprise."

"Is this the part where I ask if I'm being kidnapped?"

"You could," he said, guiding the SUV into motion, "but it would ruin the suspense."

"Just checking. I didn't pack snacks or a ransom note."

The city peeled away as we drove, the downtown landscape giving over to open sky. He kept the music low, suiting the morning, filling the silence without intruding on it. Between songs, we spoke in the way two people do when there's more comfort than curiosity. I told him I hadn't slept well all week, and he told me I'd thank him by lunchtime.

At the terminal, two intimidating, large men were waiting with a sleek midsize jet gearing up for takeoff a few yards away. The guys were familiar faces, as they were Ronan's people, exuding quiet efficiency and watchful calm. Cole nodded to each before opening my door.

"They're coming with us?" I asked, looping the strap of my crossbody across my chest. "Should I expect Ronan too?"

"Just Grim and Doom," he said. "It keeps my aunt from stressing me out."

"You have an aunt like that?"

He smiled. "You'll see soon enough."

Before I could ask more, he handed a few wrapped packages to one of the men and placed a hand at the small of my back as we boarded.

The cabin struck a balance between understatement and indulgence, its cream leather seats gleaming softly beneath warm light. The faint scent of coffee and breakfast meats drifted through the air, subtle but inviting. A folded blanket waited neatly on my seat, and beside it sat a linen lined basket filled with fresh fruit, glossy cookie croissants, cruffins dusted with sugar, and miniature jars of jam. The arrangement felt intentional enough to make me lean over and brush my lips against his.

"You planned this," I said, watching him fasten his belt.

"Planned is generous," he said. "I made a few calls."

"Calls that include pastries."

"I'm a man of taste." His mouth tilted. "Correction. Your man of taste."

Before I could reply, a small ivory card tucked beside the basket caught my eye. I picked it up and began reading.

"Brown-butter brioche French toast… herb-soft eggs… maple pepper bacon… more warm pastries…" I slowed. "Bella's pecan praline butter.'"

Steady eyes flicked toward mine.

"Cole… I don't know what to say."

He shrugged lightly. "Figured since you showed up with cake that night… I should return the favor."

My breath caught. "This isn't cake, Cole."

"No," he said. "I tried to recreate the flavors off of memory without risking your dad threatening me if I called to ask him for the recipe." He paused. "I know it's not the same but—."

"It's perfect," I murmured, folding the card in my hand.

He rubbed the back of his neck, suddenly boyish in a way he'd never admit to. "I'm hoping it comes close. If not…" His eyes softened. "We'll keep trying until it does."

The tenderness of that nearly undid me.

"Careful," I said, meeting his gaze. "I might start believing deep down you really do have a thing for me."

"That's the goal."

The jet rose through a stretch of clean sky, the clouds spreading beneath us like silk. He turned toward me, resting his elbow on the armrest.

"What are your plans for Thanksgiving?"

The question sounded casual, but it pulled something deeper. "My parents are apparently rediscovering each other and planning a trip that may end in another round of divorce threats. TJ and Evan are spending the week at his parents' house with the dogs. I was invited on a girls' trip but haven't decided yet."

"Why not?"

"I like the idea of quiet, and I'm not sure I'm ready to face old friends pretending they don't want to bring up Smoothiegate."

He studied me for a beat. "We have a home game that day. My family's coming out for it. You should join us. It's loud and full of opinions, but the catered food's apparently worth it."

I turned to him. "You're inviting me to Thanksgiving with your family?"

"I'm saying you'd fit in," he said. "And my aunts could use someone at the table who can keep up."

"Tempting."

"Don't say no yet."

"I'm not saying no."

The rest of the flight unfolded in companionable quiet, the gentle roar of the engines lulling us into an easy flow.

When we landed in Anaheim, the air was warm and crisp. A luxury shuttle waited at the edge of the runway, its tinted windows reflecting the early sun. Standing beside it was a woman with diamond studs, salt-and-pepper curls, and an expression that managed to be both welcoming and appraising.

Cole smiled as soon as he saw her. "There's Auntie Lo."

She met him halfway, pulling him into a hug. "There's my guy," she said, then turned to me. "And this must be the young woman he's been conveniently not mentioning. I'm Auntie Lo, baby. You can call me that whenever you're ready."

"I'll ease into it," I said, because claiming "Auntie" on first introduction felt like skipping a few rites of passage.

Two men joined her, both tall, broad-shouldered, and wearing matching grins that spoke of long histories and inside jokes. A woman followed behind them, her eyes bright with mischief as she held the hand of a little girl in a glittering birthday sash. The moment the girl spotted Cole, she tore away from her mother's grasp and launched herself into his arms. He caught her easily, spinning her once as she squealed with laughter, begging and daring him not to drop her.

"Bellamy," Cole said, placing a hand at my back while balancing the birthday girl on his hip, "meet my family. Auntie Lo, cousins Marcus, Darnell, and Tanisha, and the star of the day, Summer."

Summer reached out a hand, her curly braids bouncing as she tilted her head. "I'm eight. Do you like rides that go fast?"

"Only if I have someone brave sitting next to me," I replied.

"That's me," she said decisively.

"Perfect," I said. "I scream quietly, so we'll make a good team."

Laughter circled around us, open and easy. Cole caught my eye over her shoulder, and what I saw there was something soft moving through his expression, offering relief, maybe, or gratitude that this introduction wasn't a mistake.

We bypassed the main gates for a quieter side entrance reserved for VIP guests. A woman in a tailored blazer and bright sneakers greeted us with a practiced but genuine smile. "Good morning, I'm Lydia," she said. "I'll be your guide today. We'll start with something light to eat, then head into the park before the big crowds hit."

"Music to my stomach," Auntie Lo said, already eyeing a nearby kiosk.

Lydia led us toward a small courtyard that overlooked the carousel and smelled like sugar, espresso, and cinnamon. A pop-up café had been arranged for special guests, including an espresso bar and a counter filled with pastries that looked too pretty to eat. The trays gleamed with hand pies, fresh fruit, and miniature muffins that made even the adults stop and reconsider breakfast discipline.

Cole took a plate from one of the attendants and handed it to me. "Breakfast of champions," he said.

The crust was buttery, the filling warm and sweet, and before I knew it the world went quiet except for the sound of Summer giggling at her reflection in a nearby window.

"This is criminal," I said, taking another bite. "You shouldn't introduce a woman to pastries this early in the relationship."

"Then I'll take the risk," he replied easily.

Summer tugged at his hand. "Uncle Cole, we have to hurry before the lines get long!"

"Can't argue with leadership," he said, tossing the wrapper in a bin and letting her drag him toward the first attraction.

Auntie Lo looped her arm through mine as we followed behind. "He hasn't been here since he first entered the league," she said quietly. "Said he'd bring his own family one day. Guess we all came close enough."

"That's sweet," I said, watching him laugh when Summer pointed at a crew working on a parade float that had been wheeled into position.

"Sweet is one word," Auntie Lo said with a knowing smile. "That man's heart stays busy."

Cole slowed his stride to wait for us. "Y'all talking about me?"

"Always," his aunt said, handing him a napkin and pointing out the powdered sugar dusting on his beard.

He grinned and looked at me. "Don't believe everything she says."

"I don't," I said, smiling back. "But I like hearing it anyway."

By midmorning the park pulsed with life. Music drifted above the crowd, weaving through the scent of roasted nuts and funnel cake. A burst of laughter flared behind us when a costumed character crouched to play peekaboo with a child, joy catching on the air like sunlight.

Summer clutched Cole's hand and swung their arms, declaring herself parade leader. Lydia cut a path ahead, flashing a badge that opened gates before we even slowed. "This way," she called over her shoulder. "Premium access and better snacks."

"Better snacks?" I perked up.

"See? That's how you get her attention," Cole said. "Mention food."

"Food *is* attention," I said, nudging him.

Auntie Lo heard and grinned. "That right there is why I already like her."

Summer demanded something with sprinkles, which led us to a dessert stand where cupcakes glittered in impossible colors. Cole slipped his card to the cashier before I could reach for mine. His expression warned me not to argue. I ignored it. He ignored my ignoring.

Summer insisted we all taste her cupcake "for research." Cole leaned down, pretending to grade it on a ten-point scale, until icing caught at the corner of his mouth. I reached up automatically, but he caught my wrist, eyes locking on mine.

"You missed a spot," he said quietly. Then he leaned in and kissed me, soft, restrained, too brief to scandalize a theme park but enough to change the air around us.

The noise of the crowd blurred. All that existed for a moment was his breath near my cheek and the warmth still blooming between us.

Auntie Lo's voice cut through. "If y'all are done flirting over frosting, this child's got rides to ride."

We followed, laughter trailing behind us like proof we'd been caught.

Inside the royal boutique, Summer sat perfectly still in her glitter-dusted chair, chin lifted like a princess who'd been through this coronation thing before. Stylists floated around her in pastel aprons, brushing shimmer over her cheeks and pinning rhinestones into her curls until she looked like she belonged in a parade down Main Street. She watched her reflection as if meeting her animated counterpart.

Tanisha and Auntie Lo were still out at one of the shops next door, hunting for souvenirs and pretending they did not have opinions about this makeover. Which meant Summer had her three uncles and me all to herself.

"You should do something too," she said, eyes narrowing at me in the mirror. "You can't join the royal family without sparkle."

"She's right," the stylist said, already reaching for a brush that looked suspiciously like a wand.

I caught Cole's reflection before I answered. He leaned against the far wall with quiet authority, a man who had clearly never stepped inside a room this pink. His arms were crossed, but the smirk gave him away.

"Think shimmer suits me?" I asked.

His gaze lifted. "Everything suits you once you stop trying to argue with it."

"Careful. That almost sounded like game."

"Almost?" he said, brow raised.

The stylist brushed soft gold across my eyelids, a shimmer that caught the light every time I blinked. When she placed a small tiara over my braid, Summer gasped and clapped her hands.

"Now we match!"

"That makes us princesses," I said.

Summer lifted her chin, posture perfect. "I'm a *queen*," she corrected me. Then she pointed toward the mirror. "Uncle Cole, Uncle Darnell, and Uncle Marcus, you're the royal guard."

Cole groaned behind us. "Guess that makes me the glitter security detail."

"Exactly," she said with complete satisfaction.

Cole sighed. "Perfect. Armor and glitter. My dream assignment."

"You'd still make it look good," I said.

His smile turned crooked. "You'd find a way to test it."

The stylist tried not to laugh, her mascara wand pausing midair.

Summer caught us in the mirror. "Are you two flirting in the royal court?"

Cole straightened like he'd been caught sneaking out of detention. "No, Your Majesty. Just following royal orders."

Summer eyed him with mock suspicion. "Good. Because in this castle, only fairytales end in kissing."

I met his gaze in the mirror, the tiara gleaming between us. "You heard the queen."

"I always do."

We stepped out of the boutique glittering in every sense, sunlight catching the shimmer the stylists had left behind. Lydia gathered the group near the entrance, giving quick directions.

"Lunch is in about twenty minutes," she said. "Cole and Bellamy will meet us after their stop."

I turned to him. "Stop?"

He slipped on his sunglasses. "You'll see."

Security followed a few paces behind as we moved through a shaded path lined with flowering trees. The noise of the crowd faded until all that was left was the faint sound of water from a nearby fountain. The air smelled like orange blossom and sugar. At the end of the walkway, a woman in a crisp uniform stood waiting beside an unmarked door.

"Mr. Howard," she greeted Cole with a smile. "The chef is ready for you."

"The chef?" I asked.

He grinned, a little smug. "You've had your share of churros and lemonade. I wanted you to experience a little more."

Inside, the room opened wide and gleaming, stainless steel, copper, and light. The kitchen moved like a choreographed dance—flames blooming, knives working, the air thick with butter, garlic, and citrus. It smelled like home and temptation at once.

I slowed, watching. The precision of it fascinated me. A pastry chef spun sugar into delicate strands; another drizzled chocolate over something too pretty to eat.

The head chef noticed and smiled. "Would you like to see how the magic happens?"

I hesitated for a beat. "Absolutely."

She showed us to an area to wash up then handed me a white apron and guided me closer to the stove. "We're finishing your first course. You can help if you'd like."

Cole's voice came low behind me, close enough that I felt the warmth of his breath against my neck. "Go on."

The skillet hissed as prawns hit the pan. Butter foamed, the scent of lime cut through the air, and my pulse matched the thrill of it. The chef's voice was calm and precise as she described each step, but I was aware of everything else too—the heat of the stove, the pulse at my throat, the quiet pride in Cole's expression when he realized I wasn't just watching. I was learning.

When the prawns were done, she had me spoon them over coconut rice steeped in lemongrass and topped with toasted coconut and herbs. I took a small step back, smiling.

"You have good instincts," the chef said. "You knew when to stop. That's rare."

Cole grinned. "You sure this is your first time doing this? You're out here showing off."

I laughed, shaking my head. "Please. I'm usually an epic failure in the kitchen. Smoke alarms, takeout, the whole tragic pattern. But this feels… easy, somehow."

The chef glanced up from the stove, smiling like she'd overheard a familiar truth. "That's not luck. That's nerves settling. Everyone cooks better when they find their center."

"My center?" I asked, still stirring.

"Could be a person. Could be a moment," she said. "Food is a love language, and cooking's just the way some of us learn to speak it."

I felt Cole watching me again, that quiet, steady way of his that always seemed to make the air change temperature. The scent of garlic and lime lingered between us, and right away, I understood exactly what the chef meant.

She laughed and gestured toward a small table tucked in the corner. Two place settings waited, with glasses of sparkling water catching the light.

The first bite was a quiet revelation. Sweet, spicy, and clean, with a richness that made me close my eyes for half a second longer than I meant to.

"You could have warned me," I said.

"And ruin the surprise?" His tone was gentle, amused. "Never."

The next course arrived in silence—roasted vegetables glazed with chili and honey, a small filet of sea bass resting on top, crisp at the edges and impossibly tender at the center. Dessert followed, grilled pineapple layered with coconut sorbet and caramel dusted with sea salt.

By then, the conversation had slowed into something soft and unhurried. The kitchen sounds faded, leaving only the small details: his fingers tracing the rim of his glass, the brush of his knee against mine, the satisfaction that hung between us after every bite.

He leaned forward. "You've had people staring at you all day. I thought you might want a moment where the world stops watching."

Something about the way he said it slipped under my skin. "You do this often?"

"No," he said. "This one's yours."

When we finally stood, I thanked the chef, and Cole did the same. Then he reached for my hands, threading his fingers through mine. The gesture wasn't showy, just instinctive. He led us toward the door with that unhurried stride of his, making space bend a little around him. Outside, the sunlight softened, and for a moment, walking beside him felt less like leaving and more like being chosen.

"You really went all out," I said.

He looked down at me. "Just lunch. You made it more."

When we rejoined the family, Summer was bright-eyed again, and Auntie Lo was mid-story. No one asked where we'd been, but when Cole's hand squeezed mine, the quiet between us told the truth.

Later, we were guided to a roped-off terrace overlooking Main Street, a quiet pocket above the crowds where the parade would pass directly in front of us. Servers floated through with trays of popcorn, cotton candy, and lemonade, touches that made the day feel curated instead of overwhelming.

Summer pressed against the railing, eyes wide as the music swelled. Cole lifted her to his shoulders, his hands braced at her knees, and the small weight of her trust settled naturally on him. She waved at every float that rolled by, her laughter rising with each burst of confetti.

From where I stood, I could see the pride written across his face. Something that lived in the corners of his expression when he thought no one was watching. His warmth brushed against me each time he shifted, our arms touching in small, electric intervals.

"She'll hold on to this," I said quietly, watching Summer clap to the rhythm.

"So will I."

When the next float passed, the lights flashed across his profile, catching in his eyes briefly before dimming again. The sound of applause filled the terrace, but the moment between us held its own quiet, a pause deep enough to feel.

Evening settled slowly. The first firework split the sky, spreading color across the lake and signaling that our little escape to experience a sliver of joy was coming to an end. Summer leaned against me, half asleep, while Auntie Lo sang along softly to a tune that drifted from the speakers above. Under the table where a final round of treats sat nibbled by our group, Cole's hand found my thigh, his thumb resting in a quiet space that didn't ask, just confirmed.

When the final spark faded, Auntie Lo stood and pulled me into a hug. "You did good, baby. Not everyone survives the Howard family test."

"Test?" I asked.

She winked before falling in step with the group as Doom and Grim guided us toward the exit. The family drifted ahead, still laughing, their voices mixing with the park's closing music. Cole's hand found the small of my back as we followed, a quiet touch that carried more meaning than any goodbye.

Outside, the shuttle waited to take his family to their hotel, while an SUV idled just behind it, headlights washing over the pavement in soft beams. The night air was warm, faintly sweet from the treats still baking somewhere in the park.

"You were great today," he said, his voice pitched low enough for only me to hear.

"So were you," I said. "You made the magic happen."

His smile reached his eyes, a look that carried weight without effort. "You are the magic."

It wasn't just what he said, but how he said it, each word deliberate, as if he were touching something fragile without fear. Men had admired me before, but from the surface, content to stay where it sparkled. Cole didn't look at me that way. He looked at me like a man discovering something worth keeping, his gaze lingering with quiet reverence that felt both grounding and new. The space between us shifted, a pull I could feel beneath my skin.

For once, I didn't deflect or reach for humor. I let him see what no one else had taken the time to find. And when I breathed in, it felt like he was already there. Steady, waiting, and close enough to make the night tilt toward possibility.

Chapter 18

COLE

THE APARTMENT GREETED ME WITH STILL AIR AND CITY light bleeding through the blinds.

I dropped my bag by the door and exhaled. Three games in four days. Too many flights, too many rooms that didn't feel like home, even though home usually found me in a place that felt both familiar and strange. Until recently.

Though it was past two in the morning, I sent Bellamy a text from the car on the way back from the airport letting her know that I just landed.

Finally, she replied before I reached the garage. You hungry or restless?

Both, I wrote.

Her answer came seconds later. Give me five minutes.

Five minutes later, there was a soft knock. I didn't bother asking who it was. The cadence was hers. Confident enough to mean it, careful enough to test if she was welcome.

When I opened the door, Bellamy stood there in an oversized T-shirt that hit mid-thigh, her hair loosely tied back. She appeared undecided, like she hadn't planned to come and changed her mind halfway through the thought.

"You good?" I asked.

"Couldn't sleep," she said. "Figured you wouldn't be able to either."

She was right. I stepped back and let her in. She walked past me, her bare legs catching light from the kitchen.

"You want water?" I asked, mostly to keep my hands busy.

"Sure."

I filled two glasses. She leaned on the counter, watching me with an expression I couldn't read. When I handed her the glass, her fingers brushed mine. The contact was light but deliberate. She took a sip, eyes never leaving me.

"Rough trip?" she asked.

"Rough week. Every loss feels like a write-up." I pointed toward the small cut on my lip, the souvenir from an elbow that had turned into a whistle, then an inevitable fine, then a walk to the tunnel before the clock ran out. "You watch tonight?"

"Of course I did."

"Then you saw it. The part where I stopped pretending it didn't get to me."

Her eyes searched mine. "You didn't lose control, Cole. You just ran out of room to swallow it."

That hit deeper than anything I'd heard all week.

"Still plays the same on screen," I said. "Old guy with a temper, team takes the hit, franchise reconsiders the trade."

"Or maybe they remember why they took the risk in the first place."

Silence settled, not heavy, just honest.

"I'm not here for a talk," she said quietly. "Unless that's what you need."

"That's not what I was going to offer."

"Good," she said. "Because we're not spending another minute talking about that bullshit call when there are better ways to use the night."

She set her glass down slowly. I watched her hand, watched the pulse at her wrist, the small shift of her breath. When I stepped closer, she didn't move. My fingers found her jaw, tracing the smooth line up to her ear. Her lashes flickered once, then she looked straight at me.

"Say what you want," I said quietly.

"I want you to touch me like you mean it."

"I only know one way."

The first kiss landed slow and deep, like both of us had waited through too many nights to get here. She tasted like mint and something faintly sweet, something that belonged entirely to her. She met me with equal want, opening beneath the pressure of my mouth, sliding her hands under my shirt, dragging her fingers across skin that hadn't been touched in too long.

When her nails grazed my back, control went hazy. I lifted her onto the counter. She fit there like the space had been waiting for her. The sound that left her throat nearly unmade me. Her knees framed my hips, her breath unsteady against my cheek.

"You do that thing with your mouth when you're about to say something smart," I murmured. "I want to hear it."

"Then stop standing so far away."

I stepped in. The contact drew a quiet sound from both of us. I kissed her neck, tasting skin that was already warm from wanting. Her fingers curled at the sleeve of my shirt. When I found the place just below her ear, she shivered hard enough to make my restraint falter.

"Tell me if you want different," I whispered against her ear. "Tell me if you want slow. Tell me if you want me to stop."

"I want you to keep talking," she said. "And don't stop."

The shirt came off easily. Her skin glowed under the soft kitchen light. She wore nothing beneath the fabric, and I drew a breath, then bent and kissed her, my mouth tracing every inch like I was studying something worth getting right. She arched beneath me, her breath catching on a sigh that sounded like surrender and challenge all at once.

"Bedroom," she whispered.

I carried her there. The room was dim, shadows soft across the sheets. I laid her down and kissed her again, slower, deeper, until every thought scattered. She tugged my shirt over my head, fingers trailing down my chest, mapping me with quiet intent. When she pushed my sweats down, I laughed softly.

"Come here," she whispered.

I reached for the drawer and tore the foil, and her eyes followed every motion. When I sank into her, the air left both our bodies at once. Her nails dug into my shoulders and her hips lifted to meet me. The measured pace found itself, both patient and exact. The sound of her breathing shifted, caught, broke, then built again.

"Look at me," she said.

I did. I always did.

Her body trembled around mine, her pulse racing against my skin. When she came, the quiet that followed felt like still air after a storm. I followed right after, the release leaving me breathless.

We stayed like that, tangled and spent, until the world returned to sound and shape. I pressed a kiss to her forehead before stepping away to take care of what needed to be done. When I came back, she was on her side, the sheet pulled to her waist, eyes half closed but alert.

"This isn't a good idea," she said quietly.

"No," I said, sliding back into the bed beside her. "But it's ours."

"It's ours for now. This time isn't meant for forever. I need to find my way back to whatever life is still waiting for me. I just don't know what that looks like anymore."

"You say that like I can't walk beside you while you figure it out."

Prompting a faint smile from her. "Because I don't know if you're supposed to."

I brushed my thumb along her jaw until her eyes found mine again. "Then let me decide that."

She rested her head on my chest, the words dissolving into the steady rhythm beneath her ear. Her breathing slowed before mine did.

I smoothed a hand through her hair, memorizing the weight of her, the way her body curved perfectly against mine. When sleep finally came, it wasn't deep. It hovered light and watchful, keeping me aware of everything I was holding and how easily it could slip away.

An hour later, the door closed behind her, quiet but definite. I stayed in that silence, trying to pretend it didn't feel like loss. The sheets still smelled like her. My mouth still remembered her. I pulled on sweats, headed for the kitchen, and poured a glass of water I didn't drink. The city lights reached through the window, painting thin silver stripes across the counter.

Across the hall, her voice carried faintly through the wall, playful. The dogs, probably. She was coaxing them back to sleep. Then came her laugh, warm enough to undo everything I'd built back up in the last hour.

Sex I could rationalize. Her laugh was what unspooled me.

I picked up my phone, thumb hovering over the usual middle-of-the-night distractions. Team chat, schedules, film reminders… none of it mattered. My hand drifted instead toward the one app I shouldn't touch. If I had the discipline I claimed to, I wouldn't need to.

The handle sat at the top of my DMs like it had been waiting… BeautyIzHerName.

I hadn't messaged her in weeks, told myself it was smarter that way. But after tonight, pretending distance meant control felt like a lie.

Before I could second-guess it, the screen lit up. A message appeared, like she'd caught the shift in the air and knew I was there.

@BeautyIzHerName
Still awake?

A smile found me before I could stop it.

@ChefSwishWhisk
Now I am.

@BeautyIzHerName
Couldn't sleep.

@ChefSwishWhisk
What's on your mind?

@BeautyIzHerName
Too much. Nothing I want to admit out loud.

@ChefSwishWhisk
Start small. Give me one thing.

@BeautyIzHerName
Comfort food. That's safe enough.

@ChefSwishWhisk
Comfort food's never safe. It ruins discipline.

@BeautyIzHerName
So does talking to you.

That one hit harder than it should have. I stared at the screen, heartbeat steady and fast at once.

@ChefSwishWhisk
Some things are worth the ruin.

Her typing bubble appeared and then disappeared. She offered no reply. Just silence. Maybe that was her line. Maybe it was mine.

I set the phone down, leaned against the counter, and looked out at the skyline. Even at night, the city was alive, but everything felt still. Across the hall, Bellamy was there. Warm, real, breathing the same air I was, and that felt like its own kind of gravity. In my hands was something familiar, but its safety was born out of my own fear.

Sleep didn't come easy that night. But it came with Bellamy still in my head. And I knew one thing with absolute certainty: whatever this was, it wasn't finished. Not even close.

Chapter 19

BELLAMY

THE TEXT CAME JUST AFTER NOON.

Cole: You around? I'll bring food.

It shouldn't have made me smile as wide as it did. But it did.

An hour later, he was at my door fresh from practice, carrying a grocery bag instead of takeout. There was a calm certainty in the way he stood there, like this wasn't an errand but an intention.

"You really did bring food," I said, stepping aside.

"Did you think I was bluffing?"

The line came through softer than it should have, but it stayed with me. He crossed the threshold, setting the bag on the counter, and began pulling out salmon, asparagus, garlic, herbs, and a lemon that looked curated rather than bought.

"You went shopping?"

"I go to the store sometimes," he said, rinsing the salmon. "It's where the food lives."

"But you actually brought ingredients to my house."

"I brought lunch to your life."

"I was expecting something in a container. Possibly with a logo."

"Containers are for men who play it safe."

I laughed before I could stop myself.

He turned on the stove, let the butter fall into the pan, and the air shifted. Garlic hit the heat first, then lemon zest, then rosemary. It felt indulgent, domestic, and a little too intimate for two people still pretending they were casual.

I leaned against the counter. "So this is your secret talent."

"One of them," he said, flipping the salmon. "You'll have to stick around to find out the rest."

"You're really leaning into this domestic fantasy."

He grinned without looking up. "What's fantastical about it?"

The sound of the sizzle filled the silence that followed. He moved with an easy, practiced manner that was focused and assured. When he finally plated the meal, he looked up at me. "Sit."

The word did things to me it shouldn't. I obeyed, and the first bite was obscene, with lemon and butter melting into each other and the fish perfectly crisped at the edge.

"You're showing off," I said.

"I'm feeding you," he said.

We ate side by side at the island. Conversation slid easily between us in between glances that held a little long, picking up and dropping threads the way people do when comfort is starting to settle in.

He told me about his other nieces and nephews, his late mother's obsession with sending care packages when he was in college, and how Ronan kept trying to get him into golf. Once the plates were pushed aside, the air between us had changed shape.

He leaned forward, forearms resting on the counter. "You look at me like you're waiting for the catch."

"Maybe I just know there usually is one."

His smile softened. "Bella. There isn't one." He leaned back slightly, watching me like he was making peace with something that had been sitting in him for a while. "You think I'm holding out some fine print, but I'm not. You're it. The calm I didn't know I needed." His voice lowered, rough around the edges. "I love you."

It wasn't rehearsed. It just arrived solid and real, like he'd been carrying it around, waiting for a place to put it down. I forgot how to breathe for a moment. "You love the salmon," I said finally, trying to laugh.

"No," he said. "You."

He stood, closing the space between us, and the look in his eyes made it impossible to pretend this was anything less than true. His hand found my face, thumb tracing along my jaw.

"Say something," he murmured.

I opened my mouth. "You're going to ruin me."

"That's not the plan," he whispered, and kissed me. My hands found his hoodie, tugging him closer. His tongue brushed mine once, unhurried. The air around us shifted, thickened. "Bella," he said softly, voice ragged.

And then there was a click followed by a faint beep.

"Wait! Oh my God, Evan, she's kissing him!"

We froze and my blood ran cold.

Cole stilled with his grip on my arm tightening. "What the—"

"Bellamy! Girl, you better breathe!"

I blinked, realizing Cole was hearing what I heard too. We clearly were not imagining any of this.

"What was that?"

Before I could answer, a voice filled the apartment.

"I swear, if my sister's naked ass cheeks end up on top of my marble countertop—"

"Relax… if it happens, that's just destiny being punctual for once."

"Oh, *hell* no." I jerked back, eyes darting around the room. "Why am I hearing voices?"

"Did you butt-dial TJ?" Cole asked.

We both continued to look around, pulling apart briefly before hesitantly shaking it off.

Another voice chimed in, distant but crystal clear.

"Teej, did you hit the audio again? You hit the audio again!"

Evan.

Cole blinked. "Who the hell—"

"My sister," I groaned. "And their very loud partner."

Cole and I moved around the kitchen trying to figure out where their voices were coming from, because although it looked like we were alone, we clearly were not. I turned toward the mantle and that was when I spotted a decorative corgi figurine blink green.

"Heeey, Bell Bell," TJ's voice sang from the speaker. *"You didn't tell me 34B was hanging out in our kitchen, and oooh–weeee is he ever cooking. Get it, girl!"*

Evan giggled. *"Babe, you know she's going to kill us for this."*

"Are you freaking kidding me?" I said, staring at the device. I turned it over in my hand, noting it ran on both USB and battery. "This whole time?"

"Well, not the entire *time,"* TJ answered, sheepish. *"Only when we were missing our babies and you wouldn't answer us on FaceTime."*

Evan added, *"Or when they were sleeping. Sometimes we love to just watch them sleep. They're so cute when they're at peace."*

Cole tried to smother a laugh and failed. "They straight up had you under surveillance."

"It's a dog cam," I snapped.

"Correction, Bell Bell," TJ cooed, all dreamy affection. *"It's a nanny cam we had long before you moved in. We originally used it when we started suspecting the old dog walker was slacking off. Kept it afterward because it was perfect for checking on the kids. The two of you are so stinking cute. It's just so romantical. I love* love!*"*

"Romantical," Evan echoed. *"And juicy."*

My whole insides hollowed out as I gripped the figurine that had been narrating our lives. "I am going to kill them."

Cole's shoulders shook with barely contained laughter. "Bella, maybe they just—"

"They installed a camera in my house to spy on us. On me."

"Well, technically it's not—"

"Don't finish that sentence," I said, and marched straight at the outlet behind a stack of architecture books. I yanked the plug free and held the corgi by its ceramic ears as I carried it into the kitchen.

"Bell Bell, wait, we can explain," TJ pleaded through the speaker as I turned the faucet. The water hit the figurine hard and fast, streaming down its back in a steady, vindictive sheet.

Evan's voice rose in panic. *"Babe, she's serious—"*

The speaker fizzed and popped. The corgi's blinking eye sputtered, blinked once more, and went dark. Steam rose around it like a curtain. For a second the sound was all steam, and then there was quiet again.

Behind me, Cole leaned against the counter, grinning. "You know that's property damage, right?"

"They can take it out of my security deposit," I said, and the threat came out jokey because it had to. I set the sodden figurine on the counter like it had betrayed me.

He laughed, hands raised in surrender. "I'm impressed. Terrified, but impressed."

"You should be."

He moved closer and placed a hand at my waist. "You're sexy when you're mad."

"Get out before I drown your phone too," I said.

He kissed my forehead then, soft and quick. "You're unbelievable."

"And yet allegedly you love me."

He smiled. "I do."

He left still laughing. The corgis wandered in, noses twitching, sniffing at the trash can where I'd tossed the soggy spy dog. I watched them, then looked up at the ceiling and muttered, "Romantical." I did not mean it as surrender.

When I caught my reflection in the window, I was smiling. Definitely not by accident.

Thanksgiving morning was loud before I even got out of bed.

TJ and Evan had come through two days ago, long enough to swap suitcases, grab the dogs, and leave for their trip to Colorado. The apartment had been quiet ever since, until now.

My phone hadn't stopped vibrating since after midnight, every alert another reminder that peace wasn't in today's forecast. The world had found new material to chew on, and this time, it wasn't just Cole's comeback or the way he'd rebuilt his name. It was personal.

The post itself was simple. It was nothing but an ultrasound washed with a soft filter and a caption that read, *New beginnings.*

That was it. No names, no tags, just a breadcrumb the internet devoured whole. Within an hour, every gossip blog and sports feed had already written the story they wanted to tell.

Cole Howard was in new city, with a new team, and now, possibly, had a new baby with his ex-wife Laura.

I set my phone face down on the counter, like that could silence the noise that came with it. But the truth burned beneath my skin anyway. It wasn't just about him. It was about us.

The only person I hadn't heard from was him. No good morning. No "headed to the complex." Nothing.

By eight, I'd made coffee I didn't drink and told myself not to worry, which went about as well as trying not to breathe. Nina had already left me two voice notes. One advised me to stay home to avoid the drama and the other was her changing her mind, insisting I show up in something fabulous and proudly stand beside him like I had every right to. I took her second piece of advice.

By the time I reached Vantage Arena, the city was slowly perking up. The air had that dry chill San Antonio pretends is winter. I cruised by vendors who were setting up outside as holiday music floated faintly over the crowd who were waiting to get inside. Inside, the energy was electric, as the Storm clearly wanted it known it was ready to apply pressure.

I flashed my guest pass and one of the attendants waved me through to the tunnel. The private hallways always felt colder than the court itself, with concrete floors, echoes that went on too long, and fluorescent lights that made everyone look half tired.

That was where I found Ronan. He was standing near the locker room door, bent over his phone while lost in his own pregame ritual. His expression softened when he saw me.

"He in there?" I asked.

"Yeah. Not exactly feeling chatty." He slid the phone into his pocket, studying me for a beat. "You saw it?"

"I saw enough."

He hesitated, shifting his weight like he wasn't sure if he should help or protect him from me. "If you're going to get through to him, do it before Parker starts calling people to the floor."

I nodded, pulse kicking. "Thanks, Ronan."

He disappeared inside, and a moment later, the door opened again. Cole stepped out.

The sight of him hit me in the chest. He looked carved from focus and fatigue, his jawline tight, shoulders squared, and eyes dark from a night that hadn't ended. He was beautiful in a way that hurt.

When he saw me, something flickered across his face. First surprise, then something quieter, heavier.

"You shouldn't be down here," he said.

"Neither should half the people trying to tell your story for you," I replied.

He exhaled. "You saw it."

"Everybody did."

His gaze dropped briefly before meeting mine again. "You shouldn't have to deal with this."

"Don't make it about me," I said softly. "This is about you remembering who you are."

He gave a quiet, humorless laugh. "And who's that today?"

"The man who's worked to rebuild everything they said he broke. The one who keeps showing up. The one about to play the game of his life… if he doesn't let them steal it from him."

He studied me, trying to steady something in himself. "You really came all the way down here two hours before tipoff just to give me a pep talk?"

"I came because you didn't answer your phone," I said, meeting his eyes. "And because I love you."

The words left me before I could second-guess them, but I didn't want them back.

He froze. The sound of the arena faded until it was just the two of us. His gaze deepened, unguarded in a way that felt private and dangerous.

"I'm fine," he said eventually, but it came out uneven.

"You're lying."

His mouth curved slightly. "A little."

"Good," I said. "That's progress."

"Ronan says the rookies watch me like I still matter. Problem is, I don't trust what they'll see if I let the guard down."

"They'll see you're human."

Something shifted between us then. Not loud, not visible, just a quiet turning where tension gave way to trust. His hand brushed mine, thumb tracing slow circles along my skin.

"Bella," he said, his voice rough.

"Yeah?"

"Thank you." He hesitated, then added, "I love you too."

The sound of movement filled the hall again as we noticed players, coaches, and staff move about. Cameras waiting for something worth catching lingered nearby behind the lines where they were allowed.

That was when Laura appeared.

She was smaller than she looked online, but no less rehearsed. Every step measured, every angle intentional. She moved with expensive grace that came from knowing people were watching, her handler following a few paces behind. She didn't slow as she passed, chin lifted in quiet defiance, but the subtle way her hand rested on her stomach said enough.

The faint click of camera shutters followed her, a scattered beat that echoed down the corridor. Light flickered briefly against the wall, and I couldn't tell if it was imagination or flash. Maybe they caught the movement, maybe not. But even the possibility of it was enough to tighten the air between us.

Cole tensed before he even realized it, and his head started to turn. I caught his chin gently, keeping his focus where it belonged. "Hey," I said. "Eyes on me."

His gaze snapped back, and the world went quiet again.

"She doesn't get to rent space in your head today," I said. "Not when you've got an arena full of people waiting to see you do what you love so much."

He blinked, then smiled reluctantly. "You realize you're bossing around a six-nine power forward right now?"

"Somebody has to."

That earned a real smile, one that cracked the armor he'd been carrying since morning.

"You'll be up in the suite?" he asked.

"With your family. Wish me luck."

"They already love you," he said. "Auntie Lo probably already started shopping for your Christmas present."

I tilted my head, a smile tugging at my mouth. "And you? Still love me?"

He leaned in, close enough that his breath brushed my skin. "I'd have to be a fool not to."

The answer settled between us, a truth disguised as something casual. Before I could respond, Ronan's voice carried from the open locker-room door, breaking the moment like a cue neither of us wanted to take.

Cole slid his fingers through mine, squeezing once before letting go. "Don't leave without me after the game."

"I won't."

He nodded, then turned, walking back toward the locker room.

Chapter 20

COLE

THE LIGHTS IN THE PRESS ROOM WERE BRIGHT ENOUGH to make anyone blink twice before answering. Reporters leaned forward, hungry for something that might trend before the sweet potato pie hit the table. The air was thick with the phones aimed and set to record, the soft clatter of keys on laptops, and the faint edge of curiosity that always followed a good game.

I walked in to the usual shuffle of attention, the scrape of chairs, the rustle of credentialed nerves. A few greetings. A few stares. The same faces that once couldn't wait to write me off now leaned closer, ready to take notes on the comeback.

We'd won, and I'd played the way I wanted to play. Efficient, locked in, and at peace.

The first question came from a familiar face near the front. "Cole, it's your first game against your old team since the trade. Big performance tonight. How did it feel out there?"

I could have gone through the motions by thanking the team, the fans, then said something forgettable. But that version of me stopped showing up months ago.

"It felt good," I said, leaning into the mic. "Not because of who we played, but because I got to be in the moment again. I've been

269

through enough to know that's not guaranteed."

A few reporters looked up, surprised that I'd gone off script. I kept going. I finally said what I meant—not what the team needed, not what the press expected. Just what was true.

"There was a time when every game felt like a chance to prove something. Now it's just a chance to be better than I was yesterday. I'll take that any day."

The room stilled for a beat, the quiet stretching just long enough to register. Then someone toward the back asked, "Would you call this redemption?"

"No. I'd call it peace."

When the session wrapped, I stood and pushed the chair back. "That's it for me. My family's waiting. And my woman's probably wondering why I'm late for dinner."

A few chuckled, some half-heartedly shouted follow-ups, but I was already gone. Bellamy was waiting in the hallway. The next round of questions being thrown out at the next player in the lineup echoed faintly behind me, a soft backdrop to the calm she carried. Her eyes found mine and held.

"Nice game," she said, smiling just enough to undo the last few hours.

"Nice outfit," I said, and that prompted me the eye roll I'd been waiting for.

She slid her hand into mine as we started walking, and I felt the warmth of her palm against mine. For the first time all day, it felt like breathing came easy.

Then Laura reappeared. Reggie trailed a step behind her, gaze averted, avoiding mine.

"Cole," she started, voice polished smooth, "I just wanted to—"

"Don't," Bellamy said. Her tone didn't rise. It didn't need to. She didn't even look at Laura. She just held her ground beside me.

Laura's words caught in midair. Her expression changed, becoming tight around the edges.

I looked at her then, not with anger but finality. "You should take care of yourself," I said evenly. "You'll need it."

She blinked, searching for footing she'd never find. The man beside her shifted again, guilt written across his face in plain sight. I didn't stay long enough to make it worse for either of them.

Bellamy's fingers tightened around mine as we walked on.

"Was that necessary?" she asked softly once we turned the corner.

"Probably not," I said. "But it felt final."

She smiled then, slow and knowing, a smile that settled something deep inside me. "You handled that well."

"I had motivation."

"Oh really?"

"Yeah," I said, looking down at her. "She's standing right next to me."

Her laugh was soft, rolling through the quiet like a secret. Outside, the air had cooled, that crisp edge of Texas winter moving in. I opened the door, letting her slide in first. "Auntie Lo called about fifteen minutes ago to check your arrival time," she said. "Dinner's ready."

"Good," I said, closing the door behind her. "So am I."

The rented vacation home was full throttle when we got there, all warmth and noise that made it easy to forget the rest of the world existed. Family talk and laughter always fed me better than any meal could.

Auntie Lo pulled me straight into a hug, smacked my back twice, and told me she was proud of me and not for the twenty-eight points I'd managed to pull out tonight. Bellamy followed close behind, her jacket half off and smile cautious until the kids spotted her. Then she didn't stand a chance. My nieces and little cousins, led by the authoritative spirit of Summer, swarmed her before she could even take a breath. Within seconds, they had her seated in the middle of the room, picking up whatever conversations they'd shared back in the suite at the game.

I stood back and watched, appreciating how she fit into all of this without effort. There was no performance and definitely no pretending. It was just ease.

Dinner carried on the way holidays do in big families. Slow, heavy with laughter, and full of stories no one had asked to hear again. I stayed quiet, letting the sound move through me. Bellamy sat beside me, her hand brushing mine every so often, her laughter rising soft under the rest of it. I hadn't realized how much I'd missed this—the passing of plates, the teasing, the noise of people who love you without needing to understand you—but my time with Bellamy nudged me back into a space where I felt whole again.

When the last plate was scraped clean and the kids were halfway into a movie marathon, I caught Bellamy's eye from across the room. She knew what I meant before I even stood.

"You ready?" I asked.

"Yeah," she said, grabbing her jacket. "But I'm going to your place tonight. TJ swore there aren't any more cameras, but I need to trust my own eyes."

I laughed. "So you'd rather trust me?"

"Let's not get carried away."

The drive was peaceful, with holiday lights all across the city, and their reflections drifted across her face as she looked out the window. Her hand rested on her knee, relaxed, until I reached over and caught it. My thumb brushed her palm, just enough to keep her close.

"You could stay," I said.

"I'm not spending the night," she said. "You have a six a.m. flight."

"So?"

"So I plan on sleeping until noon."

I smiled at the road ahead. "You do realize, most people in relationships eventually stay the night."

"I'm not most people," she said, but her smile told me exactly what she was thinking.

Upstairs, she turned in my arms, her hands resting flat against my chest. "Go pack before you miss your flight."

I kissed her before she could move, slow and teasing. Her tongue met mine in a rhythm we both knew too well. When she finally pulled back, her eyes held that familiar mix of affection and warning that always made me listen.

She stayed for a while. Long enough for the apartment to remember what laughter sounded like. Long enough for me to forget how heavy silence could feel. When she left, the quiet returned, but it wasn't empty this time. It carried her.

I leaned against my headboard, looking out at the city lights scattered across the distance. Gratitude had felt forced in recent years. Tonight it came easy.

Laura had never wanted this. She didn't want a family, or at least with me, and I couldn't remember a time she'd ever chosen to be around mine. Nieces, nephews, cousins—it was always a polite smile, a quick exit, a reason not to stay. The simple mess of sharing a life never appealed to her.

I hadn't learned the truth until two years into trying. The doctor had asked about timelines, and that was when she finally confessed she'd never stopped taking birth control. Said she wasn't ready. Said she didn't know how to tell me without breaking my heart or breaking what we had.

It broke anyway.

Now here I was, full and finally at peace with the sharp edges smoothed. I hadn't been saved, and I wasn't exactly fixed. Just healed enough to hold whatever came next.

The DMs

@BeautyIzHerName
Happy Turkey Day! What did you cook today?

@ChefSwishWhisk
Surprisingly nothing. I spent it with family.
Big meal. Loud house. Full belly.

@BeautyIzHerName
So you let someone else handle the kitchen? Look
at you... a walking, talking Kelly from Insecure GIF.

@ChefSwishWhisk
Something like that. My girl even joined us.

@BeautyIzHerName
That sounds like love.

@ChefSwishWhisk
It is.

@BeautyIzHerName
Is she the one?

@ChefSwishWhisk
Affirmative.

@BeautyIzHerName
Then I'm happy for you. Really.

@BeautyIzHerName
I guess that means our little pact
is null and void now.

@ChefSwishWhisk
Our friendship isn't.

@BeautyIzHerName

Good. Just promise me one thing. When you get married, I want an invite. Make it a plus-one because, full disclosure, I'm in love too.

@ChefSwishWhisk

Then congratulations. He treating you right?

@BeautyIzHerName

He is. So send it to Bellamy+1.

@ChefSwishWhisk

Bellamy?

@BeautyIzHerName

Yeah... my name.
Sorry, did I make this weird?

@BeautyIzHerName

I just thought someone who's helped me this much deserves to be on a first-name basis even if we're shelving the other personal formalities.

@BeautyIzHerName

As a friend.

@BeautyIzHerName

Hello?

@BeautyIzHerName

Chef?

Chapter 21

BELLAMY

THE KNOCK CAME JUST AS THE MESSAGE SENT.

My phone was still in my hand, the chat with ChefSwishWhisk open on the screen. The typing dots had appeared, disappeared, then returned again as if hesitation itself were part of the conversation. I was half smiling, already composing my next line, when the sound came again. Firmer this time, and definitely impatient.

I crossed the room and opened the door to find Cole standing there barefoot in pajama bottoms and a T-shirt, a quiet storm behind his eyes. He had that look men wear when they are holding something in, when exhaustion and adrenaline start to blur together and neither one wins.

"You're still up," I said, leaning against the frame. "You have an early flight. Go to bed, goofball."

"Couldn't sleep," he said. His eyes dropped to the phone in my hand. "Guess you couldn't either."

Before I could respond, he brushed his thumb over his own screen. The phone in my hand buzzed at the same time, the sound filling the space between us. It was familiar in a way that didn't register until it did, and then it hit like a brick to the gut.

I looked down.

Wowwwww so you really fuckin
with me right now?

When I lifted my head, he was already turning his phone toward me. His screen glowed with the same thread, our words mirrored line for line. Two screens, one conversation, one secret suddenly standing in the open air between us.

We just stared at each other, too stunned to move.

"What is this?" His voice was threatening in the way truth sounds when it is still deciding whether to come quietly.

I blinked, trying to catch up. "Cole, what are you—"

"You've been messaging me." He held up the phone. "For months. That was you."

The words didn't make sense until they did. My stomach dropped so fast it felt like the ground moved. "Wait. *You're* ChefSwishWhisk?"

He didn't answer. He didn't have to. The absurdity of it hovered for a single heartbeat before everything underneath it surfaced. Hurt, confusion, and betrayal in slow motion.

"This isn't funny," I said finally.

"I'm not laughing," he said, his tone cutting through the air between us. "You knew?"

"Knew what?"

"That it was me. That I was the one you've been talking to."

"I didn't," I said quickly. "I swear I didn't."

He exhaled hard, rubbing the back of his neck like he needed somewhere to put his frustration. "Then what, this is all just some fucked-up joke? You, me, and this app? You have any idea what it feels like standing here wondering if the person I've been opening up to has been playing me the whole time?"

"I don't know how else to explain it," I said, my voice rising.

"You think I'd invent all that just to mess with you? Do you really believe I'm capable of something that cruel?"

He didn't answer. His jaw flexed once, then twice. The silence turned into something that pressed in on both of us.

"I didn't know," I said again, quieter this time. "Not until right now."

"Then why does it feel like I'm the only one blindsided?"

"Because maybe you're the only one who gets to assume the worst."

That stopped him. The heat in his eyes flickered, replaced by something less certain. "You think I wanted this?" he asked softly. "You think I wanted to find out like this if I did?"

"I don't know what you wanted, Cole," I said, forcing my voice steady. "But you came here ready to accuse me, and that says more about your fear than my intentions."

He stood there for a moment, breathing hard, torn between anger and disbelief. His phone dimmed, then went dark, and still neither of us moved.

"I need to know," I said finally. "Do you really think I did this on purpose? Because if you've already decided who I am, I can't fight a verdict you've already handed down."

He looked at me, his expression finally cracking under the weight of it. "I don't think it was a joke," he said. "I just don't know how it's real."

"That makes two of us."

He let out a slow breath that sounded like surrender even when he wasn't ready to mean it. "You really didn't know."

"I really didn't." I held his gaze. "And if I had, I probably would've ruined it before it ever got this good."

That pulled a small, pained smile from him, a ghost of the one I had fallen for.

"You realize I've been giving you advice this whole time," I said. "Telling you how to handle things, how to talk to this mystery girl you liked, and it was me the whole time."

"I didn't know this was you," he said. "But maybe some part of me did. You sometimes sounded like someone who saw through me. It just never occurred to me that you were real in both places."

"Well," I said, folding my arms, "mystery solved. We've officially been anonymously flirting with each other for months. Congratulations, we're the rom-com version of a cautionary tale."

I tried to laugh, but it came out cracked.

"I really didn't know," I repeated one last time.

The line hung there longer than it should have, somewhere between humor and heartbreak. He looked at me, not angry now, not defensive, just undone. "You know what the worst part is?"

"What?"

"I meant every word I said to you online," he said softly. "Every damn one."

Something cracked inside me. I swallowed hard. "I did, too," I said. "And now I don't even know which version of us that says more about."

We stood there in the doorway, phones in our hands like twin confessions, the air thick with everything that had been real before either of us knew it.

He looked down, then back at me. "I need to clear my head," he said quietly. "Because right now, I don't know what any of this means."

"I get it," I said. "Because I don't either."

He hesitated, like he wanted to take it back, to reach for something that would fix the night. But nothing about this could be fixed quickly.

"Just don't disappear," he said finally.

"I'm not the one who usually does," I said. "But real talk, I make no promises that I'll be here when you get back."

He nodded once, then turned, walking back across the hall barefoot, the quiet collapsing behind him until it felt like the air itself had closed the door.

When it finally clicked shut, the sound carried through the apartment like something final.

I stood there for a long moment, still holding the phone, still staring at the last message on the screen. The silence that followed felt wide enough to hold both our names.

The Pacific didn't soothe so much as it told the truth.

It moved the way honesty does. Endlessly, without apology. From my mother's porch, I could hear the surf rolling against the rocks below, the crash and retreat steady enough to make me feel both grounded and exposed. I used to think the ocean was about freedom. Now I understood it was about surrender. You couldn't fight it. You just had to stand there and let it speak.

The air here always carried the same mixture of salt and lemon from the trees that lined the backyard. I used to think it smelled like summers that never ended. Now it smelled like reprieve.

I'd been here just under a week, long enough for my suitcase to become a fixture in the corner, long enough to memorize the creak in the floor near the refrigerator and the way afternoon light drifted across the tile like a slow tide. The quiet of this house wasn't empty, it was deliberate. My mother filled it with soft sounds—a jazz station playing too low to name the song, the whistle of the kettle, the clink of her bracelets when she moved her hands.

My phone lived face down on the counter. Every so often it buzzed, flashing names I couldn't face. Cole's had stopped appearing two days ago, and that silence said more than any argument we'd had.

Mom was stirring something on the stove when she said, "You running or resting, Belle?"

"I'm not sure I can tell the difference anymore."

"Mmm." She poured two mugs of tea and joined me at the table, her bangles tapping softly as she folded her legs beneath her robe. "Then maybe that's what you came here to figure out."

She studied my face for a long moment, eyes tracing it like an old photograph.

I smiled faintly. "You make it sound easy."

"Nothing worth learning ever is." She took a sip of her tea, then looked at me over the rim of the cup. "You think your father made it easy for me?"

That drew the smallest laugh from me. "You took him back enough times to prove it wasn't."

"Enough for the neighbors to stop counting," she said, and there was humor in it, but also something fragile. "But I never regretted it."

Her gaze drifted toward the window. Outside, the light had softened to that late-afternoon palette that turned everything forgiving.

"When I got sick the first time," she said slowly, "he was the one who came. Walked right through my front door without an invitation, holding a box of hats from that outrageous boutique on Peachtree… Said if I had to lose my hair, I should at least do it in style. He brushed what was left of it every night like it was still a crown." She smiled. "Made soup that tasted like boiled paper and watched all my favorite shows with me until I fell asleep."

"And then he left," I said quietly.

"He did. That man's greatest trick is disappearing just when you start to believe he won't. But the truth is… your father never believed he deserved to stay. He's always been chasing proof that he deserves to be loved, like it's a paycheck that'll bounce if he lingers too long."

The words lodged somewhere deep. I could see him then, my father standing in a hospital doorway, guilt all over his face, holding a bouquet he probably thought was too small.

"You forgave him," I said.

"I did," she replied. "Because forgiveness is how I remember who I am, not who he was. Belle, loving someone broken doesn't make you foolish. It just reminds you we're all cracked somewhere."

"That didn't break you?"

"Every time," she said. "But sometimes breaking just means you're being reshaped."

I let that sink in. Somewhere down the block a dog barked twice then stopped, like even the neighborhood knew when to listen.

"I'm scared that forgiving Cole will make me look weak," I said finally.

She reached across the table, resting her hand over mine. "Weak is pretending you don't care so no one calls you foolish. Foolish is going back when the other person's stopped trying. But strength—strength is knowing the difference, and acting like you do." She gave my hand a gentle squeeze. "Sometimes, if both of you grow, there's room again later. But forgiveness has to come first."

That night, the house was quiet in a way that left no room for pretending. Mom had fallen asleep on the couch with a throw blanket around her shoulders and a half-finished sudoku puzzle on her lap. Beneath a stack of magazines, a folded pamphlet peeked out. *Radiation Follow-Up Schedule.*

I stared at it for a long moment, the letters blurring until they stopped meaning anything.

When TJ arrived the next morning, it took exactly five minutes for the truth to come out. The cancer had returned small, treatable, and almost finished with therapy, but back all the same.

"You should've told me," I said, anger sharpening my voice even as my throat tightened. "Did Daddy know?"

Mom nodded. "He's been by my side this entire time. Terrence only left so we could have this time together. He's staying at a hotel downtown in case I need him."

"So you *both* lied to us?"

Mom met my gaze calmly. "You were already carrying too much, baby. Sometimes love is knowing when not to add your own weight."

TJ shook their head. "That's not love, that's secrecy."

"And I am pretty certain it violates at least three of our unofficial family bylaws," I muttered.

"It's both," Mom said. "And I'm still here. So let's focus on that part."

The argument fell away. I sat beside her, our shoulders touching, and she leaned her head against mine.

"You don't have to fix it, Bellamy," she murmured. "Just be here. Both of you. That's all I ever wanted from your father, too."

So I stayed. I made tea. I sat through the same reruns of her favorite shows that I was sure my dad had watched with her too, laughed when she told the same story twice, and let TJ fuss around the kitchen like a storm that didn't know where to land. By evening, the house felt softer, but so did the ground beneath me, like any wrong move might break the calm we were all pretending to believe in.

Two days ago, I wouldn't have predicted hearing the news that Mom's breast cancer was back or that I'd be riding in the car with my parents and TJ after taking her to treatment. The quiet between us felt heavy but familiar, every sound carrying more weight than it should. Mom rested her head against the window while Daddy kept stealing glances at her from the driver's seat, his thumb tapping the wheel every time he wanted to say something and didn't.

When we pulled into the driveway, Mom exhaled softly and said, "You can drop us and go, Terrence. We'll be fine."

He smiled that familiar, half-defeated grin. "After I get you settled. I'm only heading out long enough to pick up something for dinner before y'all accuse me of hovering."

"You don't need to hover," she said, her voice gentle. "We remember what to do."

He nodded, eyes steady on her, like remembering wasn't the point at all.

A courier was knocking on the door and holding an elaborate bouquet of blush roses, white tulips, and eucalyptus spilling like ribbon. It looked too extravagant against the plain stucco house, like the day had decided to make room for something gentle.

When I reached him, he was already stepping back toward his truck, offering a polite nod before pulling away.

Mom followed me inside while Daddy steadied her with one hand and held her tote with the other. I set the bouquet on the table. The scent of eucalyptus drifted through the kitchen, clean and cool, a small token of mercy at a time when we needed one.

Tucked between the flowers was a cream envelope embossed with faint vine leaves, my name written across the front. Inside, the card wasn't long, just a quiet invitation. A weekend in Temecula Valley. Two nights in a hillside bungalow surrounded by vineyards and slow mornings. A place meant for rest.

Beneath the details, his handwriting curved steady and sure across the bottom, familiar now in a way that made my chest tighten.

For you and the woman who raised you strong. Your pops helped clear everything with your mom's doctors for the weekend, as long as she feels up to it. Rest, laugh, and take the time to eat every bizarre snack you love. I'll be here when you're ready to come home.
- 34B

I tried to laugh, but it came out uneven. That single ordinary word, *snacks*, broke something loose in me I hadn't realized was locked. A tear slipped before I could stop it. The card's edge pressed against my palm as I traced the lettering, my chest rising too shallow, air catching at the base of my throat until it felt like I'd forgotten how to breathe.

"I don't know what to do with this," I said quietly.

Mom looked at me for a long moment. "Then don't rush it. Sometimes love sounds different when it's finally safe."

The drive to Temecula took a little over an hour, but it felt like crossing into another world. The ocean slipped out of view, replaced by quiet stretches of highway and vineyards stripped bare for winter. The hills were brown and soft under a pale sky.

Mom rode beside me, scarf pulled close, watching the land roll by without saying much. TJ slept in the back seat, half buried under their hooded cashmere sweater, earbuds dangling. The car was silent except for the low thrum of tires against asphalt, but it wasn't the type of silence that hurt. It was one that let everyone breathe.

The bungalow sat on a ridge overlooking the valley, the porch framed by winter vines and the faint glow of a lantern waiting for us. Inside, the lights were soft, the hearth already stacked for a fire offering warmth that made you exhale before you even realized you needed to.

On the counter sat a wide wicker basket lined with cream linen, tied with a single strand of twine, and wrapped in cellophane that caught the light. It was filled with what could only be described as my digital snack drawer brought to life. There were dark chocolate bars, dried fruit, and bottles of sparkling water that made it all look respectable. Then came the greatest hits from my "questionable taste" archive: Oreos, chocolate-covered wasabi peas, kettle corn, a jar of almond butter, mini M&M's, and a bottle of Louisiana hot sauce.

He hadn't stopped there. Dill-pickle-flavored potato chips leaned against chocolate-dipped pretzels. A small jar of peanut-butter-stuffed dates waited beside a sleeve of graham crackers and a tiny jar of marshmallow fluff, as if he honestly believed I might start stress-roasting s'mores at any moment.

It wasn't just a basket. It was proof that every odd craving and every late-night confession I had thrown into our messages had been taken seriously. The man remembered my snack history better than I remembered my passwords.

TJ whistled. "Okay, this is extremely precise."

"This feels illegal," I said. "Like he hacked my two a.m. snack cart."

Mom smiled, reading the small note tucked beside the basket. "Somebody knows what his girl likes."

I did too.

We were halfway through unpacking when a soft knock sounded. A woman stood at the door in a crisp white chef's coat, her curls pulled into a loose bun that defied containment. She held a small bundle of rosemary and thyme in one hand and wore calm that came from knowing she was the main event.

"Good evening," she said. "I'm Chef Aisha Avery. I'll be cooking for you this weekend."

Mom's brows rose. "Cooking for us?"

"Yes, ma'am," Aisha replied. "Mr. Howard arranged for a private chef. He wanted you to have the full California experience, fresh, healing, and a little indulgent."

I froze, the name catching somewhere between recognition and disbelief.

"Wait," I said slowly. "Aisha Avery? As in *The Balanced Bite*? The chef with the viral golden curry tofu bites recipe?"

Aisha smiled like she'd heard it before but still appreciated it. "That's me."

TJ blinked. "I'm sorry, who?"

"She's one of the most influential chefs in the country," I said, suddenly aware of how breathless I sounded. "She makes healthy food look sinful. She's been on *Good Morning America*, and her cookbook debuted at number one."

TJ's grin widened. "So, Cole sent Beyoncé with knives."

Aisha laughed softly. "Not quite, but I'll take the compliment."

She gave me time to settle before finding me later on the patio with a soft smile and an invitation I couldn't refuse. "Come help me in the kitchen," she said, like it wasn't really a question. Maybe she needed the company. Maybe Cole had mentioned that I did. Either way, it felt like she was offering a place to rest the part of me still holding too much.

The next few hours unfolded in a blur of fragrant herbs, citrus, and butter. Aisha moved with easy confidence, turning the kitchen into something that felt almost sacred. Music played low, something simmered on every burner, and the air grew heavy with garlic and lime. It steadied me without asking for anything in return.

Temecula in winter carried its own kind of hush. The hills were soft and brown, the vines bare but orderly, and the air smelled faintly woodsy and like cold earth. We settled onto the enclosed patio just as the sun had slipped behind the ridge, leaving a muted glow that turned everything gold. Dinner was seared snapper with coconut rice and chili-lime butter, bright enough to cut through the chill.

Mom closed her eyes after the first bite. "If you marry that man," she said mid-chew, "I promise not to meddle."

TJ chuckled. "I, however, plan to meddle professionally."

I laughed, shaking my head, grateful just to see Mom eating, even if it was only a few careful bites. "Let's focus on getting you well before we start planning my love life."

Mom's eyelids fluttered. "Sometimes they're the same thing," she murmured, already drifting toward sleep.

When Aisha returned, she carried three small cast-iron skillets on a tray, each one bubbling with golden-brown peach cobbler topped with melting scoops of vanilla bean ice cream.

"Oh my," Mom whispered, sitting up straighter.

Aisha set one down in front of me last. "Mr. Howard made both the dough and the filling himself," she said. "He told me it was nonnegotiable. He had it frozen and flown in this morning and said you'd understand why."

The spoon slipped slightly in my hand, my chest tightening as warmth pooled under my collarbone.

TJ frowned. "What does that even mean?"

"It's"—my throat worked around the words—"a thing. Between us."

Aisha smiled. "He said he wanted you to have the good kind this time."

The memory landed hard. The late-night text about cobbler jerky, the laughter that had carried me through days when nothing else could. He remembered.

I took a small bite, sweet and buttery with just enough tartness to surprise me. "He really did this?"

Aisha nodded. "And that's not all. Tomorrow morning, a full

spa team will arrive. Massage therapists, nail techs, even someone who specializes in oncology recovery. All women, per his request. He said his only goal was to make sure everyone here feels seen and cared for in a safe space."

TJ whistled low. "He's setting an unfair standard."

Mom smiled faintly, spoon in hand. "Fair would've been too easy for that man."

I looked down at the cobbler again, trying not to let my tears fall into it, and thought that, God help me, maybe she was right.

The DMs

@ChefSwishWhisk
You there?

@ChefSwishWhisk
Can we talk when I get back to SA?

Seen at 7:28 PM

@ChefSwishWhisk
I keep starting this message over.
Nothing I try to say comes out right.

@ChefSwishWhisk
So here it is raw. I liked you before I knew.
I like you more now. You are still that one for me.

@ChefSwishWhisk
Hell, I don't just like you... I love you.
You know this. That'll never go away.

Seen at 9:47 PM

@ChefSwishWhisk
I've been calling and texting.
Hit me up when you get this. Please...

Delivered

@ChefSwishWhisk
Hello???

@ChefSwishWhisk: I can give you space.
I just don't want to lose the room we built here.

Seen at 2:14 AM

@ChefSwishWhisk
PLEASE SAY SOMETHING. ANYTHING!!!!! Even if
it's goodbye.

System Notification: User Not Available - Message failed to send.

Chapter 22

COLE

AS MUCH AS I WANTED THIS, BELLAMY WASN'T SUPPOSED to be here. Not yet, not this soon, not when I was still figuring out what to do with everything I hadn't said since Thanksgiving.

She stepped out of the elevator carrying a to-go bag and a Jawn cup that probably held her usual dirty chai latte, her other hand holding her phone in front of her as laughter spilled into the hallway. Her voice moved through a tangle of familiar sounds, her mother and father and TJ and Evan all talking over one another in that effortless way I'd grown used to.

"Mom, I'm fine. I told you, I still managed to get enough sleep even though the flight was delayed." She paused, shook her head, and laughed again. "No, I'm not—"

Then she saw me.

"Cole?"

The sound of my name in her mouth struck me right in the chest.

For a second, neither of us moved. The space between us wasn't more than a few feet, but it was full of everything we hadn't fixed. The silence, distance, and a history that refused to settle down.

She lowered her phone. "I'll call y'all later," she said quickly.

From the speaker came one last voice, her mother's. *"Tell him we said hi!"*

Bellamy groaned softly and tapped the screen, and the hallway went still again.

I took a small step forward before I could stop myself. "Hey," I said.

"Hey."

Her tone was even, but the air between us changed. I reached out before I thought better of it, my fingers brushing the sleeve of her blazer. The fabric was soft and expensive, a nod to anyone around her announcing she was stepping back into her element. For one suspended second, Bellamy didn't move. Then she took a small, graceful step back, and that inch of space between us hurt more than I wanted to admit.

"You just get back?"

She nodded. "Last night. Well, technically this morning. I've got an interview I need to get to."

There was a quiet pulse of excitement in her voice, and I found myself drawn to it.

"Work?"

"Possibly." A small smile played at the corner of her mouth. "It's just a pitch meeting right now, but it's something new. They reached out while I was in San Diego to talk about a new entertainment concept they're developing. It would be part on camera, part editorial… some lifestyle coverage, some culture… but not the messy or salacious kind. For once, I'd get to make something that feels honest. It's the first time in a long time I've felt nervous in a way that felt good."

The pride in her eyes caught me off guard. "That sounds perfect for you."

"It's starting to feel attainable," she said, and her eyes finally held light again.

"I'm happy for you," I said, and meant it.

"Thank you."

The air softened between us but stayed careful, like it might break if either of us moved too fast.

"I heard from your mom the other day," I said. "How's she doing?"

"She's okay. Still herself, which is both a relief and a nightmare." Bellamy smiled faintly. "She just finished her last round of treatment, and now we're waiting on her follow-up to find out what's next. My dad's been camped out at the house pretending to be useful. They're good, though. It's been… special."

"Good," I said quietly. "She's a force. I'm glad she's got him there."

Bellamy's smile deepened, then faded as she smoothed her blazer. She shifted her weight, and my eyes dropped to the impossible height of her heels. She was all business today in her charcoal trousers, silk blouse, and small gold hoops dangling from her earlobes.

"Thank you for everything you did for her," she said.

"It was for you, too."

She looked down for a moment. "I know. Still, thank you."

"You don't need to," I said softly. "I just wanted to help take some of the weight off your shoulders. You've been carrying too much for too long."

Her eyes lifted to mine, and the look stayed with me.

"I tried calling," I said.

"I know."

"And messaging you."

"I know that, too." She adjusted the strap on her bag. "I blocked you."

Her honesty hit harder than any insult could have. "I figured."

"I just needed to stop reaching for my phone every time it buzzed," she said. "I didn't want to talk through a screen anymore. If we ever spoke again, I wanted it to be real. Like this."

Her voice was soft at the end, but not unsure. It was the first time she'd said something that made it sound like *us* wasn't entirely gone.

The truth stung, but it was clean.

She tucked a braid behind her ear, gold catching the light, her perfume brushing the air between us that stayed long after she moved. "I should go. I'm running late."

"Bellamy."

She paused and turned halfway.

"Can we talk later? Grab a bite somewhere and just talk."

She hesitated. The old Bellamy would have deflected with a joke. This version of her just stood there, weighing something. Then she sighed. "Later."

We settled on a time. When she passed me on her way to her apartment, her arm brushed mine. It was barely a touch, but enough to recharge the air between us. The vibration of my phone in my pocket pulled me away from the trance I was left in.

Terrence: Heard my babygirl's back in town. Don't waste time, son. Pride don't keep you warm.

TJ: Daddy, did you really just start another group chat? Someone get Verizon on the line and strip this man of his phone privileges.

Mama B: Cole, do yourself a favor and mute this chat NOW.

Evan: Amen... but also, Dad's right this time.

Terrence: As I was saying. Whatever I can do to help love along, let me know.

The laugh slipped out before I could stop it. The hallway was empty now, but the quiet didn't feel lonely. It felt expectant, like the world had gone still to see what I'd do next.

The smell of grilled meat hit first, thick with smoke and spice. Bellamy walked beside me across the parking lot of Los Hermanos, her heels clicking against the concrete. Her braids brushed my arm as I guided her with a hand at the small of her back through the doorway. Inside, the air was warm and alive, rich with cilantro, lime, and charred tortillas.

Two men stood at the door, Dre and Knight, both new, both silent, built to look like living, menacing nightmares that knew its job. Ronan's head of security had vouched for them, said they were disciplined and discreet. I'd hired them because I had learned the hard way that being visible came with a cost. Crowds had started to gather again when I went out, a mix of overzealous curiosity and reckless boldness. Neither kind was what I wanted around her.

Bellamy took in the room with that slow, assessing glance I'd missed. "So this is what going out looks like for you now?" she asked, teasing. "You bring your own Secret Service?"

I looked back at Dre and Knight, both scanning the space. "Something like that. The guys said it was time I stopped pretending I could blend in."

"Well," she said, watching them take their positions near the entrance, "I'm glad you did it. It makes me feel better knowing someone's watching your back. And it also tells me you're finally doing more than store runs and treks to Vantage if you've actually put someone on payroll."

"Maybe," I said, smiling. "But mostly, I did it because I want to make sure you're always safe. I don't ever want to put you in harm's way if I can help it."

She looked up at me. "Is that right?"

"That's right."

We found a booth tucked in the corner, the table scarred from years of use. Bellamy slid into the seat across from me, smoothing her blouse. Her nails, painted a deep wine color, caught the light every time she moved. For a moment, I let myself imagine those fingers wrapped around more than just her glass because I craved her touch so much.

The server dropped off menus, but Bellamy barely glanced at hers before saying, "I already know I won't be able to decide. We should just order one of everything and, as your niece would say, call it research."

"A spread like that sounds dangerous," I said. "You sure you can back up the foodie persona you brought into my inbox?"

"No doubt," she replied with a grin. "You act like you've never seen all these curves up close and personal."

We did exactly that and ordered everything. Carnitas, birria, al pastor, barbacoa, chorizo, and pollo asado in various forms. Tamales wrapped tight in husks. Enchiladas swimming in red sauce. Roasted corn, three kinds of salsa, and two bottles of Jarritos she chose by color alone. When the food hit the table, it drew stares from the booths nearby. Bellamy leaned forward, eyes shining as she inhaled.

She took her first bite, closed her eyes, and let out a sound that made the hair on my arms rise. "This is unreal," she said. "It reminds me of my first night in San Antonio. The tacos you dropped off when I must have looked like I wanted to bite your head off. But I was starving, and to be fair, you were kind of my archnemesis."

"It's a good thing we've moved past that," I said, bumping my knee against hers under the table and earning a laugh.

"I'll admit, part of that's because of those tacos," she said. "They were the best I'd ever had. I still can't tell if it was hunger or the food."

"Probably both."

She tilted her head, studying me. "You always find food that tastes like home."

"It's a gift," I said. "Or maybe a coping mechanism."

"At least it's a healthy one."

"Define healthy."

"Edible." She grinned and reached for another taco.

"You still pretending chocolate sauce counts as a dipping condiment?"

That made her laugh and nudge my foot under the table. "You keep bringing it up like you didn't ask for seconds for your popcorn."

We ate slowly, talking between bites. The noise around us faded the way it does when the right person is sitting across from you.

She paused between sips of her drink, looking down for a moment like she was gathering her thoughts. "San Diego helped me think about a lot of things," she said. "About love. About what it looks like to forgive someone without losing yourself. My mom and dad… they've hurt each other more times than I want to count, but somehow, they still show up when it matters. I used to think that meant they didn't know when to quit. Now I think they just understand what matters enough to stay."

I didn't interrupt.

Her voice stayed calm but thoughtful. "Mom told me something while I was home. She said I got more of Daddy in me than I realize. The part that loves hard but runs fast when it starts to feel real. The part that convinces itself it doesn't need to be seen." She looked up at me, her eyes clear. "That hit me harder than I wanted to admit."

I nodded, waiting.

"I guess I'm realizing that most of the men I've dated kept me hidden. They said it was about privacy, but really it was about convenience. And I went along with it because, somewhere deep down, I didn't believe loving out loud was safe. When love is public, people watch it like sport. They cheer when it's new, dissect it when it cracks, and by the time it breaks, everyone feels entitled to your grief. One of those private things went public in the worst way possible. It was humiliating. Viral."

She gave a small, almost rueful laugh. "After that, hiding felt like protection. But sitting here now…" She stopped, her eyes searching mine. "It feels different. You're different. I can feel myself showing up again, and I didn't even realize how much I'd stopped."

For a while, the only sound between us was the scraping of a chair across the linoleum floor and the clank of a fork against a plate being cleared nearby. I reached across the table and brushed my thumb over her hand, slow enough that she could pull away if she wanted to. When she didn't, I released a breath I hadn't realized I was holding until then.

"You didn't stop showing up. You just stopped mistaking being watched for being loved," I said quietly.

Her mouth curved. "And maybe that's what makes this different." She pulled her hand back gently, taking another sip of her drink. "Speaking of your boy Ronan," she said, voice lighter again, "my meeting earlier was actually with him."

That got my attention. "Yeah? How'd it go?"

"Better than I expected. He's building something new. Said he's thinking about what life looks like after the game and wants to do something that still moves him. It's not just sports commentary. He wants to build a real platform. Interviews, podcasts, cultural stories. He's planning to bring in advisors for the next meeting to refine the vision. He wants me to be a part of it."

"That's big," I said, meaning it.

"It is. He even mentioned possibly developing one of the

pitches I brought him."

My brows lifted. "You serious? What's the pitch?"

She smiled like she was enjoying the suspense. "Can't tell you yet. You haven't signed an NDA."

"So this is what healthy boundaries look like?"

"Progress," she said, with mock seriousness. "You should be proud."

"I am," I told her. "Really."

Her expression softened. "Thank you."

We lingered until the restaurant started to empty. When we stepped back into the cool night, Dre and Knight followed at a distance, silent and alert. Bellamy noticed, glanced back, then turned to me.

"They're good," she said quietly. "I like that you're finally letting people look out for you."

"Can I count you in that number?"

Her eyes met mine, something flickering there. "Without question." Then she smiled. "Before we both pretend we're not heading to the same place, do you want some company while you overthink this evening to death?"

I blinked. "Was I that obvious?"

"You have no idea," she said, laughing softly.

When the elevator doors slid open on the thirty-fourth floor half an hour later, we stepped out. She slipped her hand into mine. I unlocked my door and pushed it open, and after nearly three weeks, she crossed the threshold into my space again.

Chapter 23

BELLAMY

KNIGHT, MY COMPANION FOR THE DAY, WHIPPED COLE'S Range Rover into his reserved spot at Vantage Arena before stepping out to open my door. I slipped out and pulled my coat tight against the December chill. With Christmas less than a week away, I was still racing to finish my shopping list. Shopping for my parents and TJ was already enough to make me break out in hives, but now that Cole's nieces and nephews had found their way onto it, I was officially in over my head.

That was why Cole had insisted I didn't go alone. Today was Knight's turn to escort me, part driver and part bodyguard, making sure I got to the arena on time for what he called his big night.

"She's in," Knight said into his earpiece as he scanned the area. He extended a hand to help me out. "Watch your step."

"Appreciate it," I said, breathless but smiling. Cole's people didn't miss a thing.

After a quick change at home, I swapped shopping bags for my game outfit of dark jeans, heeled booties, and a customized Howard jersey. My hair was freshly curled with new extensions blended through, the gold accessories pulling one side away from my face catching the light each time I turned my head.

Knight held the door open for me and the noise hit like a wave. The crowd was already electric, a sound that vibrated in your ribs. Dre met us halfway inside and the two of them fell into formation, silent and watchful. I adjusted my bag, grateful for their presence even if I pretended not to notice how seriously they took their job.

An attendant stopped me near the corridor. "Promo night," she said, handing me a glossy box with the Storm logo. "Don't forget your bobblehead."

"Thanks," I said, tucking it under my arm before stepping into the main tunnel.

From the corner of my eye, I caught Nina waving, a grin already spreading across her face. I hurried over long enough to hug her and set my bag beside her seat. She was already mid-sentence about the pregame entertainment when I told her I'd be right back and slipped away toward the locker room.

I texted Cole, told him to step out if he could because it would be worth it.

By the time I rounded the corner, he was already there. A towel hung around his neck, his game jersey on, his whole presence calm and composed in that quiet way that always undid me. He froze when he saw me, then smiled.

"Hey," he said. "You okay?"

"Hey," I said, nodding once.

I didn't overthink it. I stepped in and kissed him. Quick, certain, right there in the doorway like the rest of the world had fallen away.

He hesitated for half a breath, then kissed me back, slow enough to make my knees remember everything I'd tried to forget. When we finally broke apart, he grinned.

"That for luck?"

"For whatever you need it for," I said. "I missed you."

"Not as much as I missed you." His voice was still rough from that morning; he'd been up early helping with the Storm's toy drive.

My gaze dropped to his arm, where fresh ink peeked from beneath his compression sleeve, the surface still reddened beneath a thin gloss of protective film. "You got a new tattoo."

He looked down, smiling. The letters were simple and bold. *Bella.*

"That's permanent," I reminded him.

"So are you."

Before I could respond, one of the trainers called his name from down the hall.

"Go," I told him. "Bring us one more win closer to that trophy."

"Yes, ma'am." He brushed his thumb along my jaw, pressed one more kiss to my lips, and jogged off, towel hanging loose in his hand.

I made my way to my seat, still feeling the heat of that moment when I sat beside Nina. She passed me a drink without looking up.

"I'm just glad you're here," she said. "I was worried you'd miss it."

"Miss what?"

"The record," she said, eyes bright. "Cole's about to break it tonight."

I frowned. "What record?"

"Most assists off missed free throws," she said like it was common knowledge.

I blinked. "That's a thing?"

"Extremely," she said, leaning in. "He's been chasing it all season. Advanced stat. Analytics love it."

"Analytics," I echoed slowly.

"Synergy numbers," she said. "High-level stuff. That guy next to the camera told me ESPN already has the segment queued."

I hesitated. "That's… not real. Right?"

"Relax," Nina said, already texting and showing me. Ro, tell Bellamy tonight's the night Cole might get a banner for breaking the assists off missed free throws record.

"A banner?" I asked. "They make those?"

Seconds later, Ronan's reply popped up. Facts. History in the making.

Nina turned the phone so I could see. "Told you."

My mouth fell open. "Wait… so this is real? Like, *real* real?"

"Completely real," she said, face straight. "Cole didn't say anything? Ronan would've had the team pass out shirts with his face on them instead of bobbleheads."

I leaned forward, scanning the rafters. "But where would they even hang it? Next to the championship ones or in its own little section?"

"Probably between MVP and Team Community Outreach," she said. "It's a rare stat."

"It just feels so random," I muttered. "Do they count the bounce first, or does the assist start after the rim?"

"You think I know?" She coughed to hide a laugh. "You're asking the right questions, though."

I reached for my phone. "I'm Googling this."

Nina grabbed my wrist. "No. Don't ruin it. You have to experience it live."

I squinted. "Why do you sound like a preacher on Easter Sunday?"

"Because greatness deserves witnesses," she said solemnly.

"You're lying."

"Am I?" She sipped her drink. "Would Ronan lie?"

"Yes," I said quickly, but she was already facing the court again, grinning like the cat who'd eaten the canary.

The lights dimmed for player introductions, and I leaned back in my seat, still trying to question why my gut was churning.

"I hate that I didn't even know," I murmured. "If I'd known, I would've done something for him. Brought his family, made it a thing."

Nina smiled without looking away from the court. "Then it's a good thing you showed up. Some moments don't need planning. They just need presence."

I looked up again, half expecting to see a shiny banner with his name already waiting. There were championships, MVPs, and scoring titles, but nothing about free throws.

I pulled out my phone again, whispering, "Just a quick check," but Nina caught me mid-scroll and said, "Put it away and get your head in the game."

Below us, the players charged onto the floor. The arena shook with noise. Cole came out last, focused and steady, his teammates clapping him on the back as the music swelled.

He looked up, eyes finding mine. The grin that crossed his face wasn't for the cameras. It was for me.

And I didn't even try to play it cool.

By the fourth quarter, I was still watching the court like someone waiting for history to happen. Every time Cole touched the ball, I leaned forward and whispered, "Was that one?"

"No," Nina said without looking away. "He has to miss the free throw first, remember?"

I frowned. "Right. But he hasn't missed any."

"Which is why he's elite," she said in the tone of someone explaining quantum physics to a toddler.

I nodded as if I understood, then leaned in again. "So when do they stop the game and hang the banner?"

She looked at me over the rim of her cup. "Probably halftime of the next one."

I sat back, satisfied. "Makes sense."

When the buzzer finally sounded, the crowd erupted. The Storm had won by double digits. The news of their win flashed across the scoreboard in bold white letters, but there was no mention of a record. I clapped anyway, proud and a little confused until Nina stood and stretched.

"Come on," she said. "Let's go congratulate our statistical legend."

Nina glanced at her phone as we waited near the locker room. "They're still doing press. It might be a minute."

"That's fine," I said, clutching my unopened bobblehead box. "I can wait."

A staffer walked by and waved at Nina, saying, "Family lounge is closed for renovations tonight. You might want to wait by the tunnel instead."

"Good to know," Nina said brightly as we walked in that direction. Then she turned to me with a smile that I was starting to recognize as one Cole was always suspicious of. "I have to check on something real quick, but don't move. Stay right here."

I narrowed my eyes. "That sounded suspicious."

She placed a hand on her chest. "Girl. Why are you so paranoid tonight? Chill, I'll be right back."

Before I could say anything, she was gone, curls bouncing, leaving me standing there with my nerves and a handful of security staff pretending not to notice me.

I shifted my weight, glancing toward the doors leading to the locker room. The sound of laughter and footsteps carried through. I looked down at the box in my hand and finally lifted the lid.

Inside sat a miniature version of Cole in his Storm uniform, wearing a Santa hat and frozen midair with a tiny basketball. I laughed out loud, the sound breaking through the quiet.

"Of course," I said softly. "Of all the players to get, I get Santa Cole."

The bobblehead wobbled as if agreeing. Then the noise from the hallway faded and it clearly was not by accident. I heard the sound of footsteps approaching. Slow, steady, and familiar.

Cole stepped into the tunnel dressed in a tailored navy suit that looked criminally good on him. His collar was open, his hair still damp from the shower, a faint sheen of warmth on his skin. His clean scent reached me before he did, and when his eyes met mine, everything around us dimmed into something distant and irrelevant.

When he saw me, his expression softened, the edges of game mode falling away until all that was left was him.

I smiled faintly. "So close."

He raised a brow. "So close to what?"

I hesitated, feeling silly now that the words had to leave my mouth. "The record."

"The what?"

"The most assists off missed free throws thing." I shifted my weight, shrugging like it was no big deal. "You were supposed to make history tonight."

A slow grin spread across his face. "Bellamy… that's not a real record. It's not even a real thing."

I blinked. "It's not?"

"Not even a little." His laugh rolled out of him easily. "Who told you that?"

I groaned. "Ronan and Nina said—"

"Two reliable sources of misinformation." He shook his head, still smiling. "But if there were a record for loving you through all your gullible moments, I'd hold that one easy."

"I felt so bad," I said, rubbing my temples. "You were out there working so hard, and I kept waiting for the big scoreboard moment. I was ready to cry over imaginary stats."

His laughter softened into something quieter. "You came, though."

"Of course I came."

"Even when you thought I was one free throw away from being in the record books for something that doesn't exist?"

"Especially then," I said, meeting his eyes. "You looked good doing it, though."

He closed the distance between us. "Remind me to thank Nina for lying to you," he said.

I laughed under my breath. "You better not. She'll turn it into a national holiday."

He reached up, brushing his thumb along my chin. "And you'd show up anyway."

"Maybe I would," I said softly.

And in that quiet, with the arena nearly empty and the scoreboard still glowing above us, I realized I didn't care about fake records or playful schemes. I was just glad I hadn't missed this.

Chapter 24

COLE

"COME WITH ME."

She looked up, brow lifted in amusement. "Now?"

"Now."

Something in my tone must have told her not to argue. She slipped her phone into her coat pocket, then placed her hand in mine. Her fingers were cool from the air, soft against my palm. I led her toward the perimeter of the court.

The lights overhead dimmed until the hardwood gleamed like honey. Rows of empty seats stretched in shadow. The space felt bigger in the quiet. A quiet that awaited something.

"Cole," she said, smiling as she caught the shift in my face, "what are you doing?"

"Just showing you something."

Then came the sound. It began softly, a pulse beneath the silence that grew steady and sure. A single whistle cut through the stillness, bright and clean, hanging in the air like a call to rise.

From the tunnel, four drum majors stepped out, their white uniforms crisp enough to catch every trace of stray light. Gold glinted from their gloves as they crossed the court, each step landing in perfect time. The sound echoed through the open space, steady and precise, filling what silence left behind. They reached the center under the watchful eye of a spotlight trailing them, a soft fade that pulled everything else into focus. When they lifted their batons, the stillness that followed felt deliberate, like the world holding its breath before something began.

The whistle sounded again.

From every section above us, music began to descend. Rows of brass and woodwinds stepped down the aisles, the sound swelling with every measured movement. Their uniforms told stories without a single word. Deep maroon and white, bright gold and black, emerald green, royal blue, violet, and cream were just some of the colors surrounding us. Each hue carried the pride and legacy of generations who'd built their sound on fields and courts across HBCU campuses. Every sleeve bore a single stripe of Storm orange that pulled them together in one shared story. Ours.

The drums entered next, snare lines rolling like thunder from the upper decks. Bass drums boomed in sync, the vibration deep enough to move the air. Cymbals flashed, scattering light like sparks. The lush sounds filled every inch of the arena until the empty stands felt alive again.

Then the melody shifted. A few notes lingered in the air, soft and familiar, before revealing themselves. The first line of "Beauty" by Dru Hill rose through the brass, smooth and full, gliding across the rhythm.

Bellamy pressed a hand to her chest, eyes wide, her voice catching in her throat. The sound surrounded her from every direction as she recognized the song.

She turned in a slow circle, smiling through tears, unwilling to miss a single note. "Cole," she whispered, shaking her head. "You didn't."

I grinned. "I did."

The melody swelled, wrapping the court in warmth. Horns lifted, steady and golden. Drums rolled beneath them, heavy and proud. The music carried weight, not just rhythm but history, everything alive and certain.

Then the dance teams appeared, moving onto the court with the grace of a processional. Sequins caught the light as their bodies moved in unison, each motion measured and sure. Every step landed with quiet precision, the choreography unfolding like memory given form.

One dancer reached for Bellamy's hand. She hesitated, smiling through tears, and finally gave in, letting herself be led to center court. The musicians shifted formation around her, brass and woodwinds arcing inward until she stood surrounded by sound.

I stepped into the circle. Bellamy turned toward me, her face luminous in the soft light, her eyes bright and wet. The bands read the moment and drew back, the sound thinning until only the slow thrum of the drums remained beneath the quiet.

"If I broke a record tonight, it wasn't on the court," I said quietly. "It was the same one I break every day when I think I've reached the limit of how much I can love you, and then you show me I haven't. This isn't about stats or grand gestures. It's about you. About what you've always been to me."

The music stayed low behind us, a heartbeat made of melody.

"My Bella. My Beauty. I love you," I said. "You've changed everything I thought I knew about what love looks like when it's real. You're home to me, Bellamy Barnes. Every version of it."

Her eyes filled again. A tear slipped free as she whispered, "Cole…"

I dropped to one knee before I could think twice. The sound that left her was a mixture of laughter and sobbing. I opened the small black box, and the ring inside caught the downlight, but all I saw was her.

"Marry me," I said. "Let's build something that's ours. No halves. No hiding. Just us."

Her hand flew to her mouth. Then she nodded, her voice

breaking on the word. "Yes."

The drum majors lifted their batons, signaling for confetti like a championship had just been won, and the musicians roared back to life. Horns belted the hook, drums cracked like thunder, and dancers spun as the jumbotron flashed in bold white letters, *SHE SAID YES!*

Light shimmered across her tears as I slid the ring onto her finger and pulled her close. She laughed, shook her head, and kissed me.

At the edge of the court, her parents stood arm in arm, TJ and Evan nearby, Auntie Lo filming everything with my family cheering us on. My teammates and members of the Storm staff and coaching squad spilled from the tunnel. Somewhere, Nina was yelling something that sounded like "finally," but none of it mattered. Bellamy's hand was still in mine.

She looked up at me, smiling through disbelief. "You planned all this?"

"Had some help," I said. "Your dad wasn't wrong about men with resources doing the most for their babygirl."

The musicians launched into one final round, horns soaring, drums rolling in perfect cadence. Bellamy laughed again, spinning beneath the spotlight as I held her hand above her head, her ring flashing with every turn.

When she collapsed into me, breathless and glowing, she whispered, "You're something else."

"And you're everything," I said.

The court felt sacred. The light, the music, the woman in my arms… It all came together like something I had been moving toward for a long time. Bellamy was the one who'd brought me back to that truth without saying a word. I wasn't protecting a story anymore. I was finally living one worth keeping.

COLE

IF SOMEONE HAD TOLD ME TWO YEARS AGO THAT I WOULD spend my afternoons in a café packed wall to wall with basketball fans, a live band, and my wife hosting a podcast with her father while nine months pregnant, I would have called them delusional.

And yet, here we were.

Jawn was louder than usual. The Storm played for the championship tonight, and the café felt more like a pregame rally than a live taping. Fans in orange crowded every corner, shouting across tables between bites of wings and waffles. The air carried that edge of anticipation that came right before tipoff.

Bellamy's voice cut clean through it, smooth and bright. "This is Bellamy Howard, and I'm with my cohost and Daddy, the icon himself, Terrence Barnes. Welcome to our show *Tracks & Vibes*, where we talk music, culture, and the soundtrack of life."

The crowd answered like a stadium. Cheers, laughter, phones flashing. I'd played in arenas smaller than this room felt right now.

She shifted in her chair, one hand braced against the curve of her stomach, and still managed to smile like she was born for the mic. Her dad grinned beside her, feeding off the attention. "See," he told the audience, "this is what happens when you grow up backstage.

Eventually you grab the mic for yourself."

Bellamy didn't miss a beat. "Or I just got tired of waiting for you to pass it."

The café broke into applause. Even I couldn't stop the smile.

This place, the same café where she went viral singing "Survivor" with Nico and Javon as backup dancers, thanks to one of Ronan's dares, was now home to her show. Somewhere between the scandal and the second chance, she'd found her voice again.

And she had never sounded better.

From my spot near the edge of the stage, I kept one eye on her and one on security. Her due date was close enough that I had been on alert all week. When she pressed a hand low against her belly, I straightened, ready.

She caught me and mouthed, *I am fine.*

I wanted to believe her. But then something shifted in her expression, small but clear. I'd seen pain sneak up enough times to know what it looked like. Before I could make a plan, she exhaled, eyes squeezed shut, and I was already moving.

By the time I reached her, she was breathing through it, one hand gripping the table. "Sweetheart," I whispered.

"I'm fine," she said automatically, though her fingers trembled.

"Fine doesn't make your hand shake."

Jackie was already at her other side, calm as always. "Talk to me, baby."

Bellamy's voice dropped to a breath. "I think it's time."

The café fell silent for half a second before Terrence jumped to his feet like someone just cued the encore. "You heard her, folks, it's happening!"

The crowd erupted. Phones rose, people shouted blessings, someone cried near the bar.

Bellamy groaned through a laugh. "Daddy, can we not

livestream my labor?"

"All right, all right," he said, waving the crowd down. "Make way for the future MVP."

I tried not to smile as I helped her stand. "You good?"

"As good as a woman in active labor can be with a live audience."

"Then we're leaving."

Jackie was already giving orders. "Keys. Car. Now."

Terrence, bless him, tried to help. "Y'all need me to drive?"

"Absolutely not," I told him without looking up.

Jackie leaned across the car window. "Terrence, ride with TJ and do *not* go live with this."

He sighed like a man cheated out of destiny. "This would make one hell of a bonus episode on Patreon."

Bellamy laughed between contractions, holding my hand as I helped her into the back seat. She was sweating, focused, still beautiful.

"You breathing okay?" I asked.

"Trying," she said, shutting her eyes as another wave rolled through. "If this kid shows up during the game, they're definitely yours."

I couldn't help but laugh. "Then we'll both have our rings tonight."

She opened one eye. "You just made that sound romantic and competitive."

"You've got this, baby."

She squeezed my hand, voice trembling. "Cole, thank you."

"For what?"

"For being here. For showing up the way you do."

Her words caught something deep in me. All I could do was hold her tighter. "Always," I whispered. "You and this baby are my whole world."

And for a moment, all the noise outside faded. The shouts, the horns, the shenanigans of my father-in-law being my father-in-law disappeared.

Just her hand in mine.

Just our breath syncing as another contraction built.

Just the sound of a life beginning, and the peace of knowing I was exactly where I was supposed to be.

I woke to a quiet that felt like permission. The hospital machines moved in steady, unobtrusive patterns. Light filtered through the blinds, thin and careful. For a moment, the world was nothing more than the bed, the bassinet, and the two of them.

My daughter rested against my chest, heavy with newborn sleep. Her hand curled around my finger like she was tethering herself to the only place she had ever known. Bellamy slept too, her breathing soft and even, her hair a halo of curls against the pillow. She looked like the woman I'd married and also like the person who kept remaking me into someone who could live in stillness.

It was unreal how much I studied her face, like memorizing a playbook I never wanted to lose. I traced the line of her nose, the way she drew in a breath as if calculating something fierce and precise. The faint shadows beneath her eyes were proof of everything she'd carried to bring our daughter into the world. The memory of it returned in sharp fragments. We were walking the hallway, pacing slow circles between contractions, both pretending patience we did not feel. The argument started over something small. Timing. Whether I should stay or go. Her contractions had slowed, and when I asked if it was really labor or just another false start, it came out wrong, too blunt, too afraid. I was scared of losing her. She was scared I would lose myself again if I missed the game. We were both fighting ghosts, calling it love.

She'd told me to go. I remembered every word, the way she'd said, "Go, Cole. Our kid is not coming out anytime soon." It was not defiance. It was faith. She gave me the permission I did not know I needed. I thought she was being stubborn, but she was being generous. She saw how the world wanted to remind me who I used to be and refused to let that define me again.

I'd made my plans carefully. Asked a trainer to keep my phone close while I was on the court. Kept the car ready for a quick exit in the dock. Mapped out a route to the arena that could be broken off at any moment. I could not be two places at once, but I could shorten the distance.

In the end, I barely remembered the game. Winning felt distant, ceremonial. What mattered during those minutes as we fought for it was the phone in my hand between quarters and the thought of how quickly I could get back.

When I returned, Bellamy's shoulders had softened like someone finally letting go of watch duty. "Took you long enough," she'd said, her voice part accusation, part relief, and her belly still swollen with my child.

The rest of it had happened in motion. The nurses moving with quiet precision, her hand finding mine, our daughter's first cry, the weight of her placed on Bellamy's chest. I'd once thought my life was built around people on their feet cheering through every play. The first time I held our child, I understood that the moments that matter most did not ask for an audience.

People talked about fathers finding mythology in those first hours. For me it was simpler. A collection of small, undeniable truths. She did not look exactly like me. Her hair was dark and fine, her skin already the warm tone of Bellamy's cheeks. When she woke and settled again with one small sigh, I realized the world had given me an apprenticeship in tenderness. There was purpose in the steadiness of my arms that felt quietly electric.

Bellamy and I were married in a garden the way people who had been public and private in equal measure learned to do. It was quiet, with a guest list full of those who had already seen us at our worst and still believed in our best. Terrence tried to take over the music, Nina made a cake that could have fed the entire city, and Ronan gave a speech after swearing he would not. Bellamy's laugh carried through all of it, bright and steady, her hand never leaving mine.

When she danced with her father, the band began a song I did not recognize at first, although I did not need the history to understand what it meant. Later she told me he wrote it for her before she was born, that they had danced to it at her parents' first wedding. Watching her move with him that night, I could see the years folding in on themselves. The pride in her smile, the ache behind it, and the grace that met both halfway.

She once swore that if love ever felt like nineties R&B, she did not want it. Said it was too big, too messy, too full of promises that never held. But there she was, swaying with her father to a song from that very era, and it was not a cliché. It was healing. Proof that the music she once tried to distance herself from still carried parts of her DNA, pieces she did not know she wanted to claim. Watching her, I realized it was not just a dance. It was a bridge between the little girl who once stood on her father's shoes and the woman who'd finally stepped into love that was her own.

People asked what changed in me. The easy answer was everything. The harder truth was that it did not happen in a straight line. I was still the man who woke at odd hours to study film or who couldn't help coaching a rookie mid-dinner. But Bellamy had taught me to see what mattered beneath all of that. That love was not the conclusion; it was the thread that ran through every part of a life. Bellamy had taught me patience, not as endurance but as grace. She'd taught me that real apologies lived in your habits, not in your words.

There were myths worth keeping and others worth letting go. For years, I'd kept my silence because words felt loaded. Now I used them for the ordinary things, the small truths that made a life, like promising diaper duty at two in the morning. I would learn the lullabies even when I couldn't hit a single note. I would show up for the quiet, steady work of fatherhood the way I'd once showed up for practice.

The stakes were higher now. This wasn't another season to prepare for. It was a life that asked for a different kind of stamina.

Bellamy stirred beside me, hair in every direction, a sleepy smile tugging at her mouth.

"You're talking to yourself again," she murmured.

"Habit," I said. "You keep falling asleep before the good parts."

She blinked toward the bundle in my arms. "You look good holding her."

"You say that like you're surprised."

"I am. You used to hold grudges the same way."

I laughed quietly. "She's lighter."

Bellamy shook her head, smiling. "You're ridiculous."

"So you've said," I whispered, kissing her hair.

She closed her eyes, her hand finding mine. "You're impossible."

"Still here," I answered.

Morning spilled through the curtains, soft and slow. She leaned into me, our daughter warm between us. It finally felt like the world had caught up to the joke only we understood.

Some quiet still needed a witness. She was mine. I was hers.

AUTHOR'S NOTE

I can't believe this book took almost three years to finish. Life kept pulling me aside with grief, change, anxiety, and those long dramatic pauses where you wonder if the words packed up and left for good. But every time I returned to this story, something in these characters tugged me back in. A layer I had not seen before. A softness I wanted to protect.

ClickMate began as a love letter to the things that raised me… nineties rom-coms, nineties R&B, and basketball that felt like culture as much as sport. That era had its own ease, and pieces of it slipped into the way I wanted to write this story.

Somewhere along the way, the book became more than nostalgia. It turned into a story about starting over when everyone swears they already know who you are. About forgiveness that refuses to be neat. About love that shows up imperfect, late, and still right on time.

To everyone who waited through the stalls and silences and believed this book would find its way home, thank you. You carried me farther than you know.

And to anyone reading who is a little scared to try again or to let someone stay long enough to matter, I hope this story reminds you that love does not need to arrive early to be real.

—Tia